To Lynn,
Don't say
a solicitor!

GW01471471

WAITING

BRIEFS

DESMOND WRIGHT

17.11.98

Cromwell Publishers

First published in 1998 by
Cromwell Publishers
Eagle Court Concord Business Park
Threapwood Road
Manchester M22 0RR

Printed in Great Britain by
In-House Printing, Huddersfield

Bound in Great Britain by
J E Ingle & Son Ltd, Leeds

Paperback ISBN 1 901670 70 5

I would like to thank my mother and father, Maureen and John, who gave me life, and my wife, Dipinder, who saved it.

Also Sharon Quance, who typed the manuscript, and Mrs Cook who did not.

I wish also to thank my work colleagues at Desmond Wright & Co. No pirate captain ever had a better crew.

CHAPTER ONE

Half a kilo of heroin meant half a decade in prison. Shit, it would be a different world when he came out. A new century an all.

The passengers crowded around the carousel jostling for position but there was as yet nothing to jostle for. Bindi stood back from the crowd, slipped off his Armani sunglasses and put them in his top pocket while trying hard to stop those runaway thoughts from racing the Monaco Grand Prix around the twists and turns of his troubled mind. The flight was being unloaded by the baggage handlers as Bindi tried to avoid flight.

Bindi felt himself gradually losing authority over his own body; his feet shuffled his body weight from one foot to the other, his eyes kept darting to and fro and he felt a nearly overwhelming need to pee. He fiddled frantically with the folder holding his travel documents issued by the Shahanshah travel agency in Southall.

It was all right on the aircraft since he had spent the flight engrossed in "Waiting Briefs" a book about drug dealing in Southall and about a young lawyer's first experience of sex. He couldn't remember how it ended but the book had made him smile. He now tossed it into a litter bin because, like a finished can of baked beans, it was now empty for him. He tried to walk naturally back to the carousel but it became unnatural precisely because he tried.

Why hadn't it started moving? Is the luggage being checked before it is put on? Why is that Customs Officer standing by the exit door?

All throughout the long and lonely wait Bindi saw the wall cameras seemingly positioned to pick on him and record a video tape of his movements for posterity and particularly for policemen.

A slight shudder and the mobile rubber belt commenced turning. All the passengers moved towards the starting grid by the luggage belt and Bindi positioned himself between an elderly stooped male wearing a turban and holding a knobbly walking stick and a fit young lady wearing a red saree and a sad smile. The carousel did two complete turns before anything appeared at all. A purple rucksack was first, followed swiftly by a large brown box covered with black tape, then the suitcases arrived to an audible sigh. Everyone pushed each other for pole position but most were disappointed as the carousel produced all the unwanted items first. Indeed the large brown box was commencing its fourth circuit when Bindi spotted his fold-over suitcase.

Ice cold fear splashed over his internal organs carried by the adrenaline which accelerated around his arteries as his mind moved into top: leave it, leave it, leave it. Go, go, go. Walk away and ring tomorrow at left luggage. No, they always put sniffer dogs on left luggage. Joshi, who used to work at the airport, told him that. Can a dog smell gear through the cloud caused by my bag of spices? Why chance it.

Bindi stayed and the suitcase came closer. Pick that up and pick up half a decade inside. One simple, straight forward act: lifting a piece of luggage off a carousel and Bindi would spend his youth slammed up, crushed down and confined without sunshine for year after year.

6

He would definitely let it go as it glided level with him and he half turned away but then, almost automatically, he grabbed the handle of the suitcase and swung it around with him until it landed softly on the luggage trolley. He started pushing it immediately grateful for something to lean on.

It was only when he came up to the passport desk that he realised how ruthlessly he had been driving his trolley, forcing a young mother to collide with her own child and cutting up an elderly lady who cursed him in Hindi. The sweat formed a thin film between the palm of his hand and the rubber handle of his trolley.

"Passport, Sir."

Bindi tried to smile as he handed over the wrong document. He quickly corrected himself and then dropped everything as it was handed back to him. The reality of this run was very different from the thought of doing it. The sharpest corner was yet to be negotiated: H.M. Customs & Excise. He should have emphasised all this when buying the stuff off Rohit Alam. He could have paid less if he had told old Rohit exactly what it felt like to bring it through. Admittedly it was not his own cash and that was some consolation although he still cursed himself for not buying it cheaper.

Rohit Alam had not really taken any risks at all. True, he had come over the border to meet Bindi in his family's village. Half the Punjab was in Pakistan anyway and it was easy enough nowadays to cross over to the Indian part. This was the hard part of the job: Heathrow Customs.

His heart was pounding away like an old steam engine as he powered his trolley into the Green Channel. He took the entrance corner on the inside and pushed himself forwards before he could change his mind. The crowd thinned out as it passed the line of desks positioned each side of the corridor and Bindi looked quickly up and down the two rows at the empty tables. Empty! No Customs Officer in sight. The relief crashed over him like the crest of a wave. He stumbled and almost tripped over his own stupid feet.

"Sorry, sorry" he told himself, "but I've just smuggled through half a kilo of gear and I'm feeling light headed"!

A barrier of people, awaiting his arrival, cheered his safe return. He waved in return like a Bollywood star - in his dreams. He was, however, through, passed the people waiting for passengers off the Delhi flight and out into the freedom of the public concourse. I am THE MAN!

Balwinder Singh Gill put aside his luggage trolley picked up his suitcase and headed out the automatic doors to the passenger pick up point. He had never been so overwhelmed with emotion at seeing Joshi's BMW and his big, fat face smiling at him out of the driver's side window, the sound of Alisha's song "Made in India" blasting out from Joshi's mobile discotheque.

Joshi squeezed out the car and waddled over to meet his friend, the music spreading out from the open door to drown the sound of passing planes. Together they put the suitcase in the back of the BMW. They were both smiling like two children (or indeed adults) watching a Mr. Bean video. As Bindi sat down with a sigh in the passenger seat he slowly began to regain his self-respect. He breathed in and out deeply and then closed his eyes.

"How was it?" said Joshi.

8

"No problem. You women worry for nothing. Bindi the man has done the deed."

CHAPTER TWO

The breasts were bouncing high today and Archie's brass telescope was carefully (Oh! so very carefully) surveying the subtle variations in nipple movement. It was the big ones he was interested in: the ones which wobbled in the cross-wind. A vicious north-westerly cut across Lady Margaret Road from the direction of the A40 and caught the unsuspecting mammon glands as they rounded the corner of Archie's office and, from where he was perched, a good seventy feet above ground level, he had an outstanding cleavage eye view. It was, in short, fine sailing weather.

Archie was what the Americans would call a "trial lawyer." There was, alas, no money in breast spotting and, he knew that he would soon have to return to the prosecution papers in a particularly seamy, brothel-keeping case, with colour photographs, plenty of colour photographs requisitioned in unprecedented numbers by an enthusiastic vice squad - together with unnecessarily graphic, verbal descriptions by the arresting officers at the scene, and that prospect, contrary to his first expectations, did not fill him with joyful anticipation but rather it upset his emotional equilibrium. Hence the breast spotting.

The brass telescope, which was supported on a delightful wooden tripod with decorative silver inlay, prepared for another sweep of its limited albeit fruitful horizon when it came to rest, unusually, upon a face and, a unique occurrence in its contemporary history, upon a male face. Indeed, it probably had not been so used since it belonged to the headmaster of a well-known public school.

The face was familiar to Archie's eye: a young moustached a-la-Mexico mouth, golden framed glasses (reactorlight rapide), ebony almost Latin hair and a firm jaw. It was the face of a young man who Archie had intended to employ at some indistinct future date. Could it be ....? No, surely not, but then ...... Archie turned from the telescope in a bewildered state of mind and, in a rapid two fingered tattoo, summonsed his secretary on an internal number.

"Hello, Mr. Lord."

"Eleanor, when did we say that new fellow was to start here? That young chap with the face."

"Well that will make him stand out from the crowd," she teased him playfully.

"You know who I mean ...."

"Hold on," there was a humming pause, "it's reception," she explained and her voice disappeared again as abruptly as before. "Today," she continued after a muffled dialogue. "In fact he's downstairs," she concluded with glee. "Shall I send him up now."

"Repel boarders!" Archie shouted with mock-seriousness into the telephone.

"Does that mean no," she replied sweetly.

"It means, my dear, the end of life as we know it."

"No more blue tits in cold weather, Mr. Lord."

"Well, there's always you, my dear, to help me keep abreast of things so to speak" Archie dabbed his mouth with his handkerchief as he fantasised.

"And there's always your wife, Mr. Lord. Least we forget."

"As if I could," he mumbled the words more to himself than to his secretary and then he continued with the telephone conversation. "Well, send the bugger up then. Let's see if he's still the same conceited prat we offered the job to. Christ, why can't conveyancing have him?" He did not really expect an answer but he was pleased to receive the usual loyal grovel.

"Because you're the busiest partner at Messrs. Crawley and Dodgers, Mr. Lord. Now you can't deny that, can you darling?"

Mr. Christopher Larkin was a solicitor (he really was) and he had been so for nearly two whole days. Once he qualified he became a new man and as such he was determined to live a new life. This involved, understandably, a break with his old ways and, an important factor in his calculations, a complete change of habitat. One had to accompany the other. If he was to become a fast-car owning, fast-life leading, city wolf then, hardly surprisingly, he needed a city in which to prowl and growl and, accordingly, he left Afetside in Lancashire, which was a small village on the outskirts of Bolton which was itself on the outskirts of Manchester: they would only laugh at him there. Therefore he had packed his bags, kissed his mother goodbye, supped his last pint of Thwaite's ale - the last act being by far the most painful - and headed in high hopes to London town and his long awaited launch into life.

On the high-speed train journey from Manchester Victoria to London Euston, he contemplated his new employers in the confident knowledge that he had already created a good impression by his debonair "off the cuff" repartee. His joke about advising Socrates, - Christopher had specialised in the law of classical Athens at University -

had even prompted a titter of appreciation (at least he thought it was appreciation). It was true, however, that one of the partners had grimaced when he was able, entirely unaided, to quote all the recent authorities on commercial tenure - everyone should appreciate someone who really knows his stuff - but then, perhaps, that partner had suffered from post-lunch indigestion. Indeed, had Christopher stopped talking to consider the situation more carefully, then he may well have come to the conclusion that the whole interview panel suffered from some kind of similar disability and that no amount of Milk of Magnesia would ever be able to cure them of it. Indigestion being far easier to remedy than the emotional strain created by pompous young men.

Christopher wandered down to the buffet car, where a small number of jaded businessmen discussed computer systems over long tubes of tartan beer. He tried to start a conversation, when he joined the small buffet queue to purchase a cheese sandwich wrapped in cellophane, which tasted like a cellophane sandwich wrapped in cheese, but the cynical, worldly heavy weight, who he addressed his comments to, was either merely uninterested in what Christopher had to say or else wholly uninterested in him as a man or a boy or both. Perhaps it was simply that Christopher did not share the common plough of commerce and did not daily turn money around nor worry weekly about his rival's computer system. In short, it may have been that the man was not being rude nor was he being polite; he was just indifferent. Christopher did not exist as far as he was concerned; in his state of non-existence he could hardly be considered as a great conversationalist. Christopher did not mind. The man obviously did not know that he was a solicitor: a solicitor of the Supreme Court of Judicature no less. Had that fact been blazoned across his brow then he was sure that everyone would want to listen to everything he had to say.

Once Christopher had managed to choke down his sweaty sandwich and stain his red silk tie with splashes of lukewarm Scottish beer he started to think. After all, a train journey from one way of life towards another must be a time for reflection and assessment. The difficulty Christopher faced was that he had no yardstick by which he could measure the size of the break he was making in his life. Therefore he could not estimate it except by reference to the experience of others. He had tried it out first on his father as a working hypothesis.

"I'm going to London, Dad," he had announced one afternoon to the table-cloth sized Bolton Evening News, which faced him from the other side of the front sitting-room - always kept painstakingly neat and tidy by his mother just in case Her Majesty or lesser Royalty like Mrs. Stanmore-Smythe, chairwoman of the local Conservative party and secretary of the Women's Guild, should grace them with recognition - as he arrived home from a mind-stopping day of dreary intensity as an articled clerk at Bolton Town Hall (Department of Law, Administration and Waste Disposal). His father's existence behind the wall of refuge was undeniable because of the pipe smoke which emerged upwards in comfortable clouds. Finally his son's words sunk in as did the fact that they could not, on this occasion, be ignored.

Mr. George Larkin carefully folded up the Bolton Evening News in sharp, creased edges and once he had folded it up into the "normal" satisfactory square shape, of one quarter it's original size, a dimension which a lesser man would have settled for; he folded it again. And again. It then looked slightly absurd and, as this dawned on George Larkin, so did the fact that his son was watching his obsessive origami and, rather than sheepishly unfold it again, he pressed down on the newspaper with all his strength before placing it on the coffee table where, in the corner of his eye, he could see it start to unfold itself; but he chose to ignore that act of defiance since he had done all he could to force it into shape. Instead he contemplated this stranger over whom he had no control and who had started to unfold from the shape he had been crushed into. He removed the pipe from his mouth by the bowl and pointed the stem at his son as he spoke - the pipe could serve as a baton, gavel or miniature trumpet if the need arose - his wide-open farmer's eyes, with privet hedge eyebrows, tangled in intensity, met the full force of his son's pent-up, frustrated stare. "So," he said. "London," he continued in a slow measured tone as if he were imparting the meaning of life. "London," he repeated by way of emphasis "is, I hope tha knows, a very long way off."

"It's only three hours on the train, Dad."

"Aye, but not t'live there. It's a lifetime away. Why, you could be Town Clerk in Bolton, given time."

Time was one commodity Christopher did not have. His father seemed to view time as acres and acres of pasture which stretched far out to the horizon ahead of him from the great distance of the horizon behind: while beyond that was only time. To Christopher, time was a hand-brake which had been applied to stop him living. First, until he passed his "A-levels." Secondly, until he graduated from Manchester University with a degree in law and thirdly, and finally, until he obtained his professional exams and completed his two years articles. Well, now was the time for the brakes to be released so that the train could reach its fastest speeds. At over one hundred miles an hour, the Intercity express moved far too quickly for Christopher to be able to clearly discern the details of the countryside through which he passed. He was simply left with an image of shapes and colours without meaning since, at such fast speeds, he had no time to make sense of what he perceived.

Day one in the London Borough of Ealing was equivalent to day five of a tropical storm. Complete disorientation in a strange hotel where people called him "sir," which title, in itself, made him feel peculiar enough without being compounded and crippled, as he was, by a perpetual erection. It was as if his body was saying: "O.K. we've arrived, where's the orgy." Needless to say there was no orgy; indeed, the nearest he came to a sexual encounter was when he accidentally brushed hands with the barmaid when she handed him his second pint of tasteless ale. An attempt to raise the subject of the missing orgy or, for that matter, to discuss any subject at all with the barmaid was frozen solid when he referred to her in that quite proper Lancastrian form of address: "love." She gave him a double-barrelled blast of malevolent eyeballs, which almost rocked him off his bar-stool; this was the last emotion she ever showed him. From then, until he went to bed alone, she served his drinks rather like a mechanic

16

might oil a robot. Unfortunately when he stumbled down to breakfast the following morning in dire need of a, preferably female, smile he found to his dismay that the waitress in the breakfast bar wore the same body as the barmaid from the previous night and, what was much worse, she retained the same countenance. He couldn't however, complain to her about the taste of his coffee since she didn't bring him any to try. Whatever characteristics bubbled together to form the chemistry of little madam's temperament, magnanimity was clearly absent and, it could be safely asserted, forgiveness did not come naturally to her.

It was, probably, the fact that Christopher was close to starvation, that combined to deepen an already entrenched sense of anxiety, which he had stirred up to fever pitch by pot-holing in his own subconscious. An unattractive pastime but one which was inevitable when there were no mountains outside to climb. Would he really dazzle like the Sun in his new job or, like the Moon, would he break up into quarters under the strain? In any event, he made a fine first impression. Eleanor thank Jesus, Mary, Joseph and all the Saints in Christendom, actually smiled at him. His hands shook with excitement as he smiled back and he almost asked her out there and then, perhaps to marry him, but an instinct for survival stamped on his desires with a naked foot. At least he was welcome here.

"So! You're the new boy." She leaned over the typewriter and a few strands of red hair fell over her face to stab her in the eye - she brushed them aside as she spoke. "Do you wear dark glasses to look cool? Because if you do, I've got some good advice," she said in a light teasing tone.

"No, no, no," he said stupidly, Fearful that he might look less like Johnny Depp than a real prick. "They go like this with the Sun, they'll soon revert back to normal again. Anyway," he said defensively. "I've got sensitive eyes. The Optician said so, you see?" he added lamely.

"You clearly don't, not in those," she laughed. "Do you fancy a cup of coffee?" She stood up, a good head taller than Christopher, and walked around to his side of the desk. She wore a white silk blouse with a red cardigan, which went with her red hair, and a light sandy woollen skirt with the flecks of other colours woven lightly into the texture: brown, black, brick-red, blue and yellow particles could be traced "flicflac" through the cloth. The red strands seemed more prominent because of the drawing effect of the dominant cardigan colour.

"Well yes, if you think that's all right," he half-stammered and when she looked at him quizzically he continued: "I mean with whoever it is I'm supposed to be working with and that. What I mean is .... You know, ... with whoever it is who I'll be with. You see," he said and as it was quite apparent that she did not he tried to redeem the situation with the truth. It was a good move. "I'm a touch nervous about all this. First day and all that. I don't want to foul things up before I start so to speak."

"Oh that, don't worry. You're starting with the right bloke: Archie Lord. You can't possibly mess things up worse than him, he's a master of the craft of cockup."

"Oh," replied Christopher not a little crestfallen. "And he's the ......"

18

"…….. bloke you'll be working with," Eleanor finished his sentence for him. "Yes," she answered her own question. "And I'm his secretary. Besides he'll have another cup of coffee before he goes."

"Goes?" questioned Christopher.

"To Court, of course," retorted Eleanor. "Gosh! You are new to this, aren't you? A virgin novice, so to speak" she flashed a wicked, suggestive smile at him and Christopher tried hard not to blush.

"I wouldn't quite say that," he blurted out - too quickly.

"Why? Have you been to Court before?" she asked innocently and Christopher realised that he had fallen into a foolish trap of his own making.

"No, but ……" he started, only making matters worse.

"Then what did you mean?" she was clearly trying hard not to laugh as she asked the last question.

"Put him down, Eleanor," laughed Archie Lord who entered the room in search of a coffee cup.

Archibold Lord had the devil's face. A long chin which stretched his skin downward from high, prominent cheekbones. A long hooked nose overlooked by sharp diamond eyes and a high dome like brow which disappeared into a foliage of scattered silver-grey hair. It created an unavoidable and startling presence. "Hello Christopher," he thrust out a long arm which stabbed at him like an uncoiled snake. "Nice to have you aboard."

"Nice to be here," he replied stupidly as he shook the outstretched python.

"A somewhat rash assessment, I feel," laughed Archie. "Where's the coffee Eleanor, come on, shape up, only five minutes before we go over the top."

"You're always over the top and over the bloody hill as well, more's the pity," grumbled Eleanor with a half smile.

"Don't write me off yet. They made that mistake about Lazarus. Come on Christopher grab your coffee, follow me." Archie led the way through to his huge room which had two outside walls with a large window in each. It bore more resemblance to a greenhouse than an office: large pots of assorted indoor plants competed with one another to reach sunlight. They intertwined, tangled and knotted around each other so that the corner of the room between the two windows was like a miniature jungle. Archie's desk was small mock-antique with a torn red leather top which seemed to be completely dwarfed by its huge surroundings and, particularly, by the heavy basin-like leather chair, which had been swivelled around to face the window behind: so that Christopher saw only its back with, surprisingly, a large brass telescope supported on a tripod positioned close by the chair.

"Astronomy?" queried Christopher innocently.

Archie cleared his throat: "No, not exactly, no."

"Oh, just an ornament," continued Christopher as he went around one side of the desk to look at the telescope and possibly through it but Archie, who had dashed around the other side of the desk, forestalled him.

"Let's just say, I like nice things," he smiled knowingly. "This is my room. Perhaps you'd like to go around the other side of the desk, if you please."

"Oh, yes, of course, I'm sorry."

"Now, we've only got a few minutes, so drink your coffee. Have you done any Court work before, let's see? On your C.V. you said you'd done County Court applications before the District Judge. That leaves an awful lot of uncovered ground but then you're just out of Articles aren't you? And we're paying you all this money as well and you not having done a bloody thing in Court either, I don't suppose we can have some of it back until you know what you're doing? Sorry, only joking."

"Well, let me see," continued Archie, seemingly impervious to Christopher's feelings, as he fingered through a pile of files on his desk top. "I rather feel that all you can do at the moment is follow me. A sort of co-pilot until we dare let you loose to crash a few cases. Now, let me see, okay, yes that's it. We've only got a couple of remands here. More excrement than excitement today I'm afraid but it'll soon liven up, you see. I'll tell you what'll be a good idea - you do one of these remands. I say, are you all right? I mean I haven't shocked you into suicidal depression by suggesting that you carry your share of the load have I? Of course not, you're dying to make a first class fool of yourself in public. Don't worry your co-pilot will be next to you and I can resume the controls if you go into a tail-dive. It's the take off that's the problem. Once you've mastered that you're away. Provided you don't fly into a mountain or something, of course."

"Half this job is remands, they're your bread and butter. All remands are based on the proposition that Criminal Law is composed of clients who couldn't care less about their cases and can't be bothered to keep appointments with their lawyers who couldn't care less about their cases either but don't want to look stupid in Court. Hence they have to apply to remand a year old case, which has already been remanded six times, so that they can do the tricky things like take down their client's name and address and at least find out what he's charged with before the trial starts. Then, this poor old bugger, or someone like me, tries to work out what the case is about with sophisticated cross-examination of the arresting officer like: what exactly did you arrest my client for officer? Oh that's very interesting and did he do it do you know? He didn't by any chance tell you whether he had a defence did he officer because I'm dammed if I know? By the way officer do you happen to have his address so that I may submit my bill to the Law Society? That is why we remand; so that we don't have to ask questions like those. Sometimes we don't get the remand and then what do you do?" The rhetorical question hung over Christopher's head like a question mark. "A lot of noise. Plenty of objections. Don't say to yourself: Oh God, I haven't prepared lines of cross-examination, summonsed witnesses, researched law, taken proofs of evidence. Say, instead, thank God I haven't had to do any work on this case and it's the client's fault whatever happens, because he hasn't been to see me; so let's at least have some fun: advocacy without responsibility. Fun, that's what this is all about Christopher. Fun! If you're having fun the client will love you for it. He doesn't really care if he wins or loses. If he did then he'd have kept his appointments in the first place. Clients who keep their appointments are an awesome responsibility - they may truly be innocent. My God that's a worry! Clients who don't bother to come to your office just want to see a shit-hot lawyer enjoying himself by mauling the police officers. A good old verbal fireworks display."

"I don't know whether I can do that," replied Christopher with trepidation.

"You can't," snorted Archie with derision. "Not until you've been doing advocacy non-stop for ten years and, perhaps, not even then. The first qualification before you set foot through the court doors is enthusiasm. Fire in the belly. A resounding belief in the rights of the individual. Freedom, freedom to rape women, bugger children, murder the old and infirm, steal, ..." Archie burst out laughing after "steal" and as he did so he nodded his head back and forth; it reminded Christopher of a donkey baying on the farm where his father worked. "No seriously though, don't look so shocked young Christopher," he said as he wiped the tears of laughter from his eyes with his handkerchief which he then waved in the air like a flag of war. "Viva la human diversity!"

Christopher Larkin LL.B. Solicitor of the Supreme Court of Judicature, had imagined many possible "first day scenarios," which had all concluded with him being congratulated for his own brilliance and flair, but none of them had started quite like this. It was not simply the wobbly jelly of words which Archie had splattered all over the place. It was a more general ambience of anarchy. It may have been Archie's hook nose or, perhaps, the corner of a porn magazine he saw protruding from Archie's drawer - the photographs of brothel-keeping he could understand but then the magazine itself might belong to another case somewhere; although, somehow, he doubted it - or it may just have been Archie's unconventional dress: a large pink carnation together with a pink silk handkerchief flowering out of the top pocket of his white jacket spoke of flamboyant self-aggrandisement rather than civil rights; albeit Christopher had no doubt that Archie Lord was a first rate advocate, despite Eleanor's warning. Nobody would dare wear such a bright pink silk handkerchief in court unless they were the best lawyer in town or, at least, thought themselves so.

"Viva la legal aid orders." Viva la profit costs. Profit costs are all that matter," sung Archie in a rich booming voice which hit the musical notes of the Eton boat song like a sledgehammer. "Profit costs are all important. Profit costs are all that matter. Profit. Profit, costs," Archie ushered Christopher out of the building in a flurry of song with a hand blown kiss for Eleanor and a salute for the long suffering elderly and nearly deaf receptionist of Messrs. Crawley and Dodgers and Co. She, at least, was spared the pain.

Ealing Magistrates' Court was the hospital for sick causes which had seemingly no chance of recovery. They limped forward half-heartedly with their explanations: I kicked him in the head in self-defence, while he was laying on the ground, I know I was picked out on the identity parade by my mother but I wasn't there, if I can only have bail I will break a ten year drug addiction and start work as a stockbroker on Monday. If the doctors at this hospital were the lawyers, then Archie Lord regarded himself as a consultant. He administered first aid to many a hopeless cause and neatly and cleanly buried the dead ones. Are you saying he fell on the floor after attempting a Kung Fu flying kick at your body? Why does your mother hate you so? By stockbroker do you mean pawn-broker? And so, with a combination of psycho-therapy and a surgical dissection of the truth with the associated suppression of inconvenient facts, the causes looked and gradually became more outwardly presentable until, after a great deal of hard work and careful nursing, they finally walked off the operating table and into the jury room.

Christopher was lost in admiration at the adroit manipulation of method and man by the master of his craft: Archie Lord. He objected strongly in one Court and then shuffling his words like a pack of cards, he agreed to the same point in another - "the client didn't want to take that point he wanted it dealt with today," he whispered conspiratorially to Christopher behind the back of his hand - he managed to deal with attacks on his rear effortlessly, which Christopher knew by reading the file had really caught him unprepared; he dealt with applications for bail by using tatty scribbled notes alone, he smiled and joked at every opportunity he could, and he was clearly a very popular man. Even the police admired him.

"I never go to police stations," hissed Archie in a confidential aside. "The court image is the thing. It doesn't do to get your hands dirty. Besides what cricket team would choose to play away from home if they had a choice?"

It seemed to Christopher that everything Archie Lord had to say about criminal law must be true because he was so successful at it. However, when he had practised at Bolton and, on rare occasions, had come into contact with criminal lawyers at local Law Society gatherings of one kind or another, he had been told that police station visits were an essential part of their work both for the clients and for themselves as a source of new business. Yet when he voiced this concern to Archie Lord he received a rather different opinion.

"If you have to go to a police station to pick up work you've not much flair in court," he asserted pompously.

"Nonsense," the word bellowed out like a trumpet call. "What crap are you serving up to our young brethren?"

A large hulk of a man waddled down the corridor radiating assurance and contempt in equal measure. For an unexpected second or three, Archie's brilliance was eclipsed not by an obstruction of his own glowing genius but rather by the distinctive strength of character of this new arrival on the scene who so clearly caused Archie Lord, for the first time in Christopher's eyes, to feel and look exceedingly uncomfortable. "My name's Joe Bailey," a great fat banana sized grin spread across a large pumpkin head, just underneath a squash tomato nose - like a Negro, Christopher thought - while wrinkled prune eyes were preserved carefully under glass - National Health glasses, decided Christopher, the old sort with thick black frames - they surveyed him quietly and unmovingly like a lizard about to fire out its tongue and stun a passing fly. Christopher looked down to observe a huge leg of pork waiting to hold his hand. He submitted his pen-pushing fingers to the ritual crushing - a habit they had become accustomed to by his father's farming friends - and he tried hard not to grimace. Joseph Bailey's crumbled yellow checked jacket may not have been picked off the floor that very morning, after having been used to polish the tiles; but, if it hadn't, then it must surely have been purchased just recently from the local Salvation Army stores. The yellow trousers he wore - yellow trousers! - had a distinctive crease: in many different places; whereas, his tie was difficult to distinguish from a thick piece of rope which had acquired an unusual yellow plaid appearance from constant handling with nicotine hands.

"I thought you'd been struck off Joe," commented Archie gloomily.

"No, they only do that if you fiddle the books Archie. Now you know that you will be more careful won't you? All I do is insult, abuse and regularly sue police officers who may kick and squirm and write letters of complaint to the Law Society but, fortunately, they can't get me struck off for that in this Country, yet, I hope," he added ponderously. "Although to give them credit, they do try awful hard."

"Do you do crime then?" questioned Christopher nervously.

"Do I do crime?" bellowed Joe from the very depths of his lungs spewing forth fine particles of pipe tobacco as he did so and covering Christopher with the scented aroma of Golden Virginia. "I am crime in the London Borough of Ealing. Old Archie here just acts the part in my absence don't you Archie?"

"Less of the old, please. My hair may have gone grey sitting through your boring speeches year after year, or, should I say, decade after decade; but I'm still your junior by many years."

"Oh yes, of course, and by ability as well Archie Lord. Ha! Has he told you young Christopher what an arse hole he is? No, I don't suppose he has. And I suppose he hasn't mentioned his dazzling Parliamentary career?"

"No, I haven't actually," retorted Archie stuffily as he walked unsuspectingly into Joe's verbal ambush. The true artist of cross-examination never stops practising his strokes.

"That's because he hasn't had one," laughed Joe heartily. "He's lost more elections our Archie has than England's lost test matches to Australia."

"Get stuffed, Joe. If I ever do get there, I'll bring in a special statute to deal with you: the Abolition of Fat Lawyers bill will do the trick, I think."

"Ha! With all this sizeist rhetoric I may well not tell you the latest piece of gossip from the Southall streets," Joe's eyes twinkled , "the Smoke are back in business with a new load and the word has it that the Tooti Nung are not happy bunnies."

"Any arrests," asked Archie feigning indifference.

"Would I tell you if there were," winked Joe: "Archie, the Prince of Darkness."

"Hold on. Swallow your retort Joe, that was my case they called on in court five. Remand for Advance Disclosure - our last case of the morning. I'll just, wait, no, I'm forgetting something here. Here you are Christopher, your first court appearance," Archie ceremoniously handed over the dread file to his apprehensive assistant - "Oh, my God does he really want *me* to do this," panicked Christopher - while Archie winked cunningly at Joe. The latter did not return his gesture but merely watched impassively. "You've read the file, haven't you. Well, go on then, don't keep the court waiting," beamed Archie and in an aside to Joe he said: "Let's watch over our young friend's loss of virginity. Come on Joe, you might learn something."

The three magistrates did not exist for Christopher because he was too self-conscious to see them as three people adjudicating upon a cause. Instead he felt them as omnipotent Gods who were floating about in the fog somewhere above his head and were not deliberating upon his client but rather upon him personally. They had stripped him naked and were examining through a microscope his various failings in minute detail. There was a silence as he found his lonely seat in the front row. The silence continued. Someone had to do something to stop it and so Christopher stood up.

"I would like to apply for ...." he started with short, clipped, separate words which did not seem to come from his mouth and which were concluded abruptly by the court clerk with his razor tongue.

"Sit down!"

"Yes, oh right, I'll ....."

"The Defendant in this case your worships is Mr. Patrick O'Rourke of no fixed abode. Is that you, sir? (the Defendant nodded). He's charged with having on the twenty first of this month entered enclosed premises with intention to steal, do you understand?" asked the clerk.

"Yes," replied Christopher mindlessly.

"I wasn't asking you," retorted the clerk bitterly. "On account of the fact that you are qualified, I had assumed, perhaps wrongly, that this modicum of knowledge was within your grasp," the clerk glared at Christopher who felt a second skin of moisture grow over his face and on the palm of his hands which he rubbed nervously onto the kneecaps of his trousers. What would Archie do now? He turned to the row behind to see that his co-pilot had placed his hand on the top of his knuckles, which were resting on the podium in front of him. He was hiding his face. Christopher gulped and stood up once again. It was not the right move to make.

"Sit down!" barked the clerk. "I wonder sir," he continued malevolently, "whether you would kindly permit the Crown Prosecution Service to outline the brief facts before you rush in with your words of wisdom which, I can assure you, we are all as equally impatient to hear as you obviously are to orate?"

"Oh, but I ….. er …… I just wanted to ……"

"Don't we all, Mr. Larkin. Don't we all. But they say all things come to those who wait," jeered the clerk; most of the other advocates in the room, who had just noticed "the novice-bait" for the first time, started to titter. Christopher returned to his seat again and his sweaty hands clasped each other for comfort: the fingers of one hand tangled with those of the other, like Japanese wrestlers slipping and sliding but unable to lock together because of the sweat dripping off their bodies. Christopher did not hear what Miss. Alison Pull, the C.P.S. solicitor said. It could have been a lecture on the porcelain produced during the early Ming dynasty delivered in fluent Mandarin for all Christopher knew. His stomach was turning somersaults over his pancreas and his eyes had the same glazed fixed look of sheer terror and low self-esteem exhibited by a rabbit who senses the inevitable and unavoidable approach of the unseen fox. Consequently Christopher did not notice the conclusion of the C.P.S. speech. He did not notice the impatient throat-clearing cough of the clerk nor did he, alas, notice the puzzled expression of the magistrates. He did, however, hear a voice ring out from the dock behind him.

"I be thinking that my brief wants a remand for this 'onourable court to be sending him h'advance disclosure of the prosecution case against meself," announced "Paddy" O'Rourke. "And I'm thinking that we'll settle for two weeks, what have you to say to that now, my young man with the L-plates on?"

"Y-e-s," agreed Christopher amid stifled laughter and hand-muffled guffaws from his fellow professionals.

"Thank you Mr. O'Rourke," concluded the clerk with malicious glee "for representing Mr. Larkin today."

When Christopher tumbled out of the court room he avoided eye contact with everyone and forgot to approach his client, who, nevertheless, approached him and gave him an unwelcome and humiliating bear-hug: "I'll be giving me lessons in Irish blarney at the Glassy Junction Public House tonight, if you've a mind to come down an' share a glass or two," he said with beer soaked vowels.

"We can all learn a lot from you, Paddy," laughed Archie who separated the two men. "But I think it would be a good idea for you to go off and drink the first few gallons with your cronies now." Patrick bowed in reply and Joe Bailey kicked him in the bottom as he did.

"Getting ideas above your station Paddy," he joked and the two men pretended to fight. "Nicking my clients again Archie!" he laughed and let Patrick O'Rourke wander off before he winked at the broken Christopher Larkin who felt like Humpty Dumpty after the fall.

"Well, did you learn anything, Joe," teased Archie.

"Oh yes I did, Archie. I learnt a lot about you but then I knew most of it already."

"Oh suit yourself. Come on, Chris, you've had the ritual humiliation and I think I owe you a tea. You've got better things to do, haven't you, Joe. And if you haven't I'm sure you'll find them."

CHAPTER THREE

"Well, what do you expect. I should live in India is that what you're saying? For fuck's sake, I just got back in May and he expects me to go to the mother country again. Thinks I should live there, I guess. Trust that sad sod Jasbir Sood to get himself tangled up with rag tag rubbish like the Nung in the first place. Someone had to do something to stop him selling and it fell to me. It fell to me, didn't it? No other fucker was volunteering as I recall although everyone else was talking about it. Talking is our most skilful frame. Talking is what we're best at, I guess. What with Baljeet, Devvy and Nirmal inside for a long time there wasn't a lot of choice, unless you count Satish of course. But Satish, my friend, you cannot do everything, can you? So, I do it. The fucker lives, I don't know how. The kidneys, the bladder and the lung, but still he lives. He still lives now, but no-one knows where. No-one cares no more. He doesn't name me so I don't care neither. Everyone knows its me anyhow and the police, well the police they lift me: not once, not twice but three fucking times. I ask you, do they do that when we get done? Perhaps they're signed up members of Tooti Nung. Perhaps they are or perhaps they don't like the Smoke. Perhaps that's it. They don't like us because we're cleverer than them. Anyhow they lift me and, unlike you women, I keep it shut. I get my brief down to the station, I sweat it out. And I'm out. I'm out without a whisper. No witnesses, no forensic and no, NO confession. So now the police they've got other troubles and I've been to our village in the Punjab until it calms down and here I am with half a kilo of gear and you're saying I should go back again. You're wetting yourselves! Why? Just because Mukesh has blown his mouth off. What is this? I'm ashamed of you. I spit on you all."

"Cool it Bindi, cool it down," Satish lifted both hands palm up and he brought them down like a fan as if to physically cool the famous hot temper of his close friend and comrade Balwinder Singh Gill known as "Bindi" to his friends. "You're not being fair here. Okay so you've pulled off a decent run. Though where you found the money for it or the balls to bring it through I don't know. As for us, well we're at our lowest, the lowest we've been for a long time. But so are they. When Devvy and the others went down, well that was the end of the old Smoke. You carving them up pissed off the Nung. But now? There's a lot of loose ends hanging around now, lots of different gangs, and Mukesh and Anil "Jumbo" Sood have picked up what they can for their boys. You don't want to discount Mukesh - he's loony, whacko. They call him "mad" Mukesh and for good reason. He stabbed Sangi and tried to blow away Joshi here, I'm sure of it. He still has the gun and the balls to use it: he's a killer that one but he ain't been charged for fuck all. He was nicked, sure; but, like you, he ain't a great talker to the police, though they held him for three days. They also say he stabbed "Kenny" Kanth but I don't think so, Anil Sood, Jasbir's brother, did that for sure. To prove his worth, and now he'll want to prove he's a good brother too. Watch your back, Bindi. The others, well they ain't up to much, 'though they've got a lot of mouth'.

"They're rubbish, Anil's rubbish, Mukesh is trash. He's nothing. Worse than nothing. He's a bare arsed peasant whose family got kicked off their land for not paying the rent and lived off the City sewers like the trash they are. They still do. Sewer rats, that's all they are; they're not human, they're dirt. Just dirt, Filth."

"Filth with a gun though Bindi. And with the guts to use it." Satish sat back in his chair and fluttered his long, feminine lashes, which hid street-hard eyes, at Bindi and waited for the reality of what he had said to sink in. They were both sitting around a table on wicker chairs, with two other members of the Holy Smoke, in the Shahanshah. An unlikely rendezvous but one which guaranteed a certain amount of privacy nonetheless. The table was cluttered with smoking accoutrements: matches, lighters, tax free Dunhill International cigarettes and the screwed up, golden foil-coated paper from the newly opened packets. Everyone was drinking milky sweet Indian tea, that is everyone except Balwinder Gill, who had drunk enough tea on the subcontinent to last him a lifetime: he drank Nescafe black and very strong instead.

The Shahanshah was situated opposite a small green on North Road which runs parallel to the Lady Margaret Road, across the road from the Plough Public House in Southall. The café in which the boys were sat was at the end of a row of shops which included the Shahanshah Travel Agents and next door to the café an old fashioned gentleman's hairdresser shop which seemed to belong to a different time and place. Everyday the café offered a large take-away menu of sweet meats and savouries including, it boasted on its street window, Chaats (five types), Masala Dosa, Makki Kinoti and Saag. It also served cold salted lassi for hot Summer days and spicy Indian tea with fennel, cardamom seeds and milk mixed in the pot together with curious delicacies ranging from panin samosas to chilli pastries, and this guaranteed its success among Punjabi men who wanted to entertain without spoiling their appetite for home-cooking. It was also a place where Punjabi women could be safely seen in each others company without being mistaken for those who forsook reputation by frequenting the local pubs and, unlike the other local sweet centres and restaurants, it was, perhaps this was its biggest attribute, easily accessible by car. It was also free from busy bodies and informers, who frequently reported the gossip of the public bars.

Balwinder lit a cigarette and then nervously pulled it from his mouth, tapped his fingers on the table, finished his bitter coffee with a grimace, and stared at each of the three gang members in turn.

"Well, I don't know what you expect Bindi," retorted Joshi, an overweight pudding faced man in his mid-twenties with large gold rings on his sausage shaped fingers and even larger red rings on his enormous arse where the fat had probably saved his life. "To take out Mukesh is that what you expect. He blasted me with a shot-gun you know. He nearly killed me, innit. He was always a tough little nut, even at school. He's not twenty even now. And when he'd carved up Sangi; he did it proper nasty innit. Poor Sangi, he ain't come out since. He's been in shock so they say. Won't even answer his door. Lost one eye and most of his nose so they say. They say ...."

"They say this and they say that," interrupted Bindi. "I say bollocks, that's what I say. And I say we hit him before he hits us ---- and I mean us. If he doesn't hit me and if I go back to India like you say, do you really think you will all be left alone to play snooker when you want to, sell stuff when you want to, cruise around how you feel. Well do you? Devvy put the Nung off the street, wiped them out; well, now he's inside and he ain't coming out for a long time and now they think Mukesh is the man. He's got together a little tatty band of peasants and you've all had it so soft for so long that you're wetting yourself as soon as competition appears. Either that or you're listening to smart arsed , smart mouthed tricksters like Yankee Bender when you should be listening to me. Perhaps that's it. Perhaps Bender wants me to go back to India. Perhaps I cramp his style. Perhaps you all agree with bent Parminder, the great law "Bender," and perhaps you all want me out. What you all forget is that I helped to break the Nung. This isn't the old Tooti Nung that Devvy and I and the others and Satish here put off the streets permanently. The Canada Kid - was he around when we had real business to do? No, now all we're facing is a group of kids. The old Smoke members would piss them away. You, Joshi, you don't know because you were at B.A. at the time. Now you've left work or, perhaps I should say, the work left you ---- them laying people off an' all and now you've found you can make a decent screw flogging gear. And you can shift more gear than an ice-cream man can shift ices on a hot day. I'll give you that Joshi," Bindi slapped Joshi's fat face with his right hand, causing his white gold bangle to slide down his arm as he did so: Joshi glared back and then chuckled loudly: his shoulders vibrating up and down as his fat lips peeled back in a sick grin to hide his hurt and humiliation. Bindi slapped him again harder with a resounding thwack so that Joshi's whole face wobbled as if it were likely, at any moment, to fall off his head. Some other people in the café turned to look in curiosity and Bindi, who was momentarily tempted to follow up his second slap with a nose-squashing thump, smiled dangerously instead. "If Mukesh cut off your balls Joshi, no-one would notice. Now when you sell this latest stuff it'll already be cut up and messed in, so I don't want you messing it down no more. And it'll already be in ten pound deals and I don't want you breaking it down. You get too big a slice as it is. Because if you do, and that goes for you Khaki," Bindi looked at the large-eyed, lean faced young man next to Joshi. "Then I'll invite you into the gents at the Snooker Hall with Satish and some others one evening and the cleaning ladies can call the ambulance to clear away the bits in the morning: if there's any point by then."

"Cut out all this stuff," said Satish angrily. "What's got into you Bindi. You're among friends here. There's no need for all that heavy talk. Here we are, we've got some cash, we've got something to sell, we're all meeting up down the Half Way House in half an hour or so. Everyone's happy. We can pass some of your stuff round then. You and I were up half the night breaking it down and mixing it in. We'll have so much money in a few weeks we'll be using it for wallpaper," Satish laughed and looked toward Joshi and Khaki who dutifully obliged by laughing in return. Bindi looked down at the glowing ember of his cigarette and his skin was drawn tight over his cheekbones so that his facial scars stood out in long purple lines across his smooth brown skin on both sides of his face. He wore those scars proudly since the day he had won them in an altercation outside the Glassy Junction Public House when he had leapt in to rescue Devvy, a few months before the latter had, together with Baljeet, Nirmal and some friends, killed one Nung member and seriously injured three others in a notorious knife fight inside the Southall Snooker Hall, which was from that day undisputed Holy Smoke territory, and, since admission to the Hall was strictly controlled by membership only, it became the haven of the gang, until the old membership gradually drifted away, married or went to prison. Bindi was trying hard to revive it once again with mixed success.

"Surinder also brought some crack back from New York. A whole load of it. But we can't sell it here. Not for much anyhow. Yet it's supposed to be the in-thing in the States, so Parminder, I mean Bender, says. And he should know. Him having lived in Canada an' all. I can't understand it. And I'm telling you guys that if I can't move it along then no-one can. Can they? 'Kay? That's fair, innit?" Joshi looked at Bindi nervously as he spoke.

"Dickhead," jeered Balwinder Gill, "They must have seen him coming. It's got as much buzz as a flat battery. It's so bad it's probably legal. Anyway, if customers want choc-ices, do you sell them peach-melba? Well, you're the ice-cream salesman, so you tell me: do you? Do you dickhead? No of course they don't. Surinder's an idiot. Bender's a fool. Thinks he knows everything and he knows his dick's for peeing out of but he hasn't worked out if it'll do anything else for him yet. Sometimes I think you're all idiots and dickheads 'cept for Satish here. Why go risking your neck with customs bringing in stuff that nobody wants not even the pigs. You gotta understand market forces.

There's gotta be a demand first. No-one I know takes crack so how are you gonna sell it? Bender he listens to all the crap they tell him over there and he doesn't think. Well that stupidity is costing us and it'll cost him. He ain't sharing in yet. He's got to make a proper run with a proper drug before he's in and he's not a member of the Smoke till he's either done that or carved up Mukesh. It's his choice. No, on second thoughts count him out until he's made a run. Not from New York where he takes no risk with customs anyhow - from the sub-continent with gear or hash: black preferably. I'll take care of Mukesh since all you women would all wet yourselves thinking about it."

"I'll wet myself if I can't go, Mummy. Mummy, mummy, I w-a-n-t t-h-e t-o-i-l-e-t NOW!"

"Oh, Lacki you can wait can't you? You've been wanting, wanting all the time. Pulling me all over town, I've bought you toys. I've bought you sweets, now I want a pot of tea and you're just playing me up because you want McDonalds" an eighteen year old mother of a three year old boy was trying unsuccessfully to control him on the table next to that occupied by the boys. Joshi turned around to stab the young mother with his eyes after her robust little boy had banged against Joshi's chair in an effort to evade his mother's arms. "I'm sorry, so sorry mister," she said as she looked down at the floor to avoid his look of superior contempt.

"You should control your stupid brat," he retorted helpfully.

"Are you listening to me!" shrieked Bindi with air-cutting clarity. Joshi turned to him wearing a suitable expression of remorse and Bindi continued in a lower, harsher tone: "When I'm speaking, I expect you to listen, fathead."

The café was gradually filling up with week-day regulars and several solemn self-important businessmen, one of whom ordered by harsh command, to show off to the other equally solemn and self-important businessmen. The alpha male asserts his authority. When Bindi had first met his fellow Smokes, they were the café's only customers. Strangely enough, it was the comradeship of his peers which had been much missed by Bindi when he had been in India helping his cousin to market films from his backstreet studio in the Punjab sitting for hours at a time on the family bed outside among the chickens, the servants and the sunshine. It was a different sunshine in the Punjab: clear, crisp and dazzling unlike the sad rays which fell on Southall. True, he had felt the passionate, religious and political feelings of independence, which bubbled up in conversations, newspapers and broadcasts all around Bindi; but which, nevertheless, left him curious but completely unmoved. It seemed to him as if some of the Sikhs were lining up to die for a dream rather than for cash which was all that really counted in Bindi's world. Life in the West was far simpler for Bindi to grasp since, to his perception, it was really only about money; whereas life in the Punjab was about many other things as well. Moreover, in Southall everywhere was within walking distance and everything was familiar and fitted easily into a simpler view of the world: he knew who his friends were and even his enemies gave him comfort by being easily recognisable. He knew what he could buy and where he could buy it and, more importantly, where it could be sold. He knew what would

41

happen if the police caught him and what his rights were - he knew this although he did not know how to read and write in Punjabi albeit he could speak his parent's first language fluently - and experience had taught him that being guilty in England did not mean being found guilty: whereas, in India, innocence was rarely a successful defence without political, religious or administrative contacts, who could ease you out unscathed from the labyrinthine, bureaucratic machinery. It was, therefore, with initial contentment that Balwinder Singh Gill had met up with his friends after the anxiety and fear of the flight: carrying five years of prison time in the lining of his luggage. The relief he felt on seeing Joshi's BMW parked in the passengers "pick up" lane was almost solid to the touch. In that moment he loved his friends immensely - the moment soon passed.

Bindi brought his cup of Nescafe to his lips as his eyes flashed over the brim to out-stare the suppliant Joshi whose little eyes darted hither and thither to avoid him. Khaki, who looked as if nature had supplied him with Joshi's eyes by virtue of some perverse genetic error, nodded his thin lean face to indicate to the other that something important had caught the attention of his huge disc-like sockets. Bindi half turned in his chair and immediately nodded in reply to a half wave from his brief Archie Lord.

"Spending my money, Archie. All that cash I earned you," he shouted in a tone which was nearly, but not quite, jovial.

"*You* earned me? Don't make me laugh, Bindi. By the way, this is my new assistant, Christopher Larkin.

Christopher this is some of my best customers. Mr. Satish Brar ….."

"Mr. Balwinder Gill," interrupted Bindi with a wide forced smile. "I'm the only one you need to know. The others do as I say, ouch," he turned to Satish who had kicked him under the table. "Only joking, Satish. What's with you."

"I don't like to be made small in front of Archie or that stuffed prick he's got with him," he replied in Punjabi while outwardly he smiled and nodded to the two lawyers who smiled in acknowledgement before they sat down at a table by the window. "You're not the big-shot you like to think you are. You're not Devvy so you can stop acting like him."

"Aren't I," replied Bindi also in Punjabi, "Well, perhaps, I'll take care of mad Mukesh as I took care of Anil's brother and, perhaps, I'll put the Nung off the streets. Perhaps it needs me to pull this thing together. Perhaps you don't see that but perhaps it's true."

"Shit!" exclaimed Satish. "That stuffed prick just tried to drink his tea and missed his mouth. Ha Ha! He's just burnt his balls with hot water by the looks of it. Well if he don't know how to drink a cup of tea, I'm damned if he'll represent me."

"Let's see," Bindi turned around excitedly as did Joshi while Khaki stood up to get a better view. Meanwhile, Christopher Larkin, who was busy stuffing paper serviettes down the front of his trousers, looked towards them furtively in the vain hope that they had not seen what had happened. He was not that lucky.

"I think I've lost my balls," said Bindi in a high pitched voice to the others at his table. "Never mind I'll make some new ones out of paper."

"Notice he chooses white paper," laughed Joshi.

"Don't be crazy, he'd look really stupid with black balls," jeered Satish kicking Joshi under the table as he spoke.

"Here's one of yours; you better put it back inside your trousers," replied Bindi as he flicked a small chocolate coated peanut at Joshi. The latter flicked it back and soon peanuts were flying across the table from each direction.

"Those are too big for Joshi's balls," laughed Satish.

"They also taste better."

"How would you know."

"Filthy pig, you haven't eaten Joshi's balls, have you?"

"No wonder he walks funny."

"Come on, let's cruise," stated Bindi and he slapped his hands on the table as he spoke. "We can leave Joshi's balls behind," he stood up and lit a cigarette. "Come on," he repeated impatiently. "We've got some business to conduct."

"'Kay, 'kay," complained Joshi who moved as quickly as his fat body would allow. The group wondered out of the door, with a half wave to Archie Lord, and towards the sleek silver BMW which waited outside like a loyal stallion.

"We'll go in Joshi's BMW: silver coloured and silver fast," smiled Satish.

"Where're we gonna cruise to," grumbled Joshi. "I mean besides Half Way House. Once we've done that, I mean. We need to do something special and interesting. It gets kinda boring just hanging around till the evening. 'Kay you can push a little gear here and there and that's fine as far as it goes; but I wanta get a buzz out of living."

"Kill Mukesh," sneered Bindi under his breath as he slid gracefully along the pavement towards the BMW in long strides causing Joshi to wobble rapidly from one jellied leg to the other in order to keep up with him. "That's being alive. That's a buzz of pure electricity. That's your body so charged, it'll take you weeks to come down.

"I don't like violence," mumbled Joshi, "'Kay so I admit it."

The four young men cruised down the traffic choked Broadway thorough fare with the top down: passed fruit and vegetable stalls, which protruded across the pavement - to the kerb itself; passed Indian women with gold and silver bangles and red green and gold sarees; passed friends who called out "Hi," and sullen enemies, who glared ill-will; passed old Sikh men with turbans, beards and plenty of God; passed wealthy landlords and shop-owners, who spent the hot afternoon drinking salted Lassi and talking socio-religious politics; passed the sound of a film-track, from "Border" which was one of many thousands of popular Indian films, which blared out full volume from a general store, passed a jeweller's shop: selling tax free to overseas visitors; passed Bindi's mother .....

"Hey, what you doing?" shouted Satish. "That's your mum."

"For fuck's sake," complained Bindi about himself as he hid his own face with an open palm. "Keep cruising and hide my ciggy, I don't want mum to see me smoking. My mind's going into overdrive thinking about Mukesh and how I'm going to do him. It's either that, or it's Joshi here moaning like a woman all the time. A fat woman," he punched Joshi's stomach jokingly. "A pregnant woman!"

"I told him to take precautions but he wouldn't listen," laughed Satish.

"You should've gone on the pill Joshi," jeered Bindi, glad to change the subject from his mother who fortunately had not seen him or, if she had, affected not to.

"He did," retorted Satish. "But he thought they were Smarties and the greedy pig ate the whole packet in one go." Satish sat in the front passenger seat with Joshi whereas "Kenny" and Bindi sat behind: Joshi, the driver and victim of the verbal jest, stared gloomily at the car ahead, which had an orange flag tied to the boot aerial together with a large cardboard Kanda displayed from its rear window. Joshi studied it intently.

"What you looking miserable for?" asked "Kenny" looking through the gap between the two front-seat, head-rests at a sour-faced Joshi, who was pretending to be concentrating too hard on his driving to hear.

"What do you think?" he retorted balefully.

"Leave him alone," said Bindi with a down turned smirk on his lips, half looking back at "Kenny," "It's that time of the month, isn't it Joshi?"

"Where are we going?" asked "Kenny" more to change the subject than to request real information.

"We'll go to the Half Way House an' then cruise," replied Bindi simply. "Chill out my friends, chill out."

"Let's go to Wembley and see my cousin," shouted Satish excitedly as he reached over to fiddle with the radio-cassette player and finally managed to produce some smooth American soul sounds with a funky life-surging beat. The atmosphere in the car changed and everyone felt tough, mean and cool.

"I don't care where we end up - as long as we cruise, cruise, cruise," smiled "Kenny" with a doleful laid-back look. Everyone smiled in approval not only at what he had said but also at the way that he had said it: it was exactly right for the feelings that they had - an accurate, expression of emotion.

"C-r-u-i-s-i-n-g," drawled Bindi in reply as they all wound down their windows to let the world share the affluent sounds of perfect people in love emanating, ironically, from a car load of frustration and hate. However, both of those emotions were, temporarily, suspended by the subtle combination of melody and style: not only to listen to their superior sounds but to see the whole world watching them so listening. There was surely no other feeling quite so pleasing to both the ego and the senses.

They parked behind the Half Way House and no-one left the car. Joshi waved at someone who was clearly waiting for them to arrive. He sauntered over to the car oozing arrogance underneath a peak cap, worn sideways on.

"How's tricks," he said bending down to Joshi's level.

"Hanging in there, innit."

"Got the stuff."

"As always. Where's the cash."

"As always, man."

"You owe me, innit."

"I'll pay, how about we shoot some pool at the Glassy later."

"It's always later, well the stuff comes later then, innit"

"Suit yourself," the stranger saw the other boys and sauntered back to the Half Way House again.

"Shit," said Bindi, "Has no-one got no cash no more. Let's shoot some pool at the Club. This can get sorted later, let's chill out for a while at the Club."

The Southall Snooker Hall was the place to hang loose on a pointless afternoon, as most afternoons were. The only white people to enter the Snooker Hall were social workers or the like - trying to be ethnic. The Hall had an even more specialised clientele following the incident which led to the conviction of "Devvy" and his comrades for murder so that now the only members of the Hall were also either members of the Smoke or else affiliates, "hangers-on" or players. The Snooker Hall was owned by the five Sidhu brothers, who specialised in establishments catering for the young, Asian male, and, without any feelings of shame or remorse, they also quite happily owned a pool and weight-training centre, with a coffee bar annexe, which was frequented predominantly by the Tooti Nung. Moreover, they either owned or had shares in several other snooker halls, "entertainment" centres, with gaming machines, and public houses scattered around Southall, Wembley, Ealing and Hounslow. Officially none of the five brothers, being practising Sikhs, touched alcohol at all but unofficially three of them drank little else and one was a hopeless alcoholic; he was usually left to drink himself sober at the Snooker Hall in a caretaker role, which simply involved ensuring that no-one tore the tables, while the two elder brothers, who were rarely seen, ran all the business from their own "Accountants" firm on the

Broadway; although the firm could not boast a single chartered or certified qualification it nevertheless, assisted a large number of other local firms to avoid irksome taxation and VAT. Thus, it could not be disputed, the Sidhu brothers were exceedingly wealthy men as a result of their commercial acumen.

Marway Sidhu was precariously balanced on a bar stool drinking Teacher's Scotch and watching the bar television; meanwhile, various nephews, cousins, employees and other lackeys of one kind or another were serving him drinks as well as attending to the other customers, cooking the restricted but tasty range of snacks, waiting on the tables in the eating area and, occasionally, checking the membership cards of the rare, strange faces. One such servant of the great Sidhu empire made the mistake of approaching Bindi with the object in mind. The latter pushed him away with a two handed shove which sent him sprawling, bottom first, onto the floor.

"Hey! What is this! Have you a card indeed? Of course I haven't got a card. I'm Balwinder Gill and I don't need one. That's right, isn't it Marway."

"Bindi, Bindi, Bindi. Don't you goes pushing my peoples about do you hear," Marway Sidhu wagged one finger of a shaking hand at Balwinder Gill whilst looking at him with glassy, pickled eyes. He then turned to the man who had just stood up, who was now shaking with anger, and he put a restraining hand on his shoulder. "He's a member and you're new; so go do the washings up like I told you and in future wait until I tell you to challenge someone before you do: you've a lot to learn if you want to stay in this country and work and up to now, you're not learning so fast, now go to the kitchen. Go, Go," he commanded. "You," announced Marway Sidhu pointing to Balwinder Gill once more: "you come here: you tell me how things are at home. I haven't seen you since you came back. I hope you remember why I want to talk to you. Now, sit here, come here, sit next to me." Bindi reluctantly complied as the others wandered off to the snooker tables and joined in a group who crowded around the cigarette machine at the other end of the hall. The section where Bindi sat with Marway was partitioned off from the large spread of hall proper, which extended down one side of a small street, contained ten full sized snooker tables together with five small pool tables, an equal number of video games and half a dozen gambling machines. It was in the main hall that the other members of the Smoke were waiting for Bindi to join them; he was anxious to do just that, but he felt that he could not so easily ignore the wishes of one of the Sidhu brothers who, after all, had the power to ban him from the hall at a whim. Marway Sidhu, of course, was likewise conscious of the affiliations of most of his clienteles and he had to be equally careful not to upset a leading member of the present youthful, active gang. Moreover, many of the older family men, who played the occasional game of snooker, but, mainly, sat around the tables in the partitioned off bar-room drinking spirits out of tea cups - to keep up appearances; even they were once tearaway Smoke members themselves, in the heady days of the Nineteen Seventies and Eighties, although they were now respected workers and businessmen; even they only came to the Hall because of its restricted access: so they could enjoy a drink in company without the worry of being seen by the "respectable" local community. And most of them were related to the families of the younger members, through marriage or blood, and would not take kindly to the expulsion of one of their kin. Thus the management of the Southall Snooker Hall proceeded by intricate and tentative diplomacy among family connections so that if anything drastic had to be done, it was not done directly; but rather a "word of concern" was voiced to a father or grandfather about a son or grandson, which was usually more than sufficient to dampen the flame of a rebellious spirit. On the rare occasions that this did not quell the ardour of a troublemaker then it sometimes proved necessary to approach the real power which affected the family in order to exert influence: the rich uncle who may leave a legacy, a local shop owner who gave them credit, a leading figure in the local temple, an influential priest, a guru, a councillor, a power broker in the Indian Worker's Association or some other community leader who could bring pressure to bear. Thus the Sidhu brothers, with their knowledge of the tangled web of dependencies among the second and third generation immigrants, were able to use that knowledge to achieve something which the police were wholly incapable of: the control of public order by social manipulation. After they had taken over the club, following the conviction of "Devvy" and others for murder, they had, single-handedly, reduced the crimes of violence in Southall dramatically by the simple expedient of creating another club for the Tooti Nung. They received no government grant for this development nor was it the result of a belated visit to the region by a leading government minister or community liaison officer but, rather, it arose from their innate sense of community responsibility that could be summed up in the simple equation: peace equals profit. Indeed had their diplomatic intervention been on a much wider scale then they may well have been able to eradicate violent street crime altogether; but, of course, they only intervened where their own property was concerned. "Does your father, my friend, know that you prefer to push my cousins to the grounds rather than talk to thems like human beings - eh?," hissed Marway Sidhu into Balwinder Gill's ear, when they were sat next to each other on bar stools, and Marway had safely separated Bindi from his comrades, so that he would not have to act big in front of them.

"Well, he asked me if I was a member here. Me!"

"So? So what, does this mean that your hands must talk for your tongue? Don't let it happen in my club again - eh? Your father, my friend, spoils you. You drives in a flashy car he's bought for you. You wears smart clothes. Yours father's business does well and you would do well to spend more time helping him with it than playing at big shots on the streets. The reputations 'ofyoursfriends'" Marway slurred his words together but Bindi didn't laugh at him. "Isanegot-istical shallow thing. God is the only reality my young friend."

"Do you want another whiskey?" asked Bindi mischievously.

"If I do, I'll order it. I own thisestablisss ...... this hall and don't mock me Bindi for my own weaknesses. I know them well enough. Too well perhaps. The vice of too many material things and too little regard for the soul. Did you do as I asked?"

"Yes," lied Bindi.

"You're a bad liar. I bet you didn't even see my great uncle, did yous now? Tell me the truth?" Marway tugged his ragged beard nervously; he spoke in the manic, aggressive tones of a man who had consumed a vast amount of alcohol but who was, by experience, still in control of his faculties - but only just: as if the slightest emotional strain could cause his delicate mental functions to collapse into the abyss of unreason. "You lied just now. didn't you? Didn't you, Bindi?"

"I'm sorry Marway but I had many things to do. Many relatives to see. Anyway maybe your great uncle .... he wouldn't see me ....."

"He would! He would!" shouted Marway. "And my present for him. Dare you spend that yourself - eh? Dare you and you did."

"No! How dare you say that to me, Marway Sidhu! I gave it to my cousin, who owns a travel company in the Punjab, he was going to see your great uncle anyway, some time next week, and so it was better he gave it to him rather than I; you see that don't you?"

"No I don't. I asked you to give it to him from me personally. It meant something more that way but then no matter. You wouldn't understand that I suppose, eh? It was a very important thing for me. Not just money. Not just that. No matter. You better be telling the truth, that's all. Be off to your friends and remember I'm watching you all on here," Marway flicked a button a remote control console he had just picked up from the bar: the view on the television screen changed from a video in Hindi to security camera number one and a range of vision which extended across three snooker tables to the cigarette machine where Bindi's friends were joking and smoking in an excited group.

"Don't trust us," smiled Bindi climbing down from the stool in relief: pleased that he had at least given that explanation, which he had dreaded from the moment he arrived back in London with the gear in his suitcase. He had, of course, used the money to buy the drugs he had imported but he would quickly realise twenty times that amount, once he'd sold the gear. Then he could telegraph the borrowed money back to his cousin who could take it to Marway's great uncle and no-one would know any different.

"Trust you! I trust you and what happens. I cannot trust you yet because you have yet to learn about trust. Well if my great uncle does not receive that money soon then all the friends in the world will not protect you. Now, go on. Go off," Marway waved him away with one arm and shifted position on his stool so that he had, effectively, turned his back on Bindi's answer. The latter was going to buy a Coca-Cola; but, instead, he simply walked away with an undefined sense of guilt.

"Bindi at last," laughed Satish Brar when the former walked over to join them at the cigarette machine. "Bender here and the rest of us thought you were staying with the old men. We thought perhaps you'd aged in the Punjab. Perhaps you've been converted to the cause and are going to become an alcoholic like old Marway, the old fraud."

"Fuck them," snarled Bindi. "And fuck you too," Balwinder stuck a pointed finger in Bender's stomach as if it were a dagger. "You and your crack. What's the game.

At least I bring back something that can be sold. It's good stuff too and I took a risk getting it through. A big risk. Not just with Customs but in other ways. You see, my father won't give me no more money unless I work for him. Fuck him! There's other ways to get easy money. It comes easy today and tomorrow we'll pay! Anyway, who's going to sell the gear in the liftsmell estate - that's where the biggest and best market is ....."

"And that's where Mukesh is," interrupted Parminder Mangat - or "Bender" as he was called - in a soft Canadian drawl, he was a tough out-spoken young man wearing a rich, brown leather jacket and designer label jeans; he leant on the cigarette machine as he spoke, looking all the time at Bindi as if to say: "I'm not impressed."

"So," retorted Bindi. "I did for Jasbir Sood, didn't I? I'll do it for Mukesh as well but I'm not running this outfit on my own am I? I mean some of you have got something dangling between your legs as well, I hope. 'Cause in case you women hadn't noticed, Mukesh is younger than everyone here. At least two years young than Surinder: who's the youngest here, I think. And we're scared of him. Come on, let's sort this out once and for all."

"I don't recall saying I was scared," Parminder replied slowly. "I don't recall saying that. Did I say that?" he looked to the others and opened wide his arms and they all dutifully shook their heads in agreement. "No, of course I didn't," Parminder unzipped the top slanted pocket on his leather jacket and pulled out a packet of tax-free cigarettes, and he flicked one onto his lips but didn't light it nor did he offer the packet around. "Kenny," who was clearly impressed, supplied the flame from his gold lighter and

Parminder continued: "I know where Mad Mukesh will be tonight, namely doing a deal at Green Man flats and I know at what time, namely seven o'clock and I know how best to hit him but what I don't know is how we're going to get away with it."

"No problem," retorted Bindi with words flashed sharp and quick like a switch blade. He came up close to Parminder so that they were both staring at each other over the length of Parminder's cigarette. "We'll be drinking in the *Glassy Junction* when it happens, with Archie Lord and half his office. It's just across the road," Bindi turned so that he faced the others. "And if I was to nip out to the toilet's for a minute or two who'd notice: provided we arrange it properly," stated Bindi as he stood between Parminder and the others and gave them the benefit of his double-lip-barrelled smile. "Now," he spoke softly, sharply and distinctly: "a solicitor for an alibi - who can top that for planning?"

CHAPTER FOUR

At nine o'clock in the morning Christopher Larkin had been the finest solicitor in the realm but, by twelve noon, his ego had been mercilessly incinerated so that only the ashes remained to be blown hither and thither by the winds of derision. He had walked with Archie Lord back to the offices of Messrs. Crawley and Dodgers from the Shahanshah in a kind of crab like crawl as he tried, with only partial success, to hide the embarrassing stain on the front of his trousers, and he had listened, in an aura of abject inferiority, to the great man spouting forth on his worldly wisdom by relating what were, primarily, anecdotal stories consisting nearly wholly of dusted down relics from his own glorious past. Indeed, as Christopher learnt more about the importance of being Archie, he felt a corresponding drop in his own self-esteem so that, by the end of their afternoon promenade, Christopher wondered whether, like God, he really existed at all. Perhaps he was, instead, merely a figment of Archie Lord's fertile imagination, which Christopher secretly believed, was clearly vivid enough to create him if it could, so effortlessly, invent the amazing stories of coroner's exploding by internal combustion, witnesses being cross-examined to their graves and jurors simultaneously dying of the shock of it all. Needless to say, at the very centre of all these non-stop stories of legal heroics of Homerian greatness, was the imposing figure of Archie Lord: advocate to the Gods. Christopher's own insignificant adventures of scuttling around the corridors of Bolton Town Hall, with the occasional sojourn at the local county court at the other side of the precinct, could not properly be told least they detract from the great gospel according to St. Archie Lord. All Christopher could do was to listen in awe - diluted with a dash of doubt since Archie, like Christ, required a lot of believing.

"He's an awful bastard really," pronounced Eleanor when she was alone with Christopher: Archie, having arrived late for his afternoon appointments, disappeared with two different clients, who had a similar charge of shoplifting, in order to advise both of them at the same time and so save the need to waste his golden words. "He comes back to the office when he feels like it; often after swanning off around, with his Round Table cronies, in expensive foreign restaurants fantasising about lithesome young ladies and erotic sexual encounters: his feet are never on the ground you know?"

"How do you know what he does?" asked Christopher bluntly. He sat on the corner of Eleanor's desk and he tried to avoid looking at her unusually long legs, which were casually crossed at the heel and softly touched his thigh on the desk top. She sat back with her hands behind her head in a pose that had scant regard for traditional secretarial deference. Her face, with light red freckles, was not dainty or soft but rather sharp-featured and distinctive; combined with her carefully sculptured head of flowing red hair, which curled, with small ridges and indentations, down to her thin delicately wide shoulders, she somehow created an impression of open rebellion by her mere physical presence alone. She did not hold a pretty nor an attractive stance in the conventional sense of either of those words; but, nevertheless, she spawned a fatal fascination, to knowingly entrap the unwary in a worldly web of alleged experience and articulation, for the sheer pleasure of watching them squirm.

"Let's just say that the answers to some questions will have to be worked out by yourself. We'll make it your homework for tonight," she laughed lightly and her eyes narrowed into slits which seemed to emphasise some secret: guessed at and instantly resented by Christopher. Why Archie was surely over twenty years her senior and it seemed both unfair and unnatural that he should monopolise her as well as a wife at home; it seemed as Archie Lord had somehow belittled Christopher's virility by proxy as well as, earlier, castrating his professional competence.

"It seems as if I've a lot to learn," complained Christopher honestly and he then proceeded to tell Eleanor everything that had happened to him earlier that morning, which came as a complete surprise to Christopher's own consciousness since he had not intended to impart that information at all. Indeed his intellectual inclination had definitely been quite to the contrary: to suppress it in some dark recess of his mind where it could have laid safely buried, for his old age to reflect upon; but his words tumbled out in a nervous torrent nonetheless. Christopher missed nothing out but rather, to his own surprise, he exaggerated his own downfall by adding comments by the Magistrates', which they did not make, and increasing the depth of his own humiliation in the Shahanshah by pretending that everyone had laughed at him, which was not true, and, in this way, Christopher made Eleanor at first smile and then lapse into unrestrained, tear-laden laughter which pleased Christopher beyond measure. He had at least made someone happy if nothing else. Archie Lord, however, was unimpressed.

"What's this! Am I to do all the work in this place or do you think it might be possible to finish off that brief I gave you Eleanor? If you can find the time, that is, between listening to Christopher's wealth of experience and reading glossy magazines," Archie stood in the doorway as he spoke and whilst Christopher felt dutifully embarrassed, he noticed that Eleanor stared back at Archie unflustered and guilt-free. "I don't want to play the big bad boss," continued Archie in a more apologetic tone. "The brief is important though Eleanor ...." he pleaded.

"I think I get the message," she interrupted with a dazzling smile, putting to use hidden facial muscles and a new emotional richness in her tone of voice, which had not previously been heard in her social intercourse with Christopher, "Eleanor, get off your ass and lay your eggs - the battery hen is back at work. Just tell me one thing oh Lord. Oh Lord and master. Cans't thou spare a poor lilac girl the benefit of a few moments of your time at the Glassy Junction house tonight?"

"Eleanor, I meant to say earlier on," he looked down at his shoes for a half second before looking back up at Eleanor again. "I'm sorry but my wife ....."

"What's there to be sorry about," Eleanor cut off the end of his sentence with her scissor tongue as if she'd cut off his testicles and, indeed, her sharply spoken words had a similar effect on the recipient of them: he stared at her stupidly like a little boy, who had lost or forgotten that elusive explanation or excuse, which could have helped him evade punishment for his naughtiness. "You're going home to your wife, so what. You won't be missed Archie Lord. As a matter of fact, I was going to take Christopher here and show him the sights. You'd only be in the way in that case. You'll come won't you?" Eleanor gently kicked Christopher's thigh with her foot and, before he had time to think, Christopher nodded in agreement. He had already planned to spend the evening trying to find rented accommodation but Eleanor was plainly not to be denied. "The older generation can't stand the pace anyhow, can they Christopher? (the latter unwisely smiled, looked at Archie Lord, and his face instantly froze). Christopher knows all about the older generation because he's got a father, too. Never mind, Archie, you've always got your tomato plants and your hydrangeas. Your quiet domestic bliss in your carpet slippers and dressing gown ....."

"Leave it out, Eleanor," interjected Archie angrily. "Are you going to get some work done," he snapped at a surprised Christopher who jumped off the side of the desk at Archie's retort. "We haven't given you an office for you to laze around chatting up the secretaries all bloody day ..."

"We leave that to Archie in the office!"

"Eleanor!"

"Archie darling, before you blow the fuse in your pacemaker, I should point out that you haven't yet told young Christopher here that he even has an office. However, this comes as no surprise to those of us who have lived with your rampant egomania for the last few years; but if poor Christopher here is to be at all useful to you then I suggest, with the utmost respect oh Lord and master, that you stop, for one ever so small moment, thinking about your glorious self and spare a passing thought for a poor destitute lilac girl and her rose-cheeked chimney sweep here," she patted Christopher high up on his thigh in a flirtatious gesture of defiance, with the palm of her wide open hand, in full view of Archie's disapproving stare. "Who, together, seek only to serve you, but you must show us the way oh Lord and master and you must spare us the seed of your genius to sow on fertile lands."

"For Chrissake Eleanor, I ... what I mean is .... You don't seem to understand ... Oh, Christ," mumbled Archie who seemed very anxious not to leave without saying something important but, strangely, he lacked entirely the wherewithal to say it.

"Just show Christopher his office Archie, there's a dear," replied Eleanor in a slow, sad voice.

Archie Lord continued to stare at Eleanor after she had finished speaking and although once she had detected the pain in his frayed voice, she had carefully and studiously avoided his eyes, the seemingly long silence built up and created a pressure which both embarrassed Eleanor and angered her. Their eyes met, for a moment something akin to hatred, annoyance or resentment passed between them; then they smiled.

"Christopher must learn to take the rough with the smooth," said Archie, whose voice had recovered its natural rhythm, "like we all must do. Come on Chris, let me reveal the secrets of your inner sanctum to you. You'll have to forgive me for not showing it to you earlier but I think you know now just how busy I am," Archie reached out with his left arm to touch Christopher on the shoulder as he spoke to him and then he paused and half turned back to Eleanor again. "Remember the typing won't you dear," he smiled. "I wouldn't like you to forget me, you know."

"Then you'll have to refresh my memory every now and then won't you; oh Lord, master and willing slave."

"Don't count on it," Archie wagged his forefinger at her playfully. "You know what they say about pebbles on the beach."

"Oh yes," she retorted sharply. "Don't they say that the old ones which have been lying around there for some time, usually find themselves crushed under foot - eventually."

"Some of us have survived an awful lot of walking over," replied Archie with a wink.

"Some of us wouldn't tolerate it once," she rejoined and screwed her eyes up into slits as she spoke: her black eye-liner framing a pure white background to instinctive hazel-nut brown intelligence that looked out at the world in general, and Mr. Archibold Lord in particular, in fiery defiance.

"You're young yet. Give it time."

"If all age can teach me is what you know, then I'll give it a miss if it's all the same with you. Otherwise I might get bored just waiting for something to happen."

"It's worth the wait when it does though, isn't it? Some things are better done in small doses, like typing, eh Eleanor?"

"All right, daddy, message received and understood," Eleanor picked up her headphones as she spoke and placed them over her ears. She fiddled impatiently with the buttons on her playback machine and tapped her feet loudly on the pedal control underneath her desk. Christopher noticed, for the first time, just how many wires were needed to connect up the various items of electrical equipment on her desk and he felt in agreement with her muttered comment: "the battery hens back to work - cluck, cluck, cluck, cluck!"

Archie sniggered and seemed to half-sneer at her before he left the room with Christopher in his wake. He seemed to be in some turmoil as he strode down the passage, with his face creased up in concern, toward the top of the stairs leading down to the office waiting room.

"Next!" he bellowed down the stairway. "The next one for Archie Lord, please."

"Excuse me," interrupted Christopher.

"Oh," Archie put his hands on his hips and shouted down at the slowly raised head of a tall, gangly West Indian youth. "Hold it, sorry, can you give me a minute. Who's that? Is it Elroy Washington?"

"My main man," drawled Elroy in reply as he ascended the final flight of stairs in unhurried, relaxed rhythmical style. "How you doing?"

Archie slapped Elroy's outstretched hand and offered his own for a return slap in reply, in a quickly repeated gesture, which Christopher knew he had not the confidence to emulate . "Ganga?" queried Archie.

"Such a small amount, it hardly seems worth all the fuss to me."

"Just go through to Eleanor for the moment and wait for me Elroy, I'll be brief."

"I gotta a busy schedule man, things to do an' people ta see. Just see you don't keep the hottest customers waiting 'cus my business won't wait."

"The party will still be going when you get back, Elroy," laughed Archie and, after waving the tall West Indian away, he opened the door near the top of the stairs. It was not the broom cupboard nor was it the ladies toilet. However, it may well have fulfilled either role at some previous stage in its existence.

Christopher Larkin's first view of his working environment was somewhat delayed. The door handle seemed to turn easily enough in Archie's hand, but the door itself did not open without a bone-creaking, wood-splintering shoulder charge by Archie Lord, which had the effect of knocking over a huge pile of files, tearing the cardboard files themselves and ripping up some of their carefully organised contents, as the door hit the paper drift like a snow plough at full tilt. There was room (was there?) to squeeze through the gap between the fully open door and the old oak desk; jammed between the back of the desk and the back wall of an antique leather bucket chair - part of which was clearly badly torn. There was no filing cabinet - hence the pile of files: now crushed up against the wall in a hopeless mess. A partly opened sash window, perhaps the only one in the office, gave the occupant of the battered bucket chair an excellent and unobstructed view of the rear frosted glass window of the gentleman's toilet and this, probably, accounted for the triumphant crescendo of flushing water which greeted Christopher's ears on entering his new office. Indeed if he listened carefully he could detect the exact whereabouts of the pipes through which the water flowed, since they all seemed to pass through his office at some stage in their journey to and from the public sewers. It would provide an interesting pastime for him to enjoy in his few idle moments alone, provided, of course, that he could ever reach the bucket chair on the other side of his huge desk.

"We'll have to get you some chairs in here," mumbled Archie without indicating for a moment where such chairs were likely to fit in a room where space was in such short supply. "The desk is, of course, far too good for you so we hope you don't get ideas above yourself," continued Archie. "It used to be Master Crawley's desk and he died working at it. Of course he didn't use this office. This used to be .... never mind, that's not important now. You'll make us a lot of money from this room, I'm sure," Archie gave a false salesman's smile - this car really isn't going to break down on you as soon as you leave my showroom - and he tried to wave his arm around in order to illustrate the wealth of space; but, unfortunately, he immediately rapped his knuckles on the side wall and his smile turned into a painful grimace. "A fit young man like yourself will be able to climb over to the other side of the desk with no trouble at all and you can get to work in our guilty-conscience room. Ha! That name surprised you, I'll wager. Well, you must know that every solicitor in private practice has a number of files which required urgent attention several years ago. Needless to say they didn't get it. Hence the files became radio-active and no-one would dare touch them least a negligence writ sneak up on them unawares while they're reading through the papers and then thwack them on the head; so that everyone laughs and shouts: the music's stopped and you're left holding the file, stupid! - this writ has got your name on it. Bang! You're to blame sunshine. Now, all these files have passed through the urgent stage, and even through the desperate stage, so they have all been disowned by our former partners, who probably left because of them, and so together they comprise the guilty conscience of the firm which is why they are gathering dust in here. No partner dare touch them, least he is sued personally as well as the firm, but you, as an employee, cannot be so sued and hence they are now your responsibility. Salvage what you can and lose what you cannot, but, please keep us out of the shit. Now ...." Archie's monologue was stopped by a loud command from Eleanor: her unseen mouth shouting from her unseen room.

"Archie! You're wanted back at Court! They've lifted "Ruddy" Rudge on that bench warrant and he reckons you can get him bail. Personally I doubt it, but whom am I to say? "Ruddy" Rudge has faith ....." her voice trailed off to answer the mechanical, rude "buzz" of her telephone: "no, Mr. Lord's gone back to court I'm afraid. I'm sorry, I can't help what reception may have told you; He's had an urgent call ...."

"Okay," shouted Archie who interrupted Christopher's eavesdropping. "I'm on my way. You can make yourself useful young Christopher and see my afternoon appointments for me."

"In your office?" asked Christopher hopefully.

"Whatever for? You've got your own office now. May as well use it, old chap. Have a look at some of those files if you get time. A clever fellow like you will have them all ship-shape in no time. Right then, I must be off without more ado. Tally Ho!" Archie Lord gleefully charged down the stairs: away from the irksome responsibility of the office, leaving Christopher completely stranded but, nevertheless, completely in control. He wandered forlornly down to Eleanor's room and tentatively put his head around the door.

"Elroy Washington," he said in a shaky voice.

"Oh, mon!" exclaimed Elroy to a smiling Eleanor. "Have I been palmed off or have I been palmed off? Be truthful to me, girl."

"Our Mr. Larkin is more than capable....." started Miss Eleanor Redfern loyally.

.." ... of what? He sure does not look capable of very much to me. But then I'm just your hottest customer in sight 'though I'm treated like a nigger," Elroy threw his head back and laughed loudly at his last comment. "Anyone'd think I was black, the way you all carry on. Ah well, come on then, master Larkin tell me everything you knows and then ten seconds later I leave."

Christopher Larkin was about to lead Elroy out of Eleanor's office when she stopped him: "the office is through here," she indicated Archie's office. "Where do you think you're going."

"To my office," he replied.

"What!" she exclaimed. "You can't, Mr. Dodgers has been to the Star at dinner time," but, unfortunately, the significance of her last words were totally lost on Christopher; Eleanor, who had to answer yet another demand from her office telephone, was unable to expand further on her somewhat cryptic comment which was,

Christopher decided, worthy of a clue in a Times crossword puzzle. Eleanor had become instantly involved in a heated argument over the telephone which culminated in her shouting. "I tell you he's not in, he's left our company and there's no point in your coming down here now." Christopher led Elroy away from the unhappy verbal exchange and down the short corridor; he made the mistake of showing Elroy into his office first, by the gesture of a half-wave with an upturned palm; but, once Elroy had entered and effectively blocked further access, Christopher was unable to follow him in.

"Okay, so this is where I hang my coat; now where'd we do business."

"Can I squeeze past please?" asked Christopher, who was anxious not to offend the fifteen stone black man with the ten ton shoulder chip.

"You don't mean I gotta pour my problems out to you in a wardrobe, for Chrissake!"

"Excuse me, please," requested Christopher, who still managed to crush past Elroy Washington despite the fact that the latter did not excuse him at all and, indeed, moved not the smallest muscle in reply. Once he had negotiated his awkward client, Christopher had somehow to reach the other side of his desk but, by this time, he tucked his dignity out of sight in his back trouser pocket and so, without further hesitation, he clambered over the top of his desk on his hands and knees. Elroy's bottom lip fell open as Christopher, the intrepid furniture climber, dropped down the south face of Mt. Oakdesk and attempted the leather chair glacier. Alas, he would have been wise to remain at base camp instead. The leather chair was, unfortunately, jammed into an angular position and Christopher found he could not move it easily; therefore, aware of the attentions of his incredulous client, he decided to casually sit upon it as it was. That proved to be a bad move. No sooner had Christopher put his full weight upon the leather bucket chair than it started to creak under his weight. To give Christopher credit for his initiative, he immediately responded by trying to cover up the creaking sound with his own voice. "Now then, Mr. Washington, how can I help!"

The chair tilted in mid sentence: Christopher dropped down the leather slide and out of sight with a thud. Dust rose up from the floor in a mushroom cloud. A plaintive, muffled and seemingly distant cry for assistance could be heard from somewhere underneath the expansive acres of oak wood which appeared to cover all the available floor space. Elroy Washington was not impressed.

"That's right mon, bail out on the black man like all honky liberals," Elroy became angrier as he spoke and he started pointing an accusing finger at the middle of the oak desk under which he could clearly hear the rumbling movements of Christopher Larkins, which were punctuated by the occasional crack, as the head of the luckless lawyer made contact with the various hidden parts which were protruding out below the ancient piece of obsolete furniture. "You don't understand what it's like to be unwanted. Ta be police fodder, lawyer fodder an' all the time to bear arms against society. Ya don't understand ....."

"But I do ...." complained a far away voice which rapidly deteriorated into a fit of coughing.

70

"What it's like to get busted every time you walk the streets. JUST BECAUSE YOU'RE BLACK!" screamed Elroy at the desk. The desk waited a few moments before a response drifted upwards.

." ...... I want to help Mr. Washing ....Aahhh! My bleeding head ......" Christopher had clearly made contact with one of the solid oak legs and the whole desk shuddered perceptively in consequence.

"Don't give me that. You're just interested in number one. In your own problems. You don't care about the problems of the black man. All you wanna do, is crawl out from under that desk, isn't it? Admit it? That's all you wanna do. Well, I'm bailing out on you an' I'm gonna find myself a brief who cares; so play the fool in someone else's time." Christopher heard the door slam as he pulled himself out into daylight and waved the cloud of dust away from his mouth and eyes. He tried to stand upright but he found that his foot was somehow twisted and jammed fast in the bottom desk drawer. All he could see was the back wall of his office and he was stuck with his bottom upright in the air and his knees rubbing on the ground. He painfully pushed his leg backwards and was thus able to turn his foot slowly and, needless to say, the rest of his body, which was still, remarkably, attached to his leg, similarly turned itself awkwardly and agonisingly around. In this way he was able to face the desk and his office door beyond. By this time a film of sweat formed a liquid vest between Christopher's shirt and his body underneath. Blood, from a cut he had sustained on his forehead, was dribbling down his cheek and over his lips, where Christopher swallowed what he could, after it had been filtered through his moustache, to

71

prevent it dripping down onto his only suit. All attempts to release his imprisoned foot had failed. Indeed, Christopher had found that his previous efforts to free himself had simply bonded him more firmly to his desk. There, in a shaky, croaky voice, he tried to summon assistance. However, a fear of ridicule or, perhaps, it would be safer to say a fear of overwhelming degradation - since mere ridicule and humiliation were an intricate part of his life - prevented young Christopher from bawling out again in panic-stricken terror: HELP! Instead, he confined himself to a more sedate: "Hello, are you there?"

"Yes, I am!" announced a large middle-aged woman in a three quarter length brown fur coat, carrying a stocky furled-up umbrella, who battered the office door to one side as she took its place in the door frame, arms akimbo with umbrella hanging from her right hand, which was pressed against her right hip; she bore a striking resemblance to a Churchill tank: her long pointed nose, fastened to her gun turret head, turned mechanically to her right and back again and then to her left and back again. An then up and down. The creaking neck seemed badly in need of oiling; but, Christopher had no doubt, the pointed nose was clearly a lethal weapon: capable of discharging high-explosive, six pounder bogeys from either large and round nostril-barrel. Two malevolent eyeballs in the Devil's green, stared down the uplifted nose and took aim. Fortunately, the first question was one which Christopher could easily answer: "Are you the worm who has ruined my life?" she demanded.

"No, ma'am I'm not," Christopher replied in a nervous broken voice betrayed the pain he felt. "Now, if ...."

"I hope you're not lying to me," growled the armoured, Churchillian war wagon: interrupting Christopher's doomed attempt to control the conversation. "But why would you be hiding underneath your desk when I entered?"

"You see, I was trying to see a large, black client and ...."

"Any .... why are you sweating profusely," she interrupted as she scoured the room with all the skill of a professional 'busybody'. "Ah ha!" she exclaimed in triumph. "No wonder the worm is worried," she bent down and lifted high the battered remains of a double-pocketed, double-sized file and proclaimed: "you have destroyed me! Twenty years I have waited for my divorce. I was lied to and cheated out of twenty thousand pounds lawyer's fees! You told me my divorce was through. You charlatan. Now I find myself prosecuted for bigamy because you have failed to properly cast us asunder!" She bent over the desk as she spoke and her body blocked out the sunlight from the window. Her arms stretched up above her head as she held high the file like a slab of marble. She brought it down with all the strength of a wronged woman who feels the wrath of all her past pains pumping through her sinews. Christopher did not cry out or even mouth a word of protest. It was, in any event, exceedingly difficult to speak with a mouthful of copy letters, paper-clips and pieces of judicial paper. Moreover, the weight of a double-sized file around his neck, which had been successfully split over his head with a sickening thud, now worn as an unwanted and entirely unexpected chain of office, did little to increase his powers of concentration. It was obviously that he was now entirely at her mercy and two decades of legitimate legal robbery required a great deal of gratuitous violence to adequately remedy. Mere concussion was clearly only the anaesthetic for a far more sophisticated operation which involved the pointed end of the furled umbrella. Christopher was temporarily saved by the sound of a motor bike back-firing in multiple bursts rather like a machine-gun staccato. The matron, kneeling on the desk and trying to aim at Christopher's delicate regions with her lancet, hesitated and then started to cough. Tears came to her eyes and her coughing fit increased to such an extent that she had to put down her umbrella and reach rapidly for her scented handkerchief. A poison gas Vindaloo, was followed by the roar of Nigeria falls as flushing water strained the ancient piping in the walls all around them. The remnants of Mr. Dodgers' meal at the Star of India may well have saved Christopher from direct action by Mrs. Vengeance but indirectly she now presented a greater threat.

Madam Churchillian Tank started to sway back and forth on the desk, with her face changing from a lobster red into a death mask purple, until finally she fell forward: her huge breasts descending upon a horrified Christopher like a mammon avalanche. He ducked to one side but found himself rapidly covered with two large pillows of jugular flesh. It could be safely stated that when Christopher had started work that morning he had not expected to find himself gasping for breath by the late afternoon between a narrow cleavage in a glorified cupboard, while his body sought to filter out the oxygen for the benefit of his bloodstream, from lungs full of air polluted by the very best

at the meeting. It'll have to take place tonight before the information leaks out from the Strand, I'll sort that out, but if you just ask the task force delta to stand by, I think I'll go myself it should be ..... hum ...... I mean, perhaps you would like to go earlier this afternoon Cynthia ...... not at all .... I'm a fair man and there should be a bit of give and take, off you go .... Are you coming to my sermon this Sunday."

"Of course sir. I enjoy hearing you speak and I learn a lot as well."

"You must be a glutton for punishment, my dear. Well, I better see what my officers have to say, I'll see you on Sunday then."

"The small conference room on the third floor of Ealing Police Station was choked with deferential impatience: four officers of the MI5 Liaison Committee had been kept waiting for above an hour but, since they were all aware that their Commander had suffered his monthly ritual of humiliation by smart-arsed, smart-mouthed brats half his age, they all deemed it prudent not to comment on the delay.

"Well then, gentlemen, I know you've been kept waiting but I can assure you it's not my fault and I would have swapped places with anyone of you: I can assure you of that. I've received a new revised list of priorities. Again! I know," the Commander raised two huge paws to forestall criticism. "It will mean re-timetabling all our work schedules but Five don't give a monkeys about us. And I know this will be the third time in as many months. You must admit though, Five is certainly consistent," he paused before delivering his joke, "in its inconsistency," all four subordinate officers dutifully laughed and the Commander continued, "but we can turn over Douglas Spencer's place at long last. I'm not taking volunteers otherwise you'll be taking away the bricks and mortar! Seriously though, it shows how we can get it right when we try. Now let's have a look at today's agenda. I'll take the minutes and I formally agree my own notes of last month's meeting. Any matters arising, no, good. Item One: the causation report for Ealing Sector."

"Now then, the Home Secretary has put pressure on Sir David Home and he's put pressure in turn on Five which has mandated me to prepare a riot profile, whatever that is, and, in particular, to analyse the influence and cause of two local gangs which I believe are known to all of you: Tooti Nung and Holy Smoke. The Home Secretary has decided in his wisdom that they are the ...... now, what was his words ..... oh, yes I have it ..... the spark to cause the forest fire. There's no smoke without fire apparently," at this comment there was forced grins from the four subordinates. "If he had spent his time reading our reports - assuming those duplicitous public school boys weren't short of toilet paper at the time then he may have come to a different conclusion but, as usual, we are ignored and so the extremist politicos are still free to roam the streets and conspire together to cause sedition; instead of being behind bars where they belong. This new regime seems to be more concerned with drugs than with society. Anyway, ours not to reason why and all that. Now, with the privilege of rank, I'm delegating this job to you Chief Superintendent Manning; but don't worry, you've got plenty of time: the Committee want the report by Monday morning. Yes. I know it's Saturday tomorrow but the Home Secretary needs to be able to converse intelligently with the P.M. on his return from Tuscany."

"With respect sir," started Chief Superintendent Manning.

"With the utmost respect, Derek," retorted Commander Godlove sarcastically.

"..... it can't be done ......"

"Just do it, look, I'm sorry to lumber you with this Derek but your reports are by far and away the best in Ealing. Just drive around the flats tonight. Take a few infra-red shots, the Home Secretary likes plenty of pictures, and cobble together the summaries we receive from the various officers of the collator's department, and, after a careful consideration of all the evidence, draw the obvious conclusion that neither gang is a cause of crime since all they're interested in is carving each other up and selling heroin. Okay?"

"I'm supposed to be taking the missus to see Cosi Fan Tutte."

"Tooti Fruiti, Round the Clock ....." interjected Trainee Investigator Barker with youthful enthusiasm.

"Not quite," replied the Chief Superintendent dryly as he raised his eyebrows. "In any event sir," he turned to address the Commander, albeit with care, because, like plutonium - 239, the Commander was likely to produce a sudden surge of energy which, if not controlled, could break away rapidly and melt down in a thermonuclear glow. "The purpose of research is not to countenance a self-fulfilling prophecy but to ....."

"The Chief Superintendent went to University," proclaimed T.I. Barker, who at twenty one was the youngest member of the meetings, "and if anyone knows about sociology it must be our Chief Superintendent Manning. He got a first class honours too!" This seemingly crass intervention managed to simultaneously flatter both senior officers by supporting the Commander's argument and yet, at the same time, praising the brilliance of the Bachelor of Arts. T.I. Barker had an open mouth policy, but, unlike many other people with the same tongue-propelled idiocy, he had the advantage of a dominant skivvy gene within the twists and turns of his DNA molecule; thus, the amino acid messenger had activated the RNA to produce nature's perfect lackey. He was arse-licking good.

The Commander nodded sagely as if someone had unravelled the dimensions of the Universe before his eyes. The Chief Superintendent twirled and twisted the neatly clipped end of his neatly clipped moustache. And then Cynthia brought in the tea. She pushed it in on a mobile tray on wheels that carried a large silver-plated tea pot, china cups and a china sugar bowl, skimmed milk in a golliwog jug and a plate of penguin biscuits for her boys. Everyone stopped playing soldiers for a moment.

"Cynthia, I thought you'd gone!" said little Commander Godlove to his nursery nurse.

"I thought you'd all appreciate this before I go," she smiled tenderly at them all before "being mother." She handed them each a cup of tea with the requisite measure of sugar for each - she didn't ask who wanted sugar and, if so, how much. These were things she always remembered -

and she ensured that everyone received one penguin biscuit each by handing them around ceremoniously like war medals - naughty Commander Godlove, like all good Christians, had been known to wolf down everybody else's share of chocolate: given the chance - then, after tucking them all in and smiling benignly, she departed.

"An excellent, first-rate woman," said T.I. Barker with his usual innate grovel.

"Yes, you don't find them like that anymore I'm afraid. They all want to be Commanders nowadays," laughed Commander Godlove. Chief Superintendent Manning shuddered and looked to the other three male officers in the room who also laughed loyally. Qualifications that assisted my promotion, he thought to himself, namely, one sociology degree from Oxford (the "other" University), one six inch penis (when erect), two testicles (normal size) .... "Now then, Chief Superintendent," Commander Godlove interrupted Derek's muse. "You must put ideas of research to one side .... how can I put this ...... I'm not quite the philistine that you might believe I am. I'm aware, of course, that real research, for want of a better word, could take months or even years. Certainly not forty-eight hours, assuming you don't sleep that is ..... haw, haw, haw .... No, what we're talking about here is a self-fulfilling prophecy if you like. The thing is Derek we all know what the answer is, don't we?" the Commander's question met with an uneasy silence .... "let me see if I can....... Yes, I have it ...... Now then, what I mean is that I know, don't we," the Commander thumped a joint of fist on the table to emphasise the point that everyone should be agreed on this, "that the two gangs I have mentioned are a public nuisance but we know that they are not a real cause of crime because they don't distribute dogma and disturb the status quo with demos and the like. Am I right Chief Superintendent ? Of course I am."

"The internal dynamics of society are at least as determinant by peer group pressure and the resultant localised change in social norms as they are by marginal pressure groups of scant relevance to the social whole," submitted the Chief Superintendent tentatively. However, he need not have worried about his challenge to the Commander's simple assumption that a handful of politico-troublemakers were behind all the world's woe, since the bewildered Commander did not comprehend a single concept from his subordinate's seemingly unerringly accurate command of fluent Cantonese.

The Commander looked at his Chief Superintendent for a dumbfounded hogs head of time or so and then cleared his throat huffily. "Well then, now that's cleared up and we're all agreed: we can move on to item two .... Oh, one thing though, Derek, you won't forget the photos will you. Get a couple of Asians all crowded together around the Half Way House or the Glassy Junction public house. Try and get a few shots of Irish boozers kicking up a fuss at closing time as well. Inner city strife, you know the scenario. Remember you'll have the Home Secretary's ear and a subtle hint of Republicanism may help us increase our man hour projections for next year's allocation. Can you deliver the report to my home in the morning? Oh, and don't forget the "By-pass demo," just squeeze in a mention somehow but plenty and I mean PLENTY, of cultural stuff about how the Holy Smoke are generally the higher caste and the Tooti Nung are the lower caste, all that stuff. They love a bit of ethnic down at Whitehall. Oh, and put in all those details about the different splinter groups in West London all committed to revolution. Like those wretched Greens, worse than the reds if you ask me. Violent revolution and that's much worse that rioting isn't it? You know like the Utopian profile you did for Hendon last year. In fact, come to think of it, include all that - just cover up the title with blank paper on the photocopier and re-title it .... er .... let me think," Commander Godlove rested his head on his forepaws and closed his eyes.

"Riot tremors?" suggested T.I. Barker who hadn't read the Chief Superintendent's paper - but then neither had anyone else, except, perhaps, the odd gifted pupil at Hendon police training school - but who had, nevertheless, grasped very quickly what it was that the Commander wanted to hear.

"Capital!" beamed Commander Godlove. "They might even increase next years allocation, eh Derek"

Chief Superintendent Manning felt a throbbing, pounding pain pass across his brow and he lifted his hand up so that he could rub his temple with a forefinger and thumb in a soft to and fro massage. "The point I am trying to make," he said in a heavy hopeless voice, the words of which dropped to the floor with a clang, like metal horseshoes, as soon as they had left his mouth, "is that the root cause of unrest is not the intellectual ramblings of a few, predominantly Class II, discontents and issues are rarely, if ever, truthfully portrayed in such stark black and white terms ....."

"We understand," interjected the Commander waving his Chief Superintendent into silence with a frantic semaphore message delivered, impatiently, with a penguin wrapper substituted for the semaphoric flag. "That there are many different shades of black. There's the West Indian black, the Asian black," spouted the Commander knowledgeably. "But what I'm discussing here is the true cause of crime. And this brings me to item two on the Agenda .....

"The point I'm trying to make sir," interrupted Chief Superintendent Manning courageously. However, it was as foolhardy to halt the flow of the Commander's waterfall of wisdom as it was to dare the devil and boldly challenge a judge in his closing speech to the jury.

"IF YOU DON'T MIND, Chief Superintendent ...."

"Our various sources produce a pattern of a predominantly harmless intervention strategy of superficial import taking into account ......"

"Nevertheless," barked the Commander resorting now to desk thumping instead of mere semaphoric message tactics. "It has come to our attention of late that some deep-rooted conspiracy has infiltrated our community. Item two gentlemen - conspiracy!" Commander Godlove had now switched to his sermon delivery, which was a highly muscular "word wallop" style, rather like a tongue Kung fu. The sheer strength of expression, rather than the words themselves, conveyed righteous intolerance, which would flatten all dissension like a verbal steam roller; and on it rolled: inexorably. "And let me tell you all, who are gathered here today, that I'm not just talking now about those two gangs who have to my knowledge regularly operated in this area and in Southall and Hounslow to the shame of all God-fearing black folk. It may be that the Home Secretary has just noticed the phenomenon courtesy of the coloured Sunday tabloid but we all, I hope, know better," the Commander once more thumped his two large "ham pie" fists upon the table in front of him and thus created a physical exclamation mark to conclude his spoken words. His fiery eyes erupted into bloody dagger stares - thus finding a convenient outlet for the swelling surge of hot internal anger which they so clearly expressed.

Chief Superintendent Derek Manning moved the weight of his body from his right buttock to his left and looked away from the molten lava glower of his missionary leader. He wanted to explain that he was not discounting the influence of the splinter groups and, indeed, his own "Utopian Report" was accepted intelligence for all Branch Officers, but he had not wanted the work of these groupings to be elevated into a kind of universal culpability for all existing wrongs. "I am talking here of blood, gentlemen," asserted Commander Godlove. "It is a problem of revolutionary proportion which will shortly spill blood on to our paving stones and blood down our gutters. Blood on our streets! We are talking here of riot, mayhem and disorder! And it is disorder, disorder I say gentlemen, which is the enemy of order!" Hallelujah! thought Derek Manning with a quiet smile. "Now then, I have here an opinion from the Attorney General on various rubbish which has been circulating in the Ealing area recently. It doesn't look as if we can prosecute for incitement or sedition, I'm afraid. I sometimes wonder whose side they're on. But I had discussed this earlier in the week with

T.I. Barker here and we've come to the conclusion that we can nobble them under s.5 Public Order Act 1986. We don't need the D.P.P.'s consent for that nor do we have to worry about the Attorney General's office. And we can seize all the literature as an exhibit and once we get a conviction - there's no jury trial so we've got a good chance - then we can destroy all the rubbish in one go" Commander Godlove's expression changed from fury to excitement, from anger to enthusiasm, from frustration to hope. He was a happy man, again. "What do you say Derek?"

"Well, I'd ..... I mean to say, sir .... What can I say, sir ..... what can I say. If I remember the section correctly it can cover the written word in a pamphlet or anything else. You need to show harassment, alarm or distress was caused thereby, don't you?"

"An officer can give evidence that the thought of violent revolution alarmed and distressed him and caused him no end of harassment. The beauty of it is that we don't need any lay witnesses! No so-called experts. Good old English common sense will do. And one police witness won't let us down. Especially a man of intellect and vision like ...."

"T. I. Barker, sir," interjected Chief Superintendent Manning with four words designed to save his career and deflect the javelin, which had been sailing through the air towards him, away from his heart.

"No, well actually I meant ...." started the Commander who had been momentarily derailed.

"That a young, bright officer would present a smart, stock-broker image for our service in court rather like the early F.B.I.: sharp, young men struggling to save society and bravely upholding our standards of decency and decorum," persisted the Chief Superintendent as a bead of sweat formed in the facial hair in his upper lip to give his tongue a fleeting salty taste of despair. It was quite clear to him at least that whichever police officer was foolish enough to stand up in a witness box in this country and say that a political leaflet had caused him such harassment, alarm and distress so that somebody should be convicted of a criminal offence, was likely to have his career terminated amid a media witch-hunt and while Commander Godlove's crusade may well continue, with scant regard for the advice of anyone, Chief Superintendent Derek Manning knew precisely where his captain would be when the sharks came looking for a diet of human flesh: pushing the volunteer along the plank with his sharp sabre. "I think society is ready for a new image of younger officers. It will go well with our new image of tackling the causes of crime. And I believe that a caring youthful freshness may well help to persuade the Magistrates to convict instead of presenting an old fashioned fuddy-duddy image in court like, for example, myself. Youth and vigour are the key," continued Chief Superintendent Manning with desperation.

"Humph, I don't know," said the Commander thoughtfully.

"I know that T.I. Barker is keen to do his very best for the service. And, as you said, offered you advice on this very subject earlier in the week," Chief Superintendent Manning turned to the younger officer. "You are, as the boy scouts say, prepared for this aren't you?"

"Oh yes," enjoined T.I. Barker who enthusiastically put one foolish leg in the man-trap without a thought for the opinion of the world elsewhere.

"The art of persuasion relies heavily on originality of style as well as sincerity of expression and our emotive peer group identification often includes a youthful approach ..."

"All right, all right," the Commander put his hands up: too much sociology in one day was injurious to the health. "What do you say Barker?"

"Oh yes," repeated the Trainee Investigator as if he'd been offered the Order of the Garter.

"All right then," conceded the Commander. "Perhaps you ought to go with Derek tonight and get some idea of the area concerned."

"Incidentally," asked Chief Superintendent Manning, with such immense inner relief at having escaped a potential newspaper Calvary that he didn't even object to the T.I. Barker's presence on his evening sojourn, "Does anyone know what these leaflet's say?" Or doesn't that matter anymore, he didn't add. After all, if he lost this career where else could he go?

"Good point, Derek," congratulated his bear-like Commander as he stuck his right paw out to seemingly grab the answer out of the air. "Now let me see if I can remember," he continued. "Yes, I have it," the Commander rested his huge paws momentarily against the side of his brain casing: to warm the engine up. "Now then, what was the exact words: 'The Riot is the voice of the Unheard.' If that isn't a clarion call for revolution, I don't know what is."

"Hold on," Chief Superintendent Manning sat bolt upright in surprise as he spoke. "Isn't that a quote by Martin Luther King?"

"Is he the printer or the publisher?" asked Commander Godlove. "Only I'm pretty sure that his name doesn't appear on the leaflet"

"No, No," started Chief Superintendent Manning.

"Perhaps I could issue a warrant for his arrest," speculated the Commander thoughtfully.

"I'm afraid he's gone where the Queen's writ does not run, sir," he submitted with the tact of an able funambulist.

"Brazil?" queried the Commander.

"Heaven more likely," replied Derek Manning quietly as he wobbled on the tightrope.

"Humph! More likely Hell then, Chief Superintendent. Our enemies do not go to Heaven while we do God's work here on earth."

The Chief Superintendent stared at his Commander, who was a stern pillar of certainty, with incredulity. Did he really mean that or was there a sane, manipulative brain clicking away inside that glorious dalmatic, which covered his otherwise vulnerable consciousness? The Chief Superintendent reached for his moustache and gave it a firm twirl as he phased out his superior's glower. He was determined not to smile nor to utter any supportive words of approval, although he appreciated, only too well, that it would have been a career mistake to doubt the validity of the Commander's fax-link with God: silence seemed the best solution. Finally the Commander shook his huge bear head from side to side in clear omnipotent disappointment.

"God's will, gentlemen," he said enigmatically "is clear to those who seek it and it will never let us down: if we doubt it not. Now then, let us move onto a related topic. Item three: the propaganda of the Conspiracy. Now then, I have here a fax from Five which reads as follows," the Commander cleared his throat formerly as if he was just about to deliver a direct quotation from St. Matthew. "To Commander Godlove. Memo of information. Scale ten. Links are being drawn between some extremist groups and solicitors who specialise in subversive caseloads. In our analysis this has been a particular problem in terrorist cases but also in those with a general political import. Sometimes the lawyers get involved in the cause to the detriment of their professional obligations. Clear implications can be drawn of a wholesale perversion of the course of justice and conspiratorial perjury in "Hunt-Sab" Trials, demos and other public order cases. Full report will follow when R and D complete but interesting photograph shows a typist at Messrs Crawley and Dodgers, a Southall firm, handing out leaflets headed "the Riot is the Voice of the Unheard." Her name is Eleanor Redfern and she lives with another woman called Rita Cootes. Latter is known long term subversive: Women for the Whale, Green Peace, Socialist Worker and latterly the BBC"

"The BBC," interrupted Chief Superintendent Manning with surprise. "Don't we vet them?"

"No, not that BBC. They behave much more responsibly of late. No, I mean the Brent Black Caucus. Apparently this is what is known as an ant-splinter, splinter group which appeals across party barriers. You know the sort of thing, like the old Anti-Nazi League. Rita Coote's name appears on the leaflet T.I. Barker and myself looked at - as the printer. The publisher's name is the Brent Black Caucus. That's in Kilburn's area, I'm afraid; but Rita Cootes is very much in our sector. Her and her lesbian lover Eleanor Redfern, man haters I'll bet, were pushing out their damned leaflets last weekend ......"

"Lesbian?" queried Detective Chief Superintendent Manning. "Surely she's the red-head who's having an affair with old Archie Lord isn't she?"

"Well, she's living with another woman," retorted Commander Godlove as if that clinched the argument. "And it's common knowledge that most of these feminist, leftist type are a bit partial to each other. You only have to read our files to prove that. Well, if either of them try to push those leaflets in our area, tell the lads to give one of them a pull. Preferably the link with the lawyer's firm, Eleanor Redfern because who knows what we may find out about the devil's handiwork from a fallen angel's mouth, eh? We will get to the very root cause of discontent. Destroy the link with the lawyers. It may come to pass that we can nick some of the other links in the great chain of subversion, which is stretched unhappily across the length and breadth of this Borough so keep your ears open for any other such attempts to subvert our law. Together we can show the Home Office where the real problem lies."

Chief Superintendent Manning sighed silently. He had five years left until he could take early retirement. Keep your head down, he told himself, avoid the cross-fire and be elsewhere when the bomb goes off. Five years left and he had to have a fanatic for a boss! Briefly he remembered his youthful enthusiasm on starting with "the job" when he had believed that being in the police force was simply about nicking villains. What he hadn't realised then was that everybody was somebody else's villain.

CHAPTER SIX

A public house was a home for those who had no home. And for Patrick O'Rourke, without a home, the public house was the only home he had. Unlike many less colourful men, with a mere private house to their name, "Paddy" O'Rourke was not adverse to sharing his lounge with strangers. Indeed, to illustrate his generosity, he had let unfriendly visitors trample all over his carpet, pee on his urinal (and all over his toilet floor), stub fagerettes out on his polished tables, spew indecently over his outside wall and occupy all available seating space: forcing poor old Paddy to a stool at the bar over his lunchtime session. A quick trip to Ladbrokes to collect his winnings and he was back again, on his now lucky bar stool, having fleeced the bookmakers of their gold, he had returned like vengeful Ulysses to his rightful abode: the Glassy Junction pub near Southall Station. Alas no longer the old Railway Tavern that he remembered from his youth which was one of the few pickled memories that still bounced along the sea bed of his soaked consciousness. He happily contemplated these and other unremembered moments, the scars of a long death by internal drowning, as he commenced his second gallon of ale that day.

Paddy drunk his pint in a rare moment of silence and looked once again at the new surroundings in the old place he hung onto as a home of sorts. Fortunately the bar service was still supplied by Parminder, or Paddy to his friends, who was an Irish Sikh from Belfast now simply one of two bar managers of Glassy Junction although formerly the sole publican of the Railway Tavern.

"Same again Paddy. An Paddy 'ill have a Paddy chaser if Paddy will be so kind as to get it for Paddy."

"Why do you have to sit there," grumbled Parminder. "My real trade will be coming in shortly and you'll scare them all away with your Republican crap. You'll close me down one of these days so you will. Yesterday your so-called bungra dancing almost started a bloody riot and broke a dozen glasses. You can't equate freedom for the Punjab with the sixties Civil Rights and the B-Specials. No-one knows what your on about anyhow. Go to the bloody Irish club, you don't fit in here no more, so you don't."

"Hold on there naw one blessed moment or two, am I not a fine figure of a man? Am I not? Am I not as good as the next man? No, you'll be thinking and you'll be right Paddy boy. I'm not as fucking good. I'm fucking better. There's not a man in this Borough I could not knock to the fucking ground in less than thirty fucking seconds. And there's not a man here who can do a days work harder than this Paddy can if this Paddy puts his mind to it. 'Twas a fucking fated day that I came to this place and twas a holy mother of a day that I started backing the gee gees once again, to be sure it was. No wrong I can't do: no matter whichever what way I back them, they always accumulate out in beautiful, bloody wins. I've nearly a hundred fucking pounds in me pockets tonight and so you don't be telling me naw where and wherever you think I can't sit or what and whatever you think I can or I cannot do, because I'm telling you, that who or whoever has, or thinks he has, the fucking muscle to move me from in here to in there, I'm telling you this and for your own fucking good you better listen, I'm telling you that how or however any fucker thinks he's gonna do that to me, one thing is as certain as the redemption of the cross on which our holy saviour Jesus the Lord Christ was crucified, an' that is that YOU ain't gonna do that to ME. I'm a man of few words Paddy so I hope for the sake of your good self and your hairs on your head and from your bed, that you have the good, old Briti-shyte common sense to listen to old Paddy 'cause if you ain't then I'd better fucking warn you that my common sense was a casualty of the troubles."

"Don't push your luck with me, bogman," growled Parminder pointing a finger at Paddy's face "You ain't welcome here and can piss off down to the Republic of Kilburn as far as we're concerned an' I don't know why you keep coming here since we must have made that clear enough to you."

Paddy looked around him from his bar stool perch and, indeed, he began to wonder just that: why did he keep coming here. The sign "Jalandhar" hung from the ceiling just in front of him and beyond that was a snooker room with large coloured ceiling fans and a map of the Punjab on the inside wall. Behind him was a display of all India's current currency and the drinks themselves could be paid for by Rupees rather than pounds if the customer wanted, albeit a lot was lost in the conversion rate. Portraits on the wall displayed smiling young men playing the Tabalas and the real thing could be witnessed three times a week in a function room, on a small stage that was situate at the side of the pub. In true Indian style there was a children's room and an adventure playground at the rear as well. No-one was excluded although women on their own were a rarity. An exception was a young Anglo-Indian lady sat on her own at a table by the door.

Rita was at her happiest in a public house and the public house she was happiest in was, without doubt, the Glassy Junction and that was undoubtedly because it was more house than public. Perhaps it was the huge television screen which regularly showed live football matches courtesy of Sky TV. Liverpool FC. was her life. Perhaps it was the room itself which was wide open and friendly. In addition, the people who usually frequented the Glassy Junction were friendly and familiar to Rita so that she could engage in conversation if she wished or just sit back as at that moment to allow time to shuffle gently by at whatever pace it chose.

"A pint of bitter please Paddy," she said. Patrick O'Rourke ignored her and turned to the racing pages of "The Sun." Perhaps it was also the fact that Parminder, whose wife drank pints of lager, did not query or question her order which helped towards Rita's sense of well being at this particular public house.

When the first pint of the day arrived, the ceremony began. First, she liked to gaze at it before she broke the foam seal and allowed the golden liquid to cut through the taste and tensions of a day which had, thankfully, been safely concluded without incident. She stroked the side of her pint glass like the skin of a lover and she made finger paths through the film of condensation and then, with the utmost delicacy and care, she lifted the glass high: to watch the light filter through the clear, gold body as the little bubbles, tiny prisms refracting colour, rose slowly toward the cream textured top which rested naturally like a floating crown.

A whiff of hops.

A glugg glugg swallow.

And, finally, the lost iron flavour which returned to her like a lost lover.

"Aahh!" she sighed with contentment and licked her lips with her lips: using her bottom lip to lick her top and vice versa - a small vice only and one among many she enjoyed with both gusto and feeling in her quest to live life to the brim and overflowing.

SPLASH! Her friends Roger and Alex arrived and crowded her table.

SPLASH! They handed out gossip and jokes and shared innuendoes.

SPLASH! Bottles and glasses compete for the attention of hands which waved to express the sheer verve of youth's delightful dialogue with youth.

"Eleanor, over here," Rita waved her frantic message with both hands across a now crowded lounge bar. Her close friend arrived with a young man in tow.

"Bar fly," laughed Eleanor who was clearly excited to meet her flat mate who, whatever her faults, could never be accused of being dull.

"I might have known you'd be here already. I've a new solicitor in tow: meet Christopher Larkin. Christopher, this is a bold and brazen hussy. Exactly the sort of woman your mother will have warned you to stay away from. Am I right Rita or am I just right."

"I would say you're right unjust; but then who am I to judge myself. Where's Lord Archie then?"

"Don't ask. If I tell you I'm going to get as pissed as a rat then perhaps you'll be able to paint the picture by those numbers on your own and I won't have to cry telling you about it."

"You always do when you've had a few anyway. You thrive on insecurity and you know it. Well, come on lets all shift up and move bums, we've two more for the drinking trough and all the little piggies will have to move over. Come on Alex, shift your arse." She said to a young man who was dressed like a down market version of swampy. "I think even you can manage a short bum-wiggle you lazy sod. That's a good boy. Am I being sexist? I didn't comment on size did I? If I'd said little boy then you might all have thought otherwise."

"Your problem sister is that you confuse sexist with sexuality," retorted Alex, "you should know that it is as sexist to call a man a boy as it is to label a woman a girl. Size has nothing to do with it."

"Little do you know," enjoined Rita as the table of faces - apart from a surprised Christopher Larkin - laughed in response. "Your problem Alex is that you have a problem which is itself a problem to solve."

"Very problematic," smiled Eleanor in support.

"Phlegmatic even," teased Rita as she put her hands on the shoulder straps of her blue denim boiler suit. Christopher noticed a number of coloured badges advertising causes as diverse as Ban the Hunt and Save the Whale. A pale blue silk fichu flowered under her neck fastened with an emblem of the green flag whereas a dark crimson cravat was attached to her right hip through her belt buckle.

"Phlegm, in it? What you mean the beer," mocked Christopher who easily entered into the spirit of a spirited night out.

"A spittoon of ale, please?" demanded a rhinoceros with a human face whom Eleanor introduced to him as Roger the Rugby player. He looked at Christopher suspiciously over his sharp horn-like nose. Christopher had the uneasy feeling that he was shortly to be the victim of a minor stampede. "What's with the flute, Guv?"

"You what?" queried Christopher who, nevertheless, quickly gathered the meaning of the question by recalling an old episode of *"Minder"* on the television. "Oh," he continued running the forefinger and thumb of each hand down each respective lapel of his jacket. He searched rapidly for any explanation which, he hoped, would ingratiate him with the hard faced young man who seemed very determined to stare an answer out of him. "It's my working overalls," he replied finally with a sly smile.

"Didn't you hear me say he's the new solicitor?" retorted Eleanor.

"Lawyers. More bloody lawyers, we should do what Shakespeare advised: Kill all the lawyers."

"Present company accepted of course," stated Eleanor helpfully.

"Provided he's on our side," glared Roger who leant over the polished table like a pirate.

"I'm on the side of Legal Aid" rejoined Christopher in an effort to say something acceptable to present company.

"Then you're against us," retorted Roger the Rhino as he snorted derisively.

"Whose law is it anyway?" questioned Rita and she went on to answer her own question which was an irritating habit of hers: "The law of property. Not a law for property. For the environment. For all of us. A law of human rights that's what we need. Where's that then, eh?"

"Up my arse," suggested Roger unhelpfully. "Or it might be up your fanny but I don't know because you haven't let me look recently."

"You're a pig, Roger."

"Oink! Oink!"

"If Roger hadn't been the son of a millionaire," said Eleanor in a slow, sarcastic fashion, "do you think he'd then talk normally like the rest of us?"

"I am a cockney," retorted Roger defensively.

"Being born in a Mayfair flat doesn't qualify you to be cockney, Roger. Besides most working class cockneys would give up their accents to have the chances you've blown in life. Do you think you can order some more booze without being abusive or insulting. Poor Christopher probably wonders where he's ended up and who the hell he's mixed up with. Especially when he hears your mouth spewing out sewage!" Rita quickly quaffed a half pint in less than half a minute and continued. "Now Alex here. He's the true van-guard of the struggle. Aren't you Alex? When he's not pissed or stoned that is. Everyone's so pissed off these days that they're rarely off being pissed all the time. Anyway, Alex is an intellectual. Aren't you Alex? His dad was a traveller and campaigned against the M25 and so his credentials are impeccable," Rita turned to Eleanor and Christopher to explain: "it's rather like Eton and Harrow for the other side. Anyway, let me tell you this. Alex himself campaigns and even climbs trees himself: when he can be bothered that is and he has even produced the odd pamphlet or two. One of them was nearly readable!"

"I don't know why you don't just bite your tongue off sister and chew it around your mouth for a little while for something to do. It certainly isn't any use to you in any other way that I've noticed," complained Alex.

"Alex's problem," pronounced Rita after starting her fourth pint. "Is that he's just stopped sleeping with me or, perhaps I should say, that I've just stopped sleeping with him. And he can't handle it, can you Alex?"

It seemed to Christopher as if Roger was in a similar category: the Rita Redundancy Scheme. The way the rhino glared menacingly at Alex as if about to charge indicated to Christopher that his desire was far from dead. Rita was broad shouldered with a broad smile which flashed like a headlight on a dark Country road, catching rabbits like Roger and Alex in its beam. She clearly enjoyed being the centre of things whether it was a campaign for road closure or a former lover's re-union. A melee of words danced around the table as they tumbled out of mobile mouths to be only occasionally picked up by receptive ears but, more frequently, falling about the glasses, cigarettes and debris unheeded. Christopher Larkin who did more listening than the rest and picked up the following burst of word-fire over a subjective period of a few minutes which was, in fact, an objective flypast hour:

"Then the Bill sealed off the road and made a sudden sweep grabbing nearly all the activists whose faces they must have known; it was more than coincidence if you ask

me - course it was. My phone's tapped and yours is bound
to be and I'm sure they're tapping mine - I blow a high
pitch whistle down mine regularly. I'd piss down it but it
wouldn't go through would it? More's the pity - Where's
the beer, come on put your hands in your trouser pockets
Alex; and I don't mean to play pocket billiards either,
you've got stacks of dosh. Come on - that Trip to Kerala
sounds like a buzz I might do that would you fancy coming
Rita - A trip to Cardiff would be more up Roger's street.
He's just saying this to impress. Did you know that they
used a truncheon on Birdman? From the Newbury by-pass.
He only joined us 'cus no-one else would have him. He's
got the same internationalist perspective as John Bull and
he makes him look like a pacifist an' all. Always, always
looking for a scrap that one. Happen the truncheon would
be wasted on his head! - Gun law, that's what Archie calls
you lot - Do you believe him Eleanor? The Hunt-Sab was a
farce last Saturday. We didn't get close at all. Just stood
around waiting for the Bill to collar us like some kind of
Job creation scheme for the boys in blue. I got to spray
some scent an' that was it: bamcrushahhh! A mouthful of a
P.C.'s elbow - those officers didn't know how to bloody
tackle. Wouldn't last five minutes on the Rugger field - Oh,
Ruggar, very working class Woger. Tell me do you drive
to the hunt in Daddy's Rolls? Parked up with the squire's
car from the same series - Nothing wrong with a Roller.
You don't seem interested Chris, are we boring you?"

"What?" Christopher looked startled as he faced
Eleanor's hazelnut eyes which narrowed as they tried to
study his face. Some strands of red hair had cascaded down
her forehead to nearly cover half her face and cast the other

half in shadow. She pushed it back with her thin long fingers, like fat spider's legs, which seemed to dance independently across her skin to gather back the mislaid web of red hairs. "It's just that I didn't know you were into all this."

"This what?" she said as his leg accidentally touched hers. He left it there but she withdrew her own.

"This environment thing," he replied with a dying smile.

"Rita's my flat-mate. I guess I just sort of drifted into it but I do believe in some of it though. Don't you? They have made some changes you know. Stopped several roads. Now, banning the hunt is a Parliamentary Bill. People like Rita caused that. I just help her out occasionally. She's very committed so are most of them here, except you of course."

"Yes, except me. I must admit Eleanor I feel a bit out of place. Perhaps I ought to go."

"Nonsense. I'm ordering you another drink."

"Hey! It's the bright new law man!" Balwinder Singh Gill towered over Christopher Larkin, who had to turn on his stool to see who was drilling a finger hole in his shoulder blade. As he turned, Balwinder was so close to him that his fly zip was at Christopher's eye level. Christopher moved back - bar stool as well - but Balwinder simply closed in on him again. "Hello everyone. Are you all friends of Christopher," Balwinder shouted in a slurred voice across the table and his unembarrassed audacity commanded silence. "I'm a friend of Christopher as well. I'm Balwinder Singh Gill. My friends call me Bindi. You can all call me Bindi as well. Mmm I like your tits sweetheart," he leered drunkenly at Rita; as he stretched

105

his body over the table the skin on his face was pulled taut and the purple scars stood out prominently.

"Mmm an' I think you're a right tit too, sweet fart," retorted Rita angrily.

"Come on, Bindi. Leave it out. Come an' sit with us," Joshi put two arms around Bindi's shoulders and, surprisingly, the latter allowed Joshi to steer him away from the source of conflict, but he loudly insisted on a trip to the gentlemen's toilet, before returning to a table they had occupied opposite. The gents toilet smelt strongly of strong piss. It was an old stone urinal which seemed to soak up the smells of centuries and release them slowly back into the air again. Balwinder had stopped acting drunk as soon as he had closed the toilet door. Joshi leant against it. Bender, Satish and Bender's younger brother came out of a cubicle in response to a pre-arranged knocking signal and Bender's younger brother looked very sheepish and felt very silly. "The fucking tap won't work properly. I've smudged the make-up and can't clean it up properly."

"He looks nothing like me. He's supposed to look a bit like me at least. Why is it that no fucker in our outfit can get any fucking thing right except me. Here, never mind, wipe that smudge off with bog-paper. Here let me .... that's it. The scar's the best bit. His face is ugly and nothing like my gorgeous self. Never mind, take your clothes off. Don't look at me stupid. I'm taking mine off as well. The whole idea of using you is that you're a lanky bugger like me. We'll swap clothes for now and swap 'em back after. What do you mean after - what? That's not your business. Come on, be quick if someone comes in

106

now we'll have to hide in the sodding cubicles for ages, till they go again. That's it. Now, let me have me blade back. Don't touch it wanker: It's clean. That's why I've got these." Balwinder held up a pair of thin polythene gloves. "This is a blade purchased off a market stall in Delhi. Not a hope in hell of tracing it."

"Come on, Bindi let's go," Bender helped him pull on his brother's jumper just as his brother slipped on Bindi's Levi jacket. "You're sure you ain't been seen in there yet. You came in the back way didn't you?" Bender's brother nodded in reply to his brother's question. "Well when we come back and you've swapped over again, you go back out the back way and don't hang about waiting for me. And don't say anything in the pub, just bury your head in your arms on the table. Okay. Right then Bindi, we'll just cover you if anything goes wrong."

"No you won't. Don't be stupid. You go back to the table and get pissed. That's the best thing you can do for me but don't forget thirty fucking minutes and then back in here with your brother."

"I won't get pissed in thirty minutes" he retorted smiling.

"No, but that's time enough for Mukesh to get this," Bindi pressed a button on the side of his knife: sssssssssssssstic. The blade cut through the air to lock in a skin-tearing, flesh slashing, stabbing position. It had a sharp point with two cutting edges and it seemed clear that Bindi had spent hours, if not days, sharpening it to perfection. He wore polythene gloves on both hands which he thrust deep into his newly acquired rain-coat pockets, just as soon as he had re-set the blade on his flick knife. He did this quickly because his hands were shaking and he didn't want the others to see that and form the wrong impression. It was not that he was scared in any way. Indeed he felt super-charged and finely-tuned, like a high-powered formula-one racer, ready to move rapidly through the gears: to pump adrenaline rather than petrol into his bodily pistons and to tear the heart out of the opposition.

"Do it quickly Bindi. A few stabs," Bender demonstrated. "And back here again."

"Are you telling ME how to do a job. You tell me FUCK ALL! So back off Bender. Right then, this is it. Out the way Joshi. I'll be back here at ten past eight. Just make sure you do the same. Let's try an' do this right shall we. Okay I've gone," Bindi pushed Joshi unnecessarily since he had already stood to one side but Bindi's aggression had reached boiling point and Joshi was easy to shove around. After a rapid, serious stare at all his friends, he darted out of the door, which slammed shut behind him.

Mukesh's grandfather opened the door and entered the living room with a glance at his grandson who was moving cushions and looking hopeless and lost.

"God is everywhere and in everything but you do not understand that, Mukesh. You do not understand anything but you think you understand it all and that is the sad thing."

"Yes, grandfather, look I've got to go out in a minute. Now where's my jacket," Mukesh moved around the lounge unnaturally as if the queries of his grandfather had goaded him into making sudden jerky movements. He stared at the old man's serene face impatiently: "Well, do you know?"

"What I do not know could fill a book. A book of empty papers. I blame no-one, but, if your parents did not work, work: all the time work - then perhaps ..... Ah well you do not listen. The worldly vanity of a jacket is more important to a young man than the Puja he should perform to worship his God and to honour his parents and grandparents. But then what do I know? I am an old man."

"It was here on the settee. I left it here. I've looked in my room ...." Grumbled Mukesh who tried, unsuccessfully, to ignore his grandfather's criticism.

"You have no contact with the eternal and instead you just live for the shallow world of prakrti without the purusha. A world in which you walk as a blind man would."

"Stop ranting on, grandfather, what do you know anyway," Mukesh raised his voice angrily and danced two or three steps without joy: an expression of the pent-up frustration he felt. "Your Gods and your teachers have done nothing for you. They have kept you like a peasant without land. A sponger on my parents - your children. What kind of religion is that?"

"You know nothing as I have said but you think you know everything. It is a great shame. I am ......"

"..... a sponger as I have said grandfather. You do nothing but sit around this flat all day and pray. Oh yes you pray a lot but none of us are any better off as a result. And because you are a bored old man you try and tell me how to live my life. Well, I don't want any lessons from you, thank you very much. I don't want to be a miserable landless peasant all my life working for crust and crumbs and being broken by toil. For nothing, so that I cannot even support myself at sixty. Is that what you're going to teach me?"

"No," said his grandfather quietly. "I would teach you that every moment of time is a miracle to behold in awe. That there is a boundless joy in the simplicity of a shadow. That is what I would teach you if I could," he started to sing:

"You do not see that the Real is in your home, and you wander from forest to forest listlessly. Here is the truth! ...."

Mukesh stormed out of the lounge and slammed the door shut behind him as he cursed. Old, stupid, landless peasants, who have done nothing with their lives, except to ardently lick the under soles of other peoples muddy boots, may, perhaps, find some justification for their years of grovel by invoking divine providence: but he knew better. There was no God. He was not going to waste his life on years of pointless toil so someone else could get rich. He wanted it all. He wanted it now.

Mukesh took his father's leather jacket without consent; admired himself in the long wardrobe mirror, stuffed some packets of brown powder into his zip pocket and tried his flick knife in front of his adoring reflection: pivoting quickly on his heel and spinning his body round as he simultaneously pressed the button to activate his automatic blade. He looked heroic. The leader of the Tooti Nung.

CHAPTER SEVEN

He felt he could see through the night like a cat. Balwinder's body was so wound up with tension and his muscles so taut he felt he saw things he would not normally have seen, as he prowled across a concrete catwalk, which separated one squat grey sprawling block of flats from another. From the thin ugly walkway he looked down briefly at the public house he had recently left: its blaze of artificial light bathing the pavement of South Road.

Someone was going to be hurt tonight.
Someone was going to be cut by Bindi's blade.
Someone was going to be his next victim on his road to immortalisation.

Mukesh was going to die. A bloody flesh-tearing switch-blade was going to kill, kill, KILL. Bindi's soul screamed with the satisfaction of what was to come: repeated images of the fight yet to happen were flashed across his mind as he prepared himself to do the deed. The emotional stew, which made up his personality, was fully stirred and bubbling on top of the passionate heat of burning resentment. Resentment that he was not already acknowledged to be the natural successor to the old leaders of the Smoke. Resentment that he was not given his due. Resentment that he was not number one.

The internal fire within Balwinder's body burned away all caution and care about the possible consequences for himself (they did not exist because the world was made for him) and any consideration for other people. They did not matter since they merely existed as part of his consciousness: to be cut out, like an untoward thought, when the occasion arose. It was obvious that he was the only being who mattered; hence all that mattered was what mattered to him.

The complex of flats had been designed to re-create the community spirit and were a serious attempt at social engineering, with a conscious effort being made to break away from tower block alienation, and, as such, they were a roaring failure. The quaint nooks and crannies of the concrete paradise had been used as hiding holes for stolen goods, as drug abuse quarters, as sites for rape and mayhem or, as they were now, as the jumping board for a stabbing. They were not as commonly, if ever, used as a shelter for local gossip and no-one appeared to treat them as the idyllic modern equivalent of the country stile. They were not, alas, a place to pause and engage in idle chatter while walking up from one level of charming city dwellings to the next, higher level. The electric lighting, manufactured in resemblance to the old gas light, had long since been vandalised, so that the potential meeting places were cast in fearful darkness and the homebound flat dweller generally avoided, although did not ignore, their presence. A frightened half look over his shoulder as he turned his back on the black void to climb the next flight of stairs, was the usual reaction of the trembling passer-by. A response repeatedly witnessed by the lurking knifeman who waited patiently for his quarry.

Mukesh danced down the steps, after leaving his house, to make a quick deal at the pre-arranged place and time which he was destined not to fulfil: this transitory place and immediate time pre-empting all earlier plans, maps and personal geography of an illusory nature. Darkness reached out to claim him from the shadowy corners of his vision and, as he performed a reflex pirouette, dropping his blade almost as a part of his turn (almost pre-planned), his facial expression exclaimed: "not me! This can't happen to me."

No virgin slasher, no novice body-carver, can properly appreciate the thrill and spill of squirting blood: the forbidden juice of joy. In-out, in-out goes the sharp symbol of supremacy; the victim gasps and sighs and collapses before the high priest, who is momentarily satisfied, before a hazy fear of retribution gradually engulfs him: he is no high priest and his actions are not sanctioned by law. He is standing at the top of a flight of stairs and blood, in many shades of red, is all around him in splattered stains of dark, deep, nearly mauve-purple in the centre while spreading out through pinkish purple to red and lighter pink on the outside: a dozen such stains at a glance. Lumps of yellow on one step - what did they signify? A crumbled, broken body lay empty in a corner of the landing beneath Bindi's gaze and a cold dead hand reached inside his skull and somehow touched his mind. A kind of despairing regret, not at what he had done but, rather strangely, at how he had wasted his time, caused him to feel suddenly cheated as if he had finished with a lover who had, as always, failed to make the complete fantasy for him. Regret, he should feel better in his moment of triumph. Regret, what would his family say were he caught? Regretful, he turned and ran.

T.I. Barker was buzzing with the excitement of being involved in a real operation. Nowadays, it was rare for him, as a pen pushing liaison officer, to do anything other than paperwork, so that, when the opportunity came to act, it was a carefully savoured treat. Admittedly, there was not a lot of excitement to be relished from sitting next to his Chief Superintendent on an internally heated car seat in an unmarked Volvo - a bit harder to spot than the standard police-issue Vauxhall but, nevertheless, he had been given responsibility for the night-camera and was busy clicking away frantically for Queen and Country. The photographs being released automatically with a satisfying "burring" sound as they protruded out of a slit in the bottom of the camera.

"Have we been here long enough now, sir," he said with his eye on the view finder.

"What," retorted a surprised Chief Superintendent Derek Manning who was indignantly recalled from a light doze. He dared not ask how long they had been there already because that would betray the fact that he had gone over into restful oblivion. "I, well, I suppose so, have you got some good pictures for me?"

"I've got some heavy looking Irish men in a combination of four around a lamp post, sir."

"Lord protect us," interjected Derek Manning with a bitter smile. "From all combinations." Nevertheless, he fingered through the photographs dutifully with a sad smile. T.I. Barker handed another batch of photographs over with enthusiasm.

"And I've got a few of dubious looking Asian characters. Probably Holy Smoke," continued T.I. Barker, who had already been warned by Commander Godlove that Derek was becoming dangerously cynical in his old age.

"Sure it's not the Scotch Mist, Barker?" queried the Chief Superintendent. "They're a well known gang in M15 circles."

"Will you have time to complete this research tonight?" asked the junior officer anxious to change the subject before he was contaminated by free thought. Derek Manning reached down below his seat, pulled up a bar, and pushed himself backwards so that he could stretch his legs with a sigh. He then tapped the steering wheel thoughtfully, with both hands, like a drummer in a pop group.

"Don't use the word research, please. If you mean, am I going to cobble together the usual misinformation which we term 'Intelligence', then the answer is of course I am. You see, it's already done, And all I have to do is alter the title. Indeed, I think I have rehashed the same report ten times in as many years. Of course, I'll have to draw up a so-called conclusion, mentioning all the points requested by His Holiness, but that shouldn't take...."

"You mean Commander Godlove," interrupted T.I. Barker glancing sideways at his superior.

"Anyone who knows the answers before the question is asked must be a little bit holy, don't you think?" smiled Derek in reply.

"The Commander likes to lead from the front but it wouldn't do for us to put forward differing views, would it? I mean all of us as a whole should put forward one fully considered perspective of ......"

Paranoid prejudice, thought the Detective Superintendent to himself. He did not hear the rest of his junior officer's loyal address and, instead, he gazed out wistfully at the real world. Perhaps he had entered the police force when he had been much too young and had consequentially, too high an expectation of what could be achieved by such a career? Perhaps he should have gone to University first as his father had wanted and then, perhaps, he would never have entered the force at all. Perhaps ......

"Now, there's the genuine article," Chief Superintendent Manning nudged T.I. Barker who took a rapid shot of Balwinder Singh Gill as he dodged the traffic to cross Kings Road which, unknown to the two police officers, he had done in order to help him burn up his "high." It might well prove to be a fateful photograph had it shown more than a back on legs: of uncertain age, race or sex.

"Who's he?" enquired the Trainee Investigator after they had watched him enter the Glassy Junction Public House through the side door.

"Just another spoilt brat. If it's who I think it is, his father owns an Import-Export business: Gill's Direct Clothing Ltd., or some such. Got himself a big warehouse behind the Broadway"

"And his son?"

"Into all sorts. Drugs mostly and gratuitous violence. Do you know I had a lecturer once who tried to teach us that crime is the result of poverty and deprivation whereas, in my humble opinion, the causation is more likely to be boredom and the need to rise head and shoulder above the rest. Take your drug addict, for example, he only does it to give himself a bit of purpose. To fill in his time. He can spend an afternoon scoring and then fill a hole in the evening by cutting up his gear, rolling his own and generally constructing a use out of empty hours..."

"Shall we go now," interjected the glassy eyed Trainee Investigator who stifled a yawn as he spoke.

"Not interested, eh?"

"It's not that," assured the young officer fearing disapproval.

"No, of course not, but then you wouldn't be the first. Perhaps we shouldn't bite the hand ...... and all that. Who cares anyway. To really look at the causes as our new leader says would produce a whole new ball-game and they might not want us to play, eh?"

"Yes sir or rather No sir," replied a confused Trainee Investigator.

"Perhaps, three bags full sir would be better?" retorted the superior officer with a gentle, knowing smile. He reached down and turned the ignition key while he pressed the accelerator pedal with his right foot: to kick his purring engine into life. "Well, I think we've done our bit for the free world don't you? Let's go home and have some cocoa."

"It's murder. Nothing short of murder."

"Calm down there, Paddy. You being sat there so quiet and all. Don't show yourself up now."

"It's murder I tell you" he said to anyone who would listen. "Weren't you for hearing me. They killed Frank as sure as I'm being sat here so they did. Killed him dead. A victim of an SAS plot, I'm telling you."

"And I'm telling you to calm yourself and not to be speaking such tittle tattle. Old Frank died of the drink, so he did. And as for the SAS., I wasn't told of any bullet holes in his body which was, by all accounts, pickled in alcohol."

"Poison, that's how they did away with Frank an' that's how they'll do away with me."

"You being such a threat an' all. Don't make me laugh. Here let me collect these glasses."

"Don't they have any women in Afetside Christopher?" queried Eleanor, as Parminder took both their glasses.

"What?" - Cough, splutter, "er-hum." Christopher had been trying to listen to Patrick O'Rourke's conversation which was going on just behind him at the bar and he was silently hoping that Paddy wouldn't recognise him from Ealing Magistrates' Court that morning.

"Well you've been sat next to me like a frigid foreigner. Not exactly all wit, charm and repartee, are we?"

"Well, Southall seems a strange place to me, I must admit. Everything's upside down to what I expected. I suppose you'll laugh at me, Eleanor, if I say I'm nothing down here. Less than nothing maybe. At least up North I was known and respected. In my own small way, of course. I'm not trying to make out I was some kind of big shot or anything like that, not your Archie Lord like; but I was nobody's fool. Down here, I'm like a little boy again - getting into trouble in the schoolroom, not able to do my work properly. Perhaps I should've worn a hat with bells on and curled up shoes. And waved one of those tickling sticks about."

"The national custom of the Tundra!"

"Don't laugh. Oh, why not. Laugh away. I'm laughing too."

"Your eyes aren't laughing."

"Well, let's face it. My first day has not been an overwhelming success now has it? Or would you disagree. Come on Eleanor, disagree with me and make me feel better."

"You went to court and spoke for the first time. That's something akin to losing your virginity isn't it? Or wouldn't you know?"

"You'd be surprised at what I wouldn't know. I knew less than that drunken Irish buffoon who was talking to the barman just now. I represented him or perhaps I should say: he represented me."

"Was it really as bad as you told me in the office?"

"Worse. I've spent the last eight hours consistently displaying to my future clientele just what a first rate prat I am. I even managed to spill hot water down my y-fronts for the benefit of Holy Nung or whatever they are."

"You don't wear y-fronts do you comrade," interjected Rita with a deep and dirty chuckle. "I thought all lawyers, stock-brokers and professional pimps wore boxer shorts and red braces these days. Here let's have a peep!"

"Rita, darling, you're so coarse. Christopher and I were just discussing his first day."

"Free psychotherapy."

"Oh, I don't know about the free darling. You can buy the next round Christopher. After a good moan we feel much better, don't you think?"

"I don't. I feel as if I've picked the wrong job in the wrong place and that I should have stayed where I belonged."

"In the Tundra."

119

"Where I'm not making a damn fool of myself the whole time. I'm sure those Holy Nung are laughing at me."

"Holy Smokes, darling. They do seem to be clamouring for your attention. They keep waving and shouting your name and that Balwinder Gill, with the scar, keeps making a nuisance of himself. Oh God, he's coming over here again. Oh no he's not, he's going to the loo: thank heaven for small mercies. And Rita darling thanks heaven for large ones too. I know she does because she's told me so. Don't ever go to bed with her unless you want me to know how you perform because she's a terrible gossip."

"And you're a terrible liar and tease Eleanor. And you mustn't put this young law man off me because you fancy him yourself."

"Ha, no-one will come between my Archie and me."

"Except his wife."

"I might kill her. Would you represent me Christopher if I did. Oh, I forgot, I should've asked Paddy O'Rourke instead shouldn't I. He's the advocate round here."

"That Balwinder keeps walking passed our table and glaring at us or perhaps its me" said Christopher nervously. "He's waiting for me to spill another drink down the front of my trousers, I'm sure he's willing me to do it. He's been here all evening staring at me, winking and waving."

"Perhaps he fancies you."

"Woger, what a thing to say. And I thought that sort of thing only happened on rugby pitches. Oh, hello Paddy. Let's have more happy water please. Same again. No double rounds this time because Christopher's paying and I'm broke. Besides poor Eleanor here is likely to bring it all back up across the table if we do. Better make it one pint for her. That's it dear: lean on my shoulder if it makes you feel better. She's jilted in love you see. A terrible malady. And not helped by being entirely her own fault."

"If she's drunk, she should go home. Can't have drunken women in my establishment," said Parminder glumly. "Give the place a bad name."

"Whereas drunken men give it a good one, I suppose. In future, I'll be served by someone else, if you don't mind. But you can order us a taxi after you've emptied the dregs pans into our glasses."

"So we meet tomorrow in Southall!"

"Ys, Woger, well done. Same time. Same place. Same leaflets. Same old faces. Gives us something to do, I suppose. Keeps us off the streets. Here comes the final round. Here, you drink Eleanor's, Woger, and prove your manhood to us. That's it. Down in one. But not up with eight, please. No spewing in your neighbour's lap now. Oh, we've got a visitor. Irish nationalism personified. Hello, Paddy. We're just leaving coincidentally enough. A shame we can't stay for your account of the Troubles - again."

"This young fella here is my apprentice. He's a learning the law of speechifying from the lap of Paddy O'Rourke and I've come over from my table to address you all, so you better listen please, on the death of my friend Frank. Listen to me. Listen good. An' you'll be learning how to address a court from the heart. The heart, you hear. It's the heart which speaks for the head and that's an important bit of advice. I seem to have fallen over but I speak better lying down so I do. That's me second piece of advice. Lie if you can. But be sure to get away with it," Patrick put a clammy hand on Christopher's knee as he pulled himself upright, his large bulging eyes staring at Christopher like a pair of searchlights full of deadly urgency. "There's nothing that will be hurting a bodily frame so badly as too much truth. If there were too much of that around then we'd all be in the clink for sure. Aren't you agreeing with old Paddy Christopher? Now you listen, because Paddy may shortly be dead like Paddy from far too much Paddy and then you'll be wishing you'd listened to Paddy because Paddy, he knows a thing or two about the world whatever anyone else may say to the conny-tarry not the Conny Mary. Dear ole Conny Mary and the twelve Bens. Now, members of the jury. You should always start with these words. That's my third piece of advice. Here. Hold on. Where are you all going: listen to me now. Have you no pity."

Christopher managed to extricate himself from the clutches of a paranoid and pissed Patrick O'Rourke and smiling a diffident goodbye he followed the others outside.

The pavement was glossy with the remnants of a rainfall and it shone back the varied colours of light: yellow from the street posts, green from the pub sign - now all blurred and unreadable - amber then red from the traffic light on the corner, white from the passing cars, which ripped through the roadway water like a multiple whiplash, a false neon pink from the advertisement for an American brand of cigarettes and a rainbow amalgamation of every colour, with new ones found by that association, in the melting pot of puddles at the foot of Christopher Larkin. He noticed only the red which dominated all the other colours like the blood of violence shed in anger on the streets.

Rita stood next to him: tut, tut, tutting with impatience at the delayed arrival of the taxi cab and - next to her on the other side of Julia - Eleanor leant her head on Rita's right shoulder to receive what was, obviously, much needed support. She uttered occasional incoherent sentences of jumbled words which conveyed a mood of sadness, rejection and Lordlessness.

Christopher waited in the wet for someone to speak and, as he did so, he felt a drifting disappointment swell up and claim him: making him conscious, for the first time that evening, of a hitherto unexpressed emotion, which was more in the nature of a nagging unease, namely: he had clearly hoped for something more to happen that night. To be more precise, he had desired, for some time, a little warmth and compassion in his life and, since Eleanor had shown some small interest in him, he had felt, but not until now admitted feeling, that she might be able to supply the aforesaid commodities rather like a spiritual market trader: "I'll have half a kilo of warmth and a touch more compassion please" - "Sorry sir, we don't see old stock any more. Besides, I'm too pissed to care."

It had been too difficult for Christopher to really accept that Eleanor was infatuated with an old man - i.e., over thirty or, in Archie's case, considerably over thirty - and it was only when he was standing within earshot of her drunken ramblings that he had truly believed it. Her thoughts were not of him, at all.

In fact, Eleanor's thoughts were the stirred up remains of all the emotional stress she had consumed that day, being, principally, her titillation and rejection by the Lord of her passion. This fervour surged up within a body, which was now released from inhibition and, in particular, the constraints of socialisation imposed in late twentieth

Century London, fired her brain and tripped over her tongue like a large lump of sick.

B l a a a a !

The regurgitation of the day-time struggle, with her desire, spilled out of her mouth in an effort to untie a tight internal knot: she spewed out words by the wide, open mouthful: "And this bastard tell us, tells me, dares to tell me now, after everyfing else .... (a tear fell with diluted mascara down her cheek) .... he says he can't ...... he can't ..... won't ...... he says ..... the bastard .... can't leave her but leaves me .... well, doesn't he? What am I to ..... he says this to me Rita. Rita. He says this and he says that .... what does it all mean ...... I'll tell you what it means. It all means fuck all! (Eleanor waved her right hand downwards in a gesture of termination like a conductor finally silencing the orchestra after Beethoven's Ninth). Why doesn't he .... I'll tell you why he doesn't ..... because he doesn't care .... the bastard."

"Perhaps if you realise that instead of crawling back to him again, then we might not have to go through all this next time," counselled the now matronly Rita in the tones of a nursery nurse.

Christopher was completely ignored: not needed, not wanted and feeling pretty sorry for himself. He was contemplating his universal rejection when the taxi-cab arrived and splashed him with water as it parked up against the pavement with an impatient skid. He accepted his fate with a grimace. After all, his role in life was to be peed on.

CHAPTER EIGHT

When Christopher woke up he walked into the wall. He stood staring at it stupidly for a second or so before walking into it again. One perfectly possible explanation for this behaviour was that the world had changed while he had been sleeping and that the particles of matter, which made up the door, had grown weary of being shoved open and shut at the bidding of that unnatural, conscious matter-on-the-rampage and had, accordingly, changed themselves from an obedient door, at the beck and call of beings decidedly less important than God, into an intransigent wall. Christopher Larkin discounted that objective explanation in favour of a subjective one, which was usually more likely to be accurate, since, in Christopher's experience of existing as a two-legged conscious (or semi-conscious) piece of mobile matter, the world was an entirely subjective place. Subjectively speaking, he had been at home in Afetside when he had walked into the wall. The fact that he received a whack on the nose did not, indeed could not, affect that reality - HE was in Afetside and an open door should be where the wall was - hence, he walked into the wall again. This time the subjective reality ran up against the instinct for self-preservation and the, by now, throbbing, sore nose.

"What the hell are you playing at?" said the nose to the brain, "It doesn't even smell like Afetside." Thus an adjustment in subjective reality caused his internal bubbling, sparkling, electro-chemical relay of ionotropic response and the secondary adenylate cyclase and phospholipase C transmissions to re-align themselves - this took some considerable time and more than one thousandth of a second was lost, not to mention the odd microfarad displaced by a closing down of some of the brain's neurotransmitter receptor cells caused, not for the first time, by the presence of large quantities of that complicated depressant drug alcohol - and he (for want of a better word perhaps we should say the conglomerate of matter whose response to other matter and to itself is directed by an electro-chemical relay independent (?) of other such conglomerates and which we cannot be bothered to separately label since as a phenomena of matter it won't be around long enough to matter) felt the world change around him. His internal compass de-magnetised. He was away from home.

He turned away from the wall and looked at the small television which protruded out over the bed on a metal z-shaped, retractable arm. Beyond the television was blurred fog. He reached down for his glasses and put them on and, as if by magic, the bathroom appeared. Of course, he was in a hotel and there was no need to leave the room in order to wash, read, discharge processed waste matter from his rear orifice, pour H_2O down his top orifice - it was important not to confuse these functions - nor for nearly any other basic bodily need. Thus, the first thing he did was to leave his hotel room. He did not want breakfast brought up to his room; in fact, he did not want breakfast at all. The vindictive barmaid - cum - waitress - cum - potential S.S. recruit was likely to make another attempt to lace his coffee with brain remover.

Christopher successfully left his hotel room four times. This was not simply an attempt to improve his social skills. On the first occasion he was minus his wallet, watch and keys. On the second occasion, minus his wallet and watch. Thirdly minus his wallet and, fourthly, merely minus. Those gently souls who do not believe that this word can accurately reflect a state of mind have never suffered an overhang of drugged sub-conscious into the early hours of the following day; when it's pain-killing effects have been largely dissipated and it's pain-giving effects first fully appreciated. Christopher felt as if there was a layer of cotton wool between his consciousness and the outside perception of that consciousness; but it was not, as cotton wool normally is, to protect him but, rather, to insulate the pounding drum within his head; so that only he could hear it.

"Ouch," was his first word of the day not including the socially unacceptable expletive - even for Christopher Larkin - which was uttered when his nose was squashed. It was spoken as a response to the clang of his brain against its outer casing caused by an untoward and inconsiderate skip by his legs down several stairs in one foolish half jump.

"Mr Larkin. You're not in your room!" exclaimed Miss Sadistique.

No, don't shout - he did not reply, as the machine gun turrets, which were not positioned along the barbed wire fence which did not surround the hotel: opened up and riddled him with contemptuous stares. I should be dealing with a man, and not an excuse for one, her eyes appeared to say.

"Good heavens, you're right," he retorted looking down at himself in mock horror.

"But I've been ringing your room and you've not answered," she accused: his sarcasm clearly lost on her. It was clear to Christopher that the conversation would simply become more ludicrous unless he capitulated entirely.

"I'm sorry," he replied, with eyes cast down, in the body language of abject apology. "I didn't mean not to answer the telephone. I was simply not where it was when it rang."

"Well, try to be where it is the next time it rings. It's Mr. Lord for you."

"Are you awake?" asked the anxious voice of Archie Lord.

Was he going mad or was it part of sanity's burden to field inane questions in a clever manner? "Part of me is," he complained.

"Did Eleanor get pissed again?"

What's that to do with you, he did not retort. He needed his salary. "It's difficult to know when you're half-cut yourself," he laughed.

"Only half-cut. Listen when Archie has a session he's cut one and a half. At least," a muffle laugh echoed in Christopher's ear piece. "But never mind that now. Look I've got a problem that I need a bit of help with. You see Balwinder Gill got himself nicked last night ......"

"Not Balwinder Gill," interrupted Christopher.

"No?" questioned Archie surprised.

"No," replied Christopher confused.

"Then who?" queried an impatient Archie Lord.

"Balwinder Gill," replied an entirely nonplussed Christopher Larkin.

"Look," growled the earpiece of Christopher's telephone. "I have learnt from long and bitter experience, that the world makes a great deal more sense to everybody concerned if all the talking is done by me. Now please listen because all of this is very important. I am playing golf today. Balwinder Gill isn't playing golf. He is, however, playing twenty questions with his Uncle Bill only he isn't letting on that he knows any of the answers. Apparently, they are taking him to Ealing Magistrate's Court this morning. Yes, I know it's Saturday. That's why I'm playing golf. They have a special Saturday Court, you see. Christ, do I have to explain everything. I mean, can't anyone make logical deductions any more? Sorry Christopher, I'm a little grumpy this morning but you can make me happy by saying yes."

"Yes?" questioned Christopher.

"Good man," answered Archie Lord. "Just get yourself down there at half nine and give Balwinder a drop of bail and you'll be away by eleven. Don't forget the legal aid forms. Profit costs are all that matter. Profit costs are all important," Archie sang the last two sentences and concluded: "Profit! Profit! Costs! Tally ho, chucks away an' all that. Let me know how you get on by the way - on Monday morning. Ta Ra!"

Just go down to the Magistrate's Court and give Balwinder a drop of bail! It all sounded so simple. However, Christopher wasn't at all sure that he had agreed to give up his Saturday morning, as Archie Lord had implied, but he was pretty sure that he had no choice in any event. Christopher went back up to his hotel room, changed into his suit and ordered a taxi. He knew that he had not chance of finding the Magistrate's Court again by himself unless he stumbled into it by chance.

The taxi driver realised that Christopher lacked "the knowledge" as well and, displaying that well-known aversion of London cabbies to the exploitation of strangers, he drove young Christopher on a short sight-seeing tour: via the igloo settlements of the Arctic wasteland. Christopher had a pay for his journey by cheque or, perhaps more accurately, cheques: one for the tax fare, one for the huskies and another for the whaling course. A fourth cheque comprised of the taxi driver's equivalent of the restaurateur's corkage charge, namely, the lock fee. A tip was not, of course, compulsory, but if you wished the driver to exercise his muscle and brain co-ordination and release the central locking device then it was, perhaps, only fair that some vast emolument was properly paid thereto.

Christopher emerged from the exercise in legal robbery and found himself feeling very small in front of the very large Magistrate's Court building. Christopher felt like a walking antitheses of young Siegfried as he apologised to the doorman for his continued existence.

The wide expanse of tiled concourse inside the building was deserted and his own footfalls - an echoing slapping sound - seemed like a serious case of trespass with intent. The doorman cleared his throat and Christopher turned around to receive a piece of advice.

"Perhaps you ought to see your client, Sir. Before you go into court that is. The cells are the other way Sir. Down those gloomy steps in the corner. Dr. Arthur Leen is on the bench today Sir and, if I were you, I'd be as prompt as I could be. That is, if I didn't want to have the leading role in a human sacrifice drama Sir."

Christopher gave his, by now, customary, self-effacing, self-emasculating sick grin and plodded heavily down into the bowels of the court building where every third sound was the clang of metal on metal as doors banged, keys clunked in locks and steel tongues spat out iron words.

"No," said the gaoler to Christopher's simple request to be allowed access to the prisoner in his cell.

"The grille," he snarled in answer to Christopher's second question as to how he was to take instructions from a man he could not see.

Thus, Christopher found himself leaning against a metal door painted red and facing a complicated lacework effect of holes which had been made in a square piece of thinner metal positioned at eye level: for a dwarf. hence he had to bend nearly double to see two cold eyeballs flickering fiercely at him on the other side of the spasmodically placed holes.

"Why wasn't no fucker with me last night. I'm picked up almost as soon as I'm in bed. Dragged down me stairs, kicked in the fucking head and bundled in a police van. I ask for me brief and he's so bloody brief, it's untrue. Two minutes I get from Archie Anus over the telephone and that's my lot. Left to fend for me fucking self. Dodging the flying boots and trying to retain my right of silence. Just tell me one thing. One simple thing before we start. Where were you?"

"Well, Archie received the call and would have gone out, I think Mr Gill, if he had ...... what I mean is, if he had thought it strictly necessary, as such."

"If it's not necessary for a murder rap then tell me this please. Answer me this simple fucking question. When is it bleeding necessary? Does he only go out for treason these days. I mean is murder merely a misdemeanour for Messrs. Crawley and Dodgers. I'm facing a life sentence and all I get is a two minute summary of how great a man Archie Lord is and how I'm really lucky to have him as a brief and how he's going to look after me real good and then they send the bleeding tea-boy to court for my bail application. I mean what is this? Am I being sold short or what? I should have gone to Joe Bailey in the first place and then perhaps I'd have got some action there."

"You're charged with murder?" queried Christopher with a large hint of panic in his voice.

"Just attempted on account of the victim not being dead, yet; but I've high hopes."

"Well, now let me see," Christopher paused to think but Bindi was not a patient man.

"Are you coming in this cell or what? I mean are we going to have to talk like this the whole time. I've got things to tell you and we can't talk like this. Go and tell the jailer to shift his arse down here and open this fucking door."

"No," retorted Christopher, who did not relish the opportunity of being locked in a cell with an angry Balwinder Gill, especially when he was just starting to exhibit definite signs of falling apart: his face was red, his palms sweaty and his knee cap was beginning to wobble

132

uncontrollably. "I don't think we've time. We'll be upstairs in a moment. What did you say to the .... er .... police when you were at the .... er .... police station?"

"Nothing, of course."

"Nothing at all?"

"I may have said ouch occasionally," chuckled Balwinder with a chilling laugh.

"You say the police .... er .... well ...."

"Kicked me in the head," assisted Balwinder. "That's what I said and that's what they did."

"The police did that?" repeated Christopher incredulously, "I mean, are you sure?"

"Why not ask them," replied Bindi sarcastically. "I mean, I'm sure they'll admit it to you. Especially to you being a solicitor and all that. On the other hand, they may phrase it different. The prisoner head butted my foot in order to make good his escape, m'lud," the cold chilling chuckle punctuated Balwinder's dialogue. "But forget that now. I've got to get out of here and you've got to get me out. I shouldn't even be in here and you know that for sure."

"I do," rejoined Christopher in surprise.

"Of course, you do. This supposed stabbing. I know that because the Bill told me what had gone off. It occurred at seven o'clock last night or thereabouts. Now do you understand?"

"I'm not sure I do," Christopher's brain was still heavy with alcohol and clogged up with pain. In addition the shock to his nervous system of having to do his first bail application in a potential murder case had added to his bewilderment so that his mental processes became completely befuddled: the cotton wool had finally fouled up the mechanism.

"You are my alibi," proclaimed Balwinder triumphantly. "I don't think they've got a stitch of evidence on me unless they've verballed me up or got lucky with forensic, anyway, you know I wasn't there because I was in the boozer with you."

"Oh yes," said Christopher slowly as the events of the previous evening were played back by his memory recorder. "They've got the wrong man," he continued as the new subjective truth permeated the upper part of his temporal lobe and, in the process, upset the formerly happy arrangement of a few million neurone cells or so in his cerebral hemispheres. "You must be innocent then. How can this happen?"

"You're catching on superman and here was I thinking that you were a bit thick as well. Now, all you have to do is tell the magistrate what you know and I'll be out."

"Hold on," said Christopher who felt that events were tumbling over each other a little too quickly for his liking. "I asked you how this could happen. I mean how come they arrested you? They must have some reason for thinking it was you."

"Whose side are you on dickhead?" screamed Bindi.

"Calm down, calm down," begged Christopher. "I just want to help you as best I can that's all. I need to know everything in order to do that. Please, help me to help you."

"Are you for real? Okay, okay. You haven't done this kind of thing before, am I right? Well, I know I'm right. What's happened here is an everyday story of unlawful arrest by the old bill followed by a bit of assault and battery on an innocent member of the public; then a gratuitous dose of false imprisonment; all nicely finished off with a topping of malicious prosecution. How it came about was by the police thinking, wrongly, that I'm something to do with the Holy Smoke gang. I mean, I know some of the gang members, like, but that's as far as it goes. I'm victimised. They nicked me before because they claimed I stabbed Jasbir Sood and 'cause they couldn't pin that on me they're trying to do me for this. They are saying I've a motive to do Mukesh but I haven't. I won't say I like him but I don't dislike him either. I hardly know him. I never hang around with him or anything. We don't owe each other money and we don't share the same girl or anything. There's no connection and I've been lifted for no reason. No fucking reason at all. Now, tell that to the judge."

"Is Mukesh a member of Tooti Nung?"

"Who are they?"

"Are you saying you don't know about the two gangs in Southall. I mean I've been here forty-eight hours and I know that already," Christopher felt the first tingle of disbelief.

"Oh yeah, I guess so. But I don't want to admit anything that might make them up here think I've done it when I haven't. I've told you, I shouldn't even be here and you know that."

"Yes, okay, but I think you ought to start with the truth. That's your best defence."

"God save me. You really haven't done criminal work before, have you?"

"What do you mean?"

"Never mind, it would all take far too long to explain. Starting with the way the world's really run. You don't find that out from books and certainly not from law books. Just get me out of here and tell the magistrate the truth. And that is, in case you've forgotten, that you know I couldn't have done it."

"I'm not sure I can."

"Can you sleep at night knowing an innocent man can't - on account of his being banged up with violent villains. Come on Christopher, don't you believe in justice?"

Any criminal lawyer, with a few years experience to guide his perception of the world, would have answered quite simply: "No"; but then Christopher had still a few illusions to nurse, like delicate hot house plants, and so he was safely netted by the all enveloping will of the highly manipulative Balwinder Singh Gill.

"Yes I am," Bindi replied to the clerk's pronouncement of his name and his query as to its application. "Yes, I do," he answered in response to a similar question concerning his address. He was told to sit down. Christopher looked around him and awaited in terror the inevitable humiliation which seemed to accompany his every attempt at criminal advocacy. he didn't see justice anywhere and, had he asked about her whereabouts, he would probably have discovered that she did not work on Saturdays. Thus the field was left open for Dr. Arthur Leen JP

The learned doctor was the most senior Magistrate in the London Borough of Ealing; a position he had acquired through no other qualification save a stubborn refusal to die. One became the most senior member of the bench not, of course, by virtue of anything one did, which was

136

thought a very unreliable method of judging the mean potential of mesne judges, but rather on the same time-honoured principle by which the Kings and Queens of England had always been selected, that is, by the survival of the unfittest.

Dr. Leen had creaked into court supported by two crutches and while the clerk had, for twenty thousand pounds a year, conducted the extremely difficult legal preliminaries, like ascertaining the identity of the person before the court, Dr. Leen had breathed in and out like an old-fashioned vacuum cleaner and had stared out at a hostile world with two huge, bulging, bloodshot eyes, which were the only sign of life in a face otherwise drained of blood; his skin, apparently, having the same dried up texture as white cowhide that had been creaked and crinkled by excess exposure to the elements for the odd millennium or two. The learned doctor was clearly not impressed by what he saw.

"Let's move along shall we," he wheezed as he studied the insect life all around him. The learned doctor was not a medical man and his Ph D. was for a dusty tract on a particularly obscure point of fifteenth century philosophical theology. He had thus trained to be a priest before going, rather late in life into the army legal corps and, finally, to the bar, where, owing to a post war shortage, he had been rapidly made up to the rank of a judge advocate in military law and, in that capacity, had tried ungodly heretics as far afield as Cyprus, Malaya and Hong Kong. In the army he had learnt the four methods of punishment: death, lengthy incarceration, dishonourable discharge and fine. The army had none of the wet, nursery chastisement practised in

137

civilian life, which reflected mercy from the criminal's mirror only leaving the victim unable to see through the cracked glass, such as probation orders and suspended prison sentences - "You either suspend the damned criminal from a rope or bang him away in prison" - and community work for the learned doctor was a chain-gang of at least seven years duration administered by harsh overseers with whips and Doberman dogs. As Dr. Leen was fond of pointing out, crime was not common in the army.

There were, however, two reasons why Dr. Leen should be pleasant to Miss Alison Pull of the Crown Prosecution Service. One was her sex and Dr. Leen, for all his faults, retained all the old-world courtesy of any army officer and a gentleman. Secondly, she prosecuted. Christopher Larkin had neither of these advantages. She outlined the case for the Crown Prosecution Service by utilising the one quality appreciated by Dr. Leen: conciseness of expression.

"May it please you sir, the Crown in this case would ask for a four week remand to prepare papers. We object to bail in the meantime because of the serious nature of the offence, Attempted Murder, means that there is a substantial likelihood that the Defendant will fail to attend court if granted bail. Further we believe that there is a risk that the Defendant may interfere with witnesses or otherwise obstruct the course of justice. He is a member of the Holy Smoke gang and, it is believed, that the victim is a member of the Tooti Nung, which as you are no doubt aware sir, is the rival gang in the London Borough of Ealing. Finally, this interference would, the Crown believe, take the form of another attack on the victim and hence there is thus a fear that the Defendant will commit offences on bail."

"This was a particularly savage stabbing late at night in the common stairway well at about 7 o'clock in the evening. The victim was walking to a friend's flat when he was attacked from behind and suffered sixteen lacerations caused by a blade which was left at the scene. He has a punctured lung and several severed arteries causing heavy bleeding as well as serious damage to his kidneys, liver and spleen. He may not live, Sir. We have established that he was attacked from behind ......"

"A cowardly deed," interrupted Dr. Leen who seemed more annoyed at that piece of information than at any of the previous details.

"Yes, Sir," agreed Miss Pull in a polite rejoinder. "The police at the scene ......"

"Brave men," commented the doctor sternly.

"Yes, Sir," replied Miss Pull who looked curiously unsettled for a half moment or so while she quietly reassured herself that the magisterial doctor was really not bonkers. "Er .... then the victim is believed to have uttered the Defendant's name to one of the officers before relapsing into a coma from which he may not recover. Our enquiries are still continuing, Sir, and we await forensic evidence as well as the result of house to house enquiries in the locality. I have the Defendant's 609 which has been agreed and shows previous Bail Act offences, admittedly some time ago. Unless I can assist you further, Sir."

"Do you wish to address me, Mr .... er ...."

"Larkin, your honour."

"If you insist on addressing me then do so properly."

"I .... umm .... haven't said anything yet," complained Christopher Larkin tentatively, "have I?"

"Honour, Mr Larkin," said Dr. Leen with a rasping voice, "is something I both have and do not have. It is, alas, a title I cannot now aspire to. Kindly call me by the more informal title of "Your Most Worshipful Sir." You may use "Your Worship" for short."

"Your Worship, I ...... er ...... what I would like to say Your Worship is Your Worship that as Your Worship knows ...."

"Mr Larkin, 'Your Worship' is not a multiplier nor are your client's chances of bail the multiplicand," snarled Dr. Leen through a broken mouth smile.

Poor Christopher swallowed nothing in his dry mouth and became conscious once more of his appalling inadequacy. He felt like making a bolt for the door. The whole courtroom drifted into an unreal dimension. The side oak panels reminded Christopher of a medieval feasting hall or, perhaps, more accurately a throne room where King Arthur Leen I sat in judgement on his humble person. "Bring on the axeman," he could almost hear him command, and "Off with his most worshipful honourables!"

"I should just like to say, Your Worship, that my client would quite like to have bail," Christopher paused and then added, "please, or rather, if it please you, Your Worship."

"It most decidedly does not," growled Dr. Leen. "Your cowardly client has been identified by the victim. What have you to say about that, eh?"

"He didn't tell me, Your Worshipfulness."

140

"Ha!" snorted Dr. Leen. "He's hardly likely to is he, since he wasn't there at the time. He'd run off after doing a particularly nasty piece of work, hadn't he Miss Pull?"

"What's going on," shouted Balwinder Singh Gill from the dock. "Tell him Christopher, tell him that you were with me last night."

"SHUT YOUR MOUTH!" ordered Dr Leen while lifting up a finger like a revolver to point at the young man in the dock. He aimed it between Balwinder's eyes by looking down the barrel of his fore-finger as he continued to speak, but this time, in a deep, slow, deceptively quiet 'Peter Cushing' voice: "Because if you do not then I shall commit you to prison for contempt for the longest period I possibly can, do you hear me young man?"

"Yeah, I hear you." Balwinder looked back defiantly at Dr Leen as he answered but he did not attempt to say more.

Christopher Larkin, in the stroke of one second, recalled the emotional fall out following an event in junior school when he had waited, in abject terror, for a "good bollocking" from the Headmaster. Never, since that date, had he felt more terrified up until that particular moment in court when he sensed, wrongly but strongly, that Dr Leen's admonition was directed at him. He could no longer see much of the court room in any kind of normal perspective. It was like a bull-ring to a nervous matador, and, as such, it appeared to whirl around his body until, with an aura of detachment, he sensed his surroundings fade into a dangerous illusion.

Christopher bent over his notes to avoid the shifting searchlight eyes of the formidable doctor but his mind was no longer relaying messages from the ocular nerve endings and he saw no words; feeling, instead, the increasing isolation of relentless exposure to public ridicule. Sweat suddenly seemed to form a second skin over his body, with a thin tissue of water, some of which drip-drop-dripped from his cheeks and chin onto the paper before him with faintly audible splats. The world as he knew it - and on which he was to have occupied a leading role - came to an embarrassing, whimpering end.

It was not that Christopher had intended to break the rules. He had, very firmly, intended not to and, indeed, had almost resolved not to mention the fact that he was an alibi witness for Balwinder Gill. Somehow, somewhere in the deep recesses of his highly academic knowledge, he knew it would be wrong so to do. However, he could not quite bring this to the fore-front of his conscious mind and thus, rather than being able to say "This was wrong because ....," he was merely left, as an alternative, with a vague feeling of unease. Unfortunately, this was not enough to quell the rising sense of injustice he felt at the probable remand into custody without cause of his client, who could not have done the deed - whatever Mukesh may say to the contrary - because he, Christopher Larkin, defender of the Truth and knight errant of the order of "just natural," had seen him in the Glassy Junction Public House at the time of the attempted murder. He almost managed not to say what he finally said. While words may not be unspoken their meaning can be undone, if they are cleverly phrased. Christopher, however, lacked this skill.

"I have, as you know Your Worship, spoken to my client in the cells and, as you know ...... my client has said, just now as you know, that he .... er .... saw me, Your Worship. Yes, that's right, saw me at the time the murder was committed. Well, it may assist you to know, Your Worship, that I saw him too!"

"You were his accomplice," commented Dr Leen dryly. "Perhaps, Miss Pull, you'll let me hear your objections to bail for Mr Larkin next, if you please." Dr Leen smiled sardonically at the C.P.S. representative who blushed with embarrassment at a fellow professional who appeared to be a most unprofessional fellow. "I think, Mr Larkin, that you may have said enough, don't you?"

"I would like to say ......"

"Sit down, Mr Larkin."

"But Your Worship must listen to me," Christopher suddenly felt a strength of will arise within him to provide an emotional crutch; but while this inner strength may well provide him with much needed support when he was wise enough to know when to use it, on this occasion it undermined his judgement and gave the lie to his rational considerations. "You see, Your Worship, when my client saw me and I saw him, we were not at the scene of the crime but in a Public House called the *Glassy Junction* and so, you see, he could not have done it. The attempted murder I mean. He could not have done it because I saw him, yes I did, I saw him at that time drinking with some friends on the table opposite mine in the pub I've mentioned. Therefore, Your Worship, I would ask you to grant him bail because he did not do it and I can vouch for that, as I have said already ......"

"I feared you would say as much," complained Dr Leen. "And I fear you have said too much already. You have, I fear, started on a road that leads where you know not."

"But my client is innocent."

"Innocence," proclaimed Dr Leen with uncharacteristic patience, "is not mentioned in the Bail Act 1976. This is not the court of trial and I am not, alas, the jury. You do not appear to have mentioned any of the pertinent points appertaining to bail."

"The strength of evidence, Your Worship ...."

"Is a matter of identification which appears to be in issue. Don't interrupt me again! The victim may be wrong in his identification but then, sir, so may you. If you are, Mr Larkin, then you may well be my next customer. In any event I can assure you that I do not grant bail," Dr Leen paused for dramatic effect, "in such circumstances. BAIL REFUSED," he barked. "Goaler, take that man out of my sight before he does any more damage. Mr Larkin, leave my courtroom if you please. Only one thing on earth annoys me more than a foolish man: that is one who does a foolish act for a clever reason. I don't know what category you come into Mr Larkin but, in either case, I would hide my head for shame if I were you. May I take this opportunity of thanking you, Miss Pull, for your invaluable assistance. I am pleased that someone still knows what they are doing in our blighted profession."

Christopher did not obey the command to bow out of the royal presence of King Arthur Leen I but, rather, unaware quite what was happening, he almost blurted out: "but I've not finished ......" The game's not over. I want my Mummy (Daddy/nurse/teacher/wife/husband/

psychiatrist). It's not fair.

"It's not fair," he said aloud when Dr Leen had finally hobbled out of the courtroom on his crutches. Alison Pull cast a sympathetic glance at him while she gathered together all he papers and tried, with difficulty, to squeeze them into her leather briefcase. He stood in the same position - leaning slightly over his papers - as if he were still in the middle of his bail application. Indeed, subjectively speaking, he still was. He returned her gaze as if waking up from a dream. He noticed that among the papers she had yet to squeeze into her case, was a partially completed form headed "Report on Case." He saw that she had scribbled some comments under a sub-heading: "Defence Application."

"Am I in trouble?" he asked with an unnatural laugh. She did not answer him and so he continued, "The Magistrate said that I might be his next customer, a bit over the top don't you think?"

"Your application you mean," she retorted firmly. "Well, yes I would say it was. Quite frankly, Mr Larkin, I don't think I ought to say more nor should you."

"The silly old bugger didn't listen," grumbled Christopher with false jollity.

"Oh yes he did," she replied. "I'm very much afraid that he heard every word, so did I. Incidentally, for what it's worth, that silly old bugger, as you called him, tried to stop you from pressing the self-destruct button but you were beyond help by that stage. Take my advice Mr Laugh-in, from now on don't refuse any more help because I've got a horrible feeling that from here on you'll need all you can get."

No-one prevented Christopher from leaving the courtroom. No-one arrested him for foolish advocacy. Was there such an offence? He had not done anything wrong, had he? Obviously, it appeared that he had, but exactly what he had done and, more importantly, what the consequences were (if any) he could not determine. Both Dr Leen and Miss Pull had treated him as if he were a condemned man; but, surely, all that he had done was to represent someone to the best of his ability. Admittedly, that was not a very high standard but, nonetheless, he had not breached any code of ethics nor committed any crime, had he? He had certainly not been false to the court, nor had he represented an innocent man who he knew to be guilty. In fact, quite the opposite, he had forcefully asserted that a man he knew to be innocent, was so. No. Christopher answered his own questions and resolved his self-doubt. Surely he was just gradually learning how to assert himself in court. Everyone would understand that, wouldn't they? However, even Christopher's limited experience of the legal world did not permit him to have complete confidence in the understanding of his brethren, and, consequently, he felt a lurking shadow of unease fall across his vision of the world.

"Good day, Sir," said the doorman of Ealing Magistrate's Court, "And cheer up. It can't be as bad as all that."

"It's murder," replied Christopher ambiguously.

CHAPTER NINE

An overwhelming sense of insignificance is hard to shake off especially when it happens to be true. The world had clearly not been created, nor had mankind struggled through thousands of years of existence, solely to reach it's apex with the resounding career of Christopher Larkin. It was just as well.

Perhaps I should go home, he thought. They can't arrest me in Afetside. Christopher recalled that "home base" had always been safe in the school playground. It was a well-known fact that the person "on" could not "tig" you when you were standing on home base. Then he remembered that he had nothing to worry about, nothing to fear. No-one was going to arrest him because he had done nothing that was really wrong. The word "really" to qualify the word "wrong" implied more than mere doubt in Christopher's mind. He decided, as a rational human being, to think carefully through all his actions that morning in order to consider each step analytically and thus ascertain exactly what he had done and why. The result: he worried himself sick; and, with a pounding headache, he staggered about West Ealing town centre, with a coin in his hand, thinking: "Heads they'll nick me and tails they won't." Finally he decided not to toss the coin. The answer would come too quickly and without enough ritual if he did.

He found himself facing the "Pic 'n Mix" sweet counter in Woolworth's. He purchased $1/2$ lb. of hazelnut whirls, in pink wrappers, and $1/2$ lb. of chocolate covered nougat, in blue wrappers. He put them all in one white paper bag and, without looking, he picked out chocolates at random as he walked around the town. If his last chocolate was pink then he would be arrested; whereas, if it were blue, he would not. As he had been happily stuffing his face for the whole of Woolworth's and one floor of Marks and Spencer, he found that he preferred the hazelnut whirls to the chocolate nougat and so he decided to change the colour code: from now on, if the last chocolate was blue he would be arrested. After all, he told himself, the pyramid-shaped hazelnut whirls felt distinctly different in the crumpled white paper bag from the oblong chocolate nougat and thus, without looking, he still had no difficulty in selecting the favourably fated confectionery. However, by the time he had completed the second floor of Marks and Spencer and had travelled down the escalator, busily munching chocolate nuts, he decided the whole escapade was a complete, childish farce. He dumped the packet of sweets in a dustbin just outside the rear door of the store. It was the triumph of rationalism over superstition. He had only walked four paces - three was an unlucky number - when he demonstrated just how short-lived any such triumph was and, in a near panic, he turned quickly and dashed back to lift the dustbin lid - he saw his sweet packet turned on its side. He picked it up to find only one pink sweet left inside. He conveniently forgot the subsequent amendment to his examination of chocolate entrails and declared himself saved. Hadn't he originally decided that a remaining pink sweet would mean that he was safe from arrest.

"Down on your luck," said a granite-faced truck driver wearing a tartan checked half-coat and, before Christopher could reply that, in fact, his luck had just been interpreted

148

successfully, the man thrust a five pound note into his free hand. Christopher's other hand was holding the dustbin lid.

"No, take it back," said Christopher. "I was just trying to find some sweets."

"Well, with that you can buy some of your own," the man replied smiling benevolently; rather like Father Christmas at Harrods.

"You don't understand," replied Christopher desperately.

"Yes, I do, I understand only too well what it's like to be down on your luck. You don't need to tell me mister," he concluded and with that he disappeared round a corner with a wave.

"It's about time I bought a new suit," Christopher decided as he replaced the dustbin lid. No wonder Eleanor prefers Archie Lord, with his dazzling white two piece, a la Martin Bell, when all he can offer is the clothes he was first articled in: a drab blue affair, which his mother had reliable informed him would "set off" his eyes. His eyes had, however, stayed exactly where they were: hidden completely behind his dark - in harsh sunlight - gold-framed glasses. Surely they would have signposted his professional mystique and avoided any possible confusion with a local tramp. Still, poverty wore a very different countenance in late Twentieth Century London where all the tramps were former lawyers. He put his hand up to stroke his moustache and felt a rough-grained, sandpaper stubble around his chin. His first night away from home had shattered his usual routine; he had not shaved. Nor had he had a cup of coffee.

A cafe was what he needed, urgently.

He did not, of course, know where the cafes were in West Ealing nor, indeed, where anything else was either. Thus with no definite purpose in mind he stepped on a 607 bus and proceeded, chauffeur driven, to Southall Broadway.

He was drawn into the Indian village facade but, alas, found no warmth or compassion there; thus, feeling curiously empty inside, like the naughty boy who had not yet been spanked, he drifted into an alley way shopping precinct and then out again after taking an L-route down two passageways, he wandered into the emptiness with no initial purpose in mind but found himself, much to his surprise, heading towards the Town Hall. When he asked himself why, he was told, by himself, that it had something to do with accommodation. Being a child of the old welfare-state days part of him - approximately two hundred thousand neuro-receptor cells, particularly those responsible for utopian philosophy - nearly believed that the Town Hall might be responsible for finding him a rented flat. It was with that in mind that the other part of him agreed to go along for the walk.

"Here, have a leaflet, Sir."

Christopher did not say "stuff it." He merely felt like it. There was, however, something reassuringly familiar about the outstretched hand over and above the fact that it was, like most other hands Christopher had come across, attached to a similarly outstretched arm.

"Come on, comrade Plekhanov. If you don't take one we may as well give up," laughed Rita who wore the same dungarees she had worn the previous night but topped, this time, by a green beret. Her blonde hair flowed down on either side to frame a round, red face which may well have been described as friendly save for the occasional broken veins which seemed to indicate another reason for her sanguine appearance. Eleanor acknowledged him with a pained grimace which seemed to match her own bloodshot eyes.

"The Riot is the voice of the Unheard," said Christopher slowly reading the top of the leaflet. "And what is the voice of the Heard," he asked with a smile.

"Money," replied Rita happily.

"Talking of which, young Christopher," Eleanor produced a donation box with the words "Fighting Fund" on the front. But I voted Conservative at the last election he, fortunately, didn't say. Luckily he had an easy way out of the dilemma and won instant approval by donating the truck driver's five pound note. "Oh very good," Eleanor commented.

"Just for you," he replied stupidly.

She looked at him strangely. "Hardly," she said and she gave Rita a side-long glance.

"For the struggle," Rita retorted firmly.

Whose? He had not the courage to retort. "Of course," he said instead.

"Not for petty bourgeois romance, eh Eleanor?" mocked Rita. Eleanor pulled her face in reply and Christopher felt decidedly awkward. He changed the subject quickly.

"No Roger or Alex then?" he asked.

"Oh they were here," said Eleanor, who spoke without looking at him, which made him feel slightly uncomfortable.

"They've led the heroic vanguard to the drinking trough," asserted Rita who looked at him too thoroughly which made him feel even more uncomfortable.

In the interests on comfort, he decided to leave. "Well, good luck with the leaflets then," he said as he raised his arm in a farewell gesture.

"Wait a minute," said Eleanor impetuously. "I think I'll go ...... I mean, haven't we done enough here today Rita? These leaflets are going like pamphlets for double-glazing or loft insulation. We're not going to push out any more. Let's join the others. I could do with a hair of the dog. So could Christopher," stated Eleanor who was anxious to escape leaflet distribution.

"Well ......" he replied tentatively, not wishing to upset Eleanor. Unfortunately, Christopher's stomach felt queasy from a severe overdose of chocolate and his brain had been disorientated by the earlier actions of his mouth. Besides, the ladies seemed to enjoy needling him and he had had quite enough holes pricked into him for one day.

"I can't sister," apologised Rita. "I've some marking to do for the kiddy winkies tomorrow. I'll have to go home. You two go if you want to, I'll see you later."

"No," snapped Eleanor too suddenly. She looked at Rita sheepishly. "I've got a bottle of Teachers at home. I might make a salad or something as well."

"I might share a glass of that with you. Teachers for teachers," Rita laughed. "Do you want to come along, Teddy Hoffman. We need someone to do the work."

"Christopher's going to the pub," asserted Eleanor for the second time and, for the second time, she was wrong.

"No, that's all right," he said nervously in response to Eleanor's unease. "I've nowhere else to go, I'm afraid."

"What about the pub," snapped Eleanor.

"That was your idea," replied Christopher. "Of course if you'd rather sort things out at home on your own, I've some things I could be attending to."

"Nonsense," concluded Rita. "You're coming home with us."

Rita Cootes not only took the decisions but also did most of the talking and, unbeknown to her, most of the listening as well. Eleanor and Christopher waited at the bus stop, then on the bus and latterly in the kitchen, for her to finish. It was clearly going to be a long wait. She had the enviable disposition of always having something to say. Christopher hoped she wasn't going to ask questions afterwards. He found his surroundings far more interesting that Rita's dialectics.

The house, where Eleanor and Rita lived, was set back from the main road and the ground level windows were hidden from prying eyes by a jungle of rhododendron bushes: out of the centre of which sprouted a wide-rimmed chestnut tree, which successfully blocked out all the remaining light not already halted by the unkempt tangle of bushes; thus preventing any other species of plant life from adding a much needed delicate touch to the otherwise heavy-handed front garden.

The house itself was on three floors. The upper floor was in the process of renovation while the middle floor contained two bedrooms, a bathroom and separate toilet. The kitchen, where Rita was continuing her lecture, was at the back of the ground floor; whereas the open spaced dining area extended from there to the living room, which was to the left of the front door as Christopher had entered the house. He had barely had time to take his coat off before he had been ushered into the kitchen and set to work on cutting up red and green peppers and washing a decidedly limp lettuce. Eleanor was intensely occupied in doing something to potatoes and mayonnaise while Rita needed no props; being herself was a full-time job.

"I've six different meetings I could go to tonight. Now, I ask you what do I do? Should I put my priorities into Southall Women's Centre, the "By-pass Demo," or should I continue support for the BBC. The black struggle is, I think, one of the most exciting movements of modern times, after the women's movement; but there are only so many hours in the day and we should all seek to advance the cause of Green politics whenever and wherever the opportunity arises. Personally, I feel the environment is the starting point for all wider issues nowadays and if we don't find a way of addressing it without losing our broader perspective then we'll find out that the masses are ahead of us and joining up the Green Party in droves. I'll attend the meeting on "Man-made Extinction" I think; but it starts at five, so you better take over here Eleanor, I'll have a quick bath. Here I've done the tomatoes anyway."

Rita tossed down the knife and, with irrepressible energy, she bounced off upstairs.

"What was that all about?" queried Christopher.

"The diversification of the struggle for existence," Eleanor shrugged and her red hair tumbled down from her shoulders onto her breasts as she did so. "It's her life and she needs to feel she's doing something with it. Especially

154

when Liverpool's not playing. I admire her commitment. I just wish I had something to believe in."

"You mean you don't go in for all this struggle business?"

"No, I told you last night. I help Rita wherever I can especially if, like today, I had nothing better to do. Here, bring the salad through and I'll carry the plates." Eleanor led the way into the dining area and left Christopher standing by the table while she disappeared into the living room. Suddenly the sound of an Eric Clapton guitar riff faded quickly away into an electronic crackling which was itself replaced by the opening deep-bass bars of "Cocaine." Eleanor reappeared with the bottle of whisky and three tumblers.

"I'd better take one up to Rita," she said by way of an explanation. "She won't mind missing out of the food but she'll get all huffy if she misses the booze," she smiled and creased her eyes at the same time. Christopher felt he could relax in her face. It almost eased his troubled mind just to look at her. She was infatuated with Archie Lord, he reminded himself. Perhaps he could cut a dashing figure like Archie if he tried. He thought about this while she took two full tumblers of Teacher's whisky to her housemate. He could hear them laughing in the bathroom. They seemed to spend on inordinately long time playing with water before Eleanor re-emerged with a mischievous grin and an empty glass in either hand. By this time Eric was knock, knock, knocking on heaven's door and Christopher wished he was doing the same to the door of his hotel. He decided to play it cool. He sat, as he had once seen Archie Lord sitting, with his left leg crossed underneath his right knee. He tapped his right fingers on the table at the same time but he had to stop eating salad. It was difficult to look cool with a lettuce leaf dangling from your bottom lip or, even worse, with mayonnaise splattered down your shirt front.

"I shot the Sheriff," said Eric Clapton and Christopher Larkin together: "but it was in self defence."

It was not just that Eleanor was completely unimpressed. To say that would be to imply that she had taken some notice of Christopher's posing and had discounted it contemptuously; whereas, in fact, she had simply failed to notice it at all. She did, however, notice Rita and gave her a warm farewell hug as the latter took her own atmosphere with her to reinforce the ozone layer. Even Christopher merited a half wave which he returned nonchalantly. "Here's looking at you kid," he fortunately didn't say.

Among the many other things which Christopher did not then do; one of them was not to gracefully lean over Eleanor while she was helping herself to salad, in order to whisper a kind entreaty and praise her perfume. Thus she did not return his concern with an intimate smile nor did she look at him admiringly as he kindly removed one or two strands of hair from here eyes. The world did not stop for a heartbeat of time as their bodies swayed together in rhyme. Poetical ecstasy did not then crack open the seal of time to envelope them in a hidden refuge of mutual warmth and safety.

Among the many things Christopher did do however, was to attempt something along the lines indicated above. Between the romance and the reality lurked his inexperience. He tried to hide that within a part he created for himself: the mythical Archie Lord. The problem was that no-one had given him a script.

Christopher snapped his fingers and rubbed one open palm on his thigh while allowing his head to bob from side to side in time to the music. Eleanor had collected together a plate piled high with salad and was giving her whisky tumbler a generous refill when Christopher made his move.

His head was still bobbing as he levered himself out of his chair to "smooch" over to the table. Unfortunately, his left leg gave way under him almost immediately. That never seemed to happen in the movies. Clearly he had succeeded in stopping the circulation to his left foot and had it not been for the quick response of Eleanor in catching him as he pivoted forward then he may well have succeeded in knocking himself out as well. Crash! They both hit the floor in a complicated tangle of arms and legs.

"Take two! That was terrible, Chrissy! You have to move like Don Juan not Don Key for Chrissake! Camera one, can we have a misty filter ready for the close up scene please?"

Alas there was no Director to make reality perfect and definitely no chance of a second take. Otherwise there would have been two contiguous realities and Christopher had enough of a problem being a fool in one of them. Fortunately, Eleanor laughed but, perhaps less fortunately, the more Christopher tried to explain the louder her laughter became, until her tears carried her eye make-up down her cheeks to the tip of her chin in long black pencil-like lines. When he gave her his husky, smouldering volcanic vowels, she became nearly hysterical.

"Darling, your smile is the most wonderful ever seen on any mouth," he heard himself say as her belly heaved up and down underneath him and her hands hit the floorboards on either side of her body in a vain attempt to control her uproarious outburst. What else would Archie have said in order to seduce the now, nearly wild Eleanor? "I admire your fine eyes and copper hair my dearest darling," he ventured hopefully. At this point she started kicking her legs madly in the air.

Eleanor seemed as if she might fall apart in a paroxysm of giggling. It can be safely assumed that her reaction did not do Christopher's ego very much good. Indeed, he was silently wondering whether he ought not to follow a different role model. Coco the Clown came to mind, when Eleanor finally managed to control her own larynx sufficiently to utter a few, more or less, coherent sentences: "Oh Christopher, let me up, I haven't laughed so much in .... you're such a funnyosity. It's a wonder everybody doesn't laugh at you, all the time!"

"Thanks," replied Christopher who was reluctant to move since his head was conveniently resting between Eleanor's breasts and, he had to admit, no amount of advance planning could have placed him in such a favourable position in such a short period of time. It was even worth a small amount of ridicule; although not much more than he had already received, so far.

"Here, let me up now. You're not falling asleep on me are you?"

"Chance would be a fine thing," retorted Christopher. "Your breasts are certainly most wondrous." That did it.

Eleanor collapsed backwards in a cackling chorus of intense muscular spasm and Christopher, who had played the last line for laughs, joined in. They ended up crying their tears together as their cheeks touched and Christopher tried to brush his lips against hers. She pulled her body from underneath him causing him to topple over as she stood upright, still smiling. She brushed herself down with her two hands.

"I don't think so," she said.

"Saving it all for Archie, are you?" he retorted bitterly as he looked up at her from a carpet eye-view. "The question is, will he save himself for you? Or is he more concerned with saving his marriage?"

"Don't Christopher! You don't know what you're saying or what you're talking about. You know nothing about Archie and me so you'd be better not commenting at all. I just don't fancy you in that way. It's nothing to do with Archie or anyone else. You don't seem to know what you're doing, do you?"

"You're a fine one to talk. I guess you do. You've got it all worked out, I don't think. Following in Rita's wake as she single-handedly overturns the establishment and making yourself available for Archie when he feels like his bit of stuff!"

"Christopher, you bastard!" She stood out in the hallway as she swore: her frame framed by the door frame.

"I'm sorry. I didn't mean that."

"Yes you did. You'd better go."

He pulled himself along the carpet until he was in a kneeling position. Strangely, he looked as if he were

159

proposing to her but her facial reaction made it clear what her answer would be if he did.

"Cut it, cut it," interrupted the Director of Christopher's imagination. "This ain't working out according to my script. The public will never buy it unless you go to bed at this juncture and have graphically-described sexual intercourse in at least fifty-eight exotic positions, preferably after twelve hours of amorous foreplay."

"It's too late," Christopher replied aloud.

"It most certainly is not," snarled Eleanor. "It's not even six o'clock yet and you're not going to remain here one moment later after what you've just said to me."

"Can I start again?" he pleaded but he discovered, alas, that the segment of time he had just allowed to slip painfully by was no longer "now" - it was wholly irredeemable. Eleanor held open the front door. The Universe had not yet reached the point where consequences precede the event and so it was, temporarily at least, natural for Christopher to walk through and out into the loop of time he had left laying by the front porch; to pick up the threads of possible spatial movement and alternative matter interaction. In other words, to find something else to do and someone else to do it with. The front door slammed behind him. He was on his own again. How had that happened? He had told Eleanor sweet lies and that had not worked and so he had told her the truth and that had not worked either. It seemed that whether he lived in Afetside near Bolton or in Southall near London he would not be the lover ne plus ultra. Perhaps he should settle for a plastic red nose and a pointed three corner hat with bells on the end. Ding a ling - long - ling: here comes the clown.

He walked down the steep steps from the darkest interior of Eleanor's front garden, avoiding the man-eating tigers of Bengal, which, he was convinced, were growling unseen, and, for that matter, unheard, with their stomachs pressed hard against Rhododendron roots, their fire-filled eyes flickering fleetingly between the dense foliate layers. A sudden crackle of twigs betrayed their movement. They were too late. Christopher skipped safely down the last few steps past the policemen crowded around the front gate.

Policemen!

There were four officers in uniform looking innocently towards the top of Eleanor's chestnut tree. One of them even whistled an Eric Clapton song. Another two officers, not from Bengal after all, emerged from the rhododendron bushes behind Christopher.

Panic made a double-sheet-bend-sheepshank-running-bowline-round-turn-and-two-half-rolling-hitches knot out of Christopher's intestine. He tried to push between two officers who were blocking his way, but they restrained him gently without uttering a word. Another officer, with silver pips on his shoulder, climbed out of the passenger door of any unmarked van which had been parked on the road in front of the gate.

"Are you Mr Christopher Larkin, solicitor presently working for Messrs. Crawley and Dodgers?" he asked in a bland dull tone. Christopher nodded nervously and half swallowed: his Adam's apple had rusted in position preventing a full scale gulp.

"And did you appear this morning on behalf of Mr Balwinder Singh Gill at Ealing Magistrate's Court?" This time, the officer with the pips did not wait for an acknowledgement since he seemed to know the answer to that particular question before it was asked. "I am Inspector Conway and the gentleman in the suit just behind me is Trainee Investigator Barker. He has something to say to you which I have come along to witness."

Inspector Conway stood to one side to allow Christopher a full view of a man dressed in a navy blue suit, who did not seem much older than himself, and who had apparently followed the Inspector out of the passenger seat of the unmarked police van. He looked enthusiastic and his face was flushed with verve as he spoke.

"Mr Christopher Larkin, I arrest you for having, on diverse days within the jurisdiction of the Central Criminal Court, conspired with a Mr Balwinder Singh Gill to pervert the course of justice by stating that he was in a Public House when he was attempting to murder elsewhere. I must warn you that you are not obliged to say anything but that it may harm your defence if you do not mention when questioned something which you later rely on in Court. You are no longer a free man, Sir, and I would kindly ask you to accompany me to Southall Police Station. This way, if you please."

"But, I ...... er .... I mean, you can't do this, can you?"

"Will you please note down the suspect's response. Grab him lads," T.I. Barker said with glee as he supervised the joyful , physical removal of Christopher Larkin from the pavement and into the back of the police van where he landed with a thud. His face was pushed down onto a

162

bumpy aluminium floor while his hands were handcuffed behind him. One officer seemed intent on crushing his spine by surf-boarding his back - pulling his neck towards the small of his back, which he was kneeling on at the same time - while another office searched his pockets.

"Don't find anything that isn't already there," warned the young Trainee Investigator. "And let him up now, if you please." The young Detective stared at Christopher without blinking. "Welcome to the Metropolitan Police Force, Sir," he said with a forced smile. "We hope to make your stay with us a memorable one!"

CHAPTER TEN

At first the world came into focus around Mukesh as a distorted, enlarged close up - it was as though his eyes had been replaced by two magnifying glasses - he felt somehow desperate and insecure; not in pain but closeted in the all enveloping duvet of modern drugs. He wanted his Mummy. He wanted her as he had not wanted her for a decade: close to him, to hold his hand.

When Mukesh had been asked for his address by the Registrar he had given the street where he had lived in as a child: an address in Wolverhampton. He had said then that he wanted his mummy (now!) and, finally, she came to see him together with his father and grandfather. He reached out to them but they were no longer there. Had they ever been? He floated away into his paternal auntie's house: she was making tea - plenty of sugar and milk stirred up together in the pot - and cooking special sweetmeats, at which she excelled. As her favourite nephew, he was given a big solid piece of coconut cream mixture with chocolate on the top. He wished he could stay with his auntie forever. She wanted him to. He nearly did, but then after he had finished his sweets he stood up to leave, she waved at him to sit down again; but he had to leave through the same door he had entered. It was as if he had no choice. He had to say goodbye to her. He had to see his mummy again.

"Your auntie's dead," his mother said.

"She's waving goodbye," he replied dreamily.

After forty eight hours in intensive care the consultant could safely take Mukesh off the critical list. He lay on his bed in a state of semi-being: his childhood memories more vivid to him that the "real" events taking place immediately around him. However, he never thought he was going to die. He willed himself to understand. He pulled himself through the seductive sludge of dreamland and back into consciousness again. It was as if he was doing a thousand press-ups: only much harder, much more physically demanding. It was too much: he drifted back to the back streets of Wolverhampton with his older friend Sammy. You see, Mummy, Sammy is ten years of age.

"Mukesh, Sammy's not here. We're living in Southall now. the doctor he says you'll be all right," his mother continued talking but he now saw only her lips moving as if God had just turned down the sound; he gave her a big happy smile. Her voice drifted slowly back again. He saw his grandfather, with his long white beard, looking at him from a distance ... . "and then you'll be able to come home. Everything's going to be all right. You're going to be all right. The doctors say so. Some policemen want to talk to you. They tried to speak to you before but you passed out on them. You told them who had done this to you. They've arrested him ......," his mother faded out of the picture as if someone had erased her image with an India rubber. In her place stood a white police officer with a chubby face and stern eyes.

"You told us, Sir, that Mr Balwinder Singh Gill had attacked you. Is that right?" Mukesh nodded in reply to the officer's question. "We would like you to sign this simple statement which says only that for now. We will talk to you again when you've recovered properly. The doctors say that you can understand me, is that right?" Mukesh nodded

165

again and he took the pen which the officer handed to him; he was able to make out the simple assertion on the simple statement; he scrawled his name on the bottom. The officer disappeared. Everyone disappeared, except Sammy. They played together on the building site close to Mukesh's home in Wolverhampton; Sammy stole the dumper truck, again. Mukesh sat in the front on top of a pile of soggy sand. He had a big contented smile on his dirty face. He had never been happier.

Balwinder Singh Gill had never been more miserable. He may have been marginally better off in a prison or young offender's institution but, in common with many other remand prisoners, he found himself back where he had started from: in a police station. And, to make it worse, he was remanded, due to prison over-crowding, back into Southall Police Station where his local reputation ensured that every possible step was taken to make his visit an unpleasant one.

His cell, like all police station cells, was intended for overnight prisoners only and hence it lacked all the basic amenities: hot and cold running water, bath, shower, pillow, furniture, radio, television, reading materials of any kind: what he did have, however, was a one inch mattress and abundant aggravation of every possible kind. The toilet could only be flushed from the outside, presumably to prevent prisoners from disposing of any drugs which may have been concealed internally, and the custody officer had been far too busy so far to perform this extremely complicated and painstaking task; hence, after twelve hours, the cell began to smell distinctly like the gentleman's urinal in Yates' Wine Lodge. The heady stench of piss, unmitigated by any access to fresh air, not only caused Balwinder to feel queasy but also, he was convinced, contributed to his gritty throat infection and his consequential rasping cough. Despite this, Balwinder had stripped down to his boxer shorts in order to seek some relief from the oppressive, dry heat. It goes without saying that he had no control over the temperature of his cell since it was, of course, in the nature of imprisonment to be deprived of all control over your environment. Obviously, he could not see out of it either. The thick, opaque glass let the light in only; and light, in this context, which was so distorted as to carry no visual image of the outside world; it's messenger function being thus castrated; so it operated only on the higher frequencies as Eunuch light. Balwinder could tell it was daytime but that was all. It is a constant surprise to the occasional prison visitor, brought up on a diet of Wild Western romance or the rich Victorian novel where hands can reach out between bars and accost the outside world, that the modern prisoner is so completely and successfully isolated from everyone and everything around him. Balwinder Singh Gill was no exception and, although he had initially protested by continually pressing his bell; which had been disconnected by the jailer in any event, and kicking the door to his cell, he had gradually become more and more subdued as the futility of his actions impressed itself upon him. He was not allowed to smoke in his cell, nor was he allowed his watch and so the hours drifted slowly and imperceptibly by - or did they? Perhaps time had been suspended altogether. Perhaps that too could be achieved by a Home Office directive? In any event, the effect on Balwinder was strangely disorientating. As if he had been totally forgotten.

He tried to take his mind off his plight and off the twisted, tortured figure of Mukesh. Was it really a human body he had stabbed? Once the taboo had been lifted; once one had experienced the ease with which human skin could by cut, carved open and the flesh exposed. Once it had been done once ...... Well, it became easy to do again - didn't it? Yes, he replied to himself, and now with any luck Mukesh was lying on some bed somewhere: dying, slowly. Or, perhaps, already dead. Now, that was a thought. He tried to smile joyfully but, somehow, he could manage only a decidedly sick grin on nervous twitching lips. He may have killed a man. That would put him in the same league as Baljit, Devinder and Dhillon: the heroes of the Smoke. That would also put him in prison for life: convicted, only if convicted. he began to panic. Not enough is being done for me. Not enough preparation is being done on my case. My solicitor didn't get me bail: ergo, my solicitor is a prick. Hence, I am going to lose my case because of my solicitor. Conclusion: I must change my brief.

Briefly, these considerations tumbled over each other in Balwinder's consciousness and from tiny pin-point thoughts, which danced around his mind like butterflies, they became a firm opinion, which alighted onto his cerebral electro-chemical relay system and re-aligned millions of cells, so it could now be said, with as much certainty as the principle of universal uncertainty permitted that this was the final judgement of Balwinder Singh Gill on his solicitor. He sighed heavily with the effort of it all.

No-one could say whether his consciousness was connected by invisibly strands of energy to the consciousness of other human beings and so, it might properly be said, that when the name of Christopher Larkin was heard, at that very moment, by Balwinder Singh Gill, it was "a coincidence": whatever that may mean.

Had Christopher Larkin come to Southall Police Station to visit him? Perhaps his earlier judgement had been wrong? However, before his nerve endings re-fired his electrical impulses and sent messages scurrying to the furthest corners of his consciousness: to appeal to his newly formed decision at first instance, his ears picked up some dialogue which reinforced rather than undermined his previous cogitation.

"Mr Christopher Larkin, you have been arrested for Conspiracy to Pervert the Course of Justice, thus I am authorising your further detention at this police station while enquiries are conducted into these matters. You have a right under s.58 Police and Criminal Evidence Act 1984 to consult privately with a solicitor free of charge at any time. You may exercise ....."

"I know but all this is wrong," interrupted Christopher desperately.

"As I was saying," continued the custody Sergeant who was, of course, well aware that Christopher Larkin was a criminal solicitor, using the former word both as a noun and adjective, but who, nevertheless, took a perverse delight in pedantically reading him his rights, enjoying the presumption of ignorance it implied. "You may exercise your right to consult a solicitor at any time either now or before you leave the police station. You also have the right

169

to have someone reasonably named by you notified that you are here. If that person cannot be contacted you may choose up to two alternatives. And, in addition, you may make one telephone call, by virtue of the code for the Detention, Treatment and Questioning of suspects at a police station. That right, as I have said, is in addition to the right to consult privately with a solicitor at any time and the right, already specified to have someone notified of your detention. You also have the right to consult the Codes of Practice whenever you choose. Here is a leaflet setting out your rights issued by the Law Society, you may have heard of them, Mr Larkin." (Sniggers with various officers.) "Now, we do hope you will enjoy your stay with us. I'm afraid I can't offer you a key to your door but room service will direct you there presently. First, I think a strip search is in order."

"He's been searched," snapped T.I. Barker, who like many of the most sycophantic of inferiors, was a bully given the chance. His role as liaison committee member gave him a slight edge. He intended to enjoy it. "And there's no justification for a strip search. You should know better."

"As you say, Sir. Sign here and here for your property, Mr Larkin, if you please."

"But this says I don't want a solicitor."

"Do you?"

"Yes."

"Well, I'm afraid it's not practical right at this moment because I'm too busy. Just sign that now and perhaps later on ...."

"Sergeant," interrupted T.I. Barker, "I don't know what you've been used to down here but I want all the i's dotted and the t's crossed on my jobs. And particularly as far as Mr Larkin's case is concerned. He has just said clearly and unambiguously that he wants a brief, get him one will you please."

"Yes," spat the Custody Sergeant at an officer nearly half his age. He had been a sergeant for nearly two decades now and just as he had mastered his job and was finally heading for an Inspector's ticket, they had produced a whole new set of priorities with smart-arsed, clean-cut, gutless, pen slaves like T.I. Barker to interpret them for him. It was a tragedy. In the old days they could strip a prisoner naked whenever they felt like it and poke around happily in his anal passages for drugs to their little heart's content. It was surprising what you could find if you had one or two colleagues covering for you. Nowadays, it was policy to seek the consent of a quill-tip like T.I. Barker and even then it was supposedly necessary to call out a supervising doctor and comply with a myriad of other regulations. The job had lost all its spontaneity; all it's fun. "Mr Larkin," grumbled the sergeant in a slow and deliberate manner, as if speaking tongue-in-cheek, "do you have a solicitor who you would wish to contact or shall I ring the Duty Service to arrange the attendance of the duty solicitor. You could, if you wish, consult of local Law Society Directory which I have ......"

"Archie Lord," blurted out Christopher. "I want to speak to Archie Lord. I want to speak to him now," Christopher Larkin looked at the custody officer who in turn glanced sideways at T.I. Barker.

"Isn't he one of the persons unknown on this Conspiracy rap?" queried the sergeant but T.I. Barker simply shrugged without affirming or denying the negative allegation.

"You can use the telephone through there. It's a private office and you won't be disturbed," T.I. Barker said and, after a few seconds silent consideration, he reached out to open an office door for Christopher and even obligingly closed it behind him, almost like a well-trained doorman, save for the wicked sneer on his lips.

Christopher Larkin felt more afraid than he had ever felt in his life before. More so than when he had been attacked in the school playground for not paying his dues to the school bully. More so than when he had taken his solicitor's finals. Much more so than when he had addressed Dr Arthur Leen much earlier the same day. He half-tripped with nervousness as he stumbled over his own feet to reach the only telephone in the sparsely furnished room: it was placed in the middle of an ancient, rickety table. Unknown to Christopher, as soon as he lifted up the receiver, T.I. Barker lifted another receiver in another room on the same party-line. He had, after all, only promised a private office.

"Hello, Archie Lord speaking," said the man himself as he answered the telephone.

"Archie, it's me. Help. I need help. I've been arrested."

"Sorry to hear of your problems but I don't do police station calls," said the sophisticated voice blandly.

"It's me," repeated Christopher urgently. "Me!"

"That's not you is it," replied Archie.

"Yes," rejoined Christopher.

"What on earth are you doing? Weren't you supposed to be getting Balwinder Gill a drop of bail? Did you say that YOU were actually arrested?"

"Yes," pleaded Christopher.

"You personally?"

"Yes."

"Arrested?"

"Yes."

"Good heavens, just for applying for bail for a chap?"

"Yes."

"What's the charges?"

"Yes."

"What?"

"Mr Lord, I'm bewildered and confused. Come down here please," Christopher almost choked out a voice blocking sob but he managed, somehow, to swallow back his emotions.

"Look, Christopher, old fellow. I'm sorry but I really can't come down right now. Actually, to tell you the truth, we're in the middle of a little soiree with a few of my wife's academic friends. But don't feel guilty about interrupting us. The soufflé will be ruined, of course, but that's not your problem. Now, perhaps if you kindly tell me what exactly it is that you've been picked up for?"

"Conspiracy-to-Pervert-the-Course-of-Justice," blurted out Christopher in a regular blancmange of jellied words.

"Mmmm," considered Archie Lord for want of anything better to say. "It sounds like you're in trouble."

"What should I do?" he shouted.

"Well, first of all stay calm. I don't think it would be in your best interests to have me represent you in this matter

Christopher, old boy. You see it wouldn't look too good for our firm to defend you on a Conspiracy to Pervert the Course of Justice. The fact that we work together and all that. By the way," he said suddenly as if ready to impart some urgent and useful advice.

"Yes," said Christopher hopefully.

"They didn't mention my name at all, did they?"

"No," replied Christopher, not a little crestfallen.

"Oh well, that's the main .... I mean ...... You see the sense in what I say."

"About what?" queries Christopher sulkily.

"About it not being such a good idea for me to come down there and all that. Bad form, I think, in the circumstances. Besides I don't think I'd even get paid. The Legal Aid Committee and bound to query a form submitted on behalf of one of my own employees. Not that that is in any way and important consideration. Actually though, come to think of it, I know something that might be very important. Critical, in fact."

"What?" interrupted Christopher: his ear pressed hard against the telephone received to pick up any scrap of Archie's vast experience which the latter may condescend to drop his way.

"I hope you don't misunderstand me here Christopher, but, in the circumstances, with a Conspiracy charge hanging over you and all that, it might be better if you didn't come into work for a while."

"Am I s' s' sacked?" stuttered a gobsmacked Christopher Larkin.

"Good heavens, no. Merely, shall I say, temporarily suspended. And on full pay too."

Crash! Christopher threw the receiver back onto it's cradle. The shit. The utter, unreserved, unmitigated shit! Almost as soon as the receiver had hit the cradle, T.I. Barker entered the room with a sly smile playing over his lips, which were barely under his control, and a half-humming, mumbling tone, like a sardonic whimper, coming from deep inside his larynx.

"What shall I do?" Christopher asked him, stupidly; knowing, the moment that he had asked the question, that he could not trust the answer.

"You shall come along with me, Sir," obliged T.I. Barker whose smile had transformed into a full-frontal gloat.

"I want another solicitor, please," he begged.

"Out of the question I'm afraid for the moment. You can't keep ringing up different solicitors all the time. That would be unreasonable. I've allowed you a private consultation with the solicitor of your choice and now I'm going to ask you some questions. If you would be good enough to accompany me to the interview room, Sir." T.I. Barker held the door open and Christopher had to physically touch him as he squeezed by: the alpha male looking down his nose at him contemptuously from a clear head and shoulders' advantage.

The Trainee Inspector was halted in his attempt to leave the custody complex together with his important prisoner. "You can't take him out of the complex yet, Sir," the custody sergeant proclaimed delightedly.

"What's this?" retorted T.I. Barker in a hostile manner.

"You've not signed for him yet on the Custody Record. This ma n remains my responsibility until then."

"All right," he whiplashed the words off his tongue leaving them dangling in the air like the "Y'nik" sound of the whip. "All right. Where's his Custody Record?"

"It's not as simple as that. I have to be satisfied that the investigation is being conducted expeditiously at all times and that you, Sir, are familiar with the Codes of Practice and agree to observe them during the suspect's interview," smirked the custody sergeant.

"That was a bad decision you made sergeant," quipped his T.I. Barker.

"What's that?" queried the custody officer suspiciously.

"Not to be a traffic warden. Missed you vocation in life, if you ask me."

"I didn't," he retorted dryly but, nevertheless, some of the other officers guffawed loudly at their sergeant's expense and the latter blushed as much as his dried, wrinkled face would allow. T.I. Barker, having established control over the situation proceeded to snatch the Custody Record from the sergeant's desk without asking him first and then he stamped the requisite authorisation on Christopher Larkin's Custody Record, which he then signed with an arrogant scrawl, and, as much as the words rolled like barbed wire out of his throat, he complied with the sergeant's proper request by signing a stock formula of words, just as, many centuries earlier, important legal principles became diluted into repetitive slogans which would be missed off the old Writ at the litigant's peril; thus, law becomes reduced to mumbo jumbo.

"All right, let's go," T.I. Barker grabbed Christopher lightly on the arm - an imposition Christopher much resented as yet another small dent in the much misused armour of his pride - and marched him down towards to interview rooms which had been built as self-contained, sound-proof, recording rooms which were somewhat similar to miniature studios, at the other end of the long corridor containing twenty-four-cells. He had not even passed the first cell door before he heard the unmistakable voice of Balwinder Gill.

"What fucking use is a fucking brief who gets himself fucking nicked. I fucking ask you! Loser Larkin!"

No-one rebuked the maker of the comment and Christopher himself, arm in arm with his arresting officer, did not feel in a position to dispute it.

"Did I hear the name Larkin?" a large pumpkin-sized head stuck out, without its' body, from behind a solid metal cell door which was slightly ajar. Christopher did not recognise the squashed nose and thick, black-framed National health glasses at first glance, since the head, although undoubtedly big, was still ten cell doors away, at the other end of the long corridor, in the same direction they were walking. "Is that Mr Christopher Larkin whom I had the pleasure of meeting yesterday," continued the almost jolly voice emanating from an already large mouth which, nevertheless, increased in size proportionally as the two men approached, according to the natural laws of perspective.

"It is!" shouted Christopher who had the good sense to recognise a friend.

"And what's that to you," whined T.I. Barker who had tried to growl at the, by now, recognisable features of Joseph Bailey - the self-termed "solicitor of the supreme court of clowns and local beer soak" - but who had, alas, found that his vocal chords were not up to such a formidable challenge when they faced such a formidable adversary.

"I am Mr Larkin's solicitor," announced Joe boldly.

"No you're not," complained T.I. Barker who had almost by-passed the fat solicitor when the latter, in a crafty by-play, blocked his way both physically and legally.

"Are you denying me access to my client, T.I. Barker?"

"He's not your client."

"Yes I am," confirmed Christopher quickly.

"C-u-s-t-o-d-y o-f-f-i-c-e-r," bellowed Joe Bailey.

"Who's that?" came the faint reply from an unseen voice in the custody complex, which was at the far end of the corridor.

"All right," snapped T.I. Barker loudly for his sergeant to hear, "but what about the prisoner you've just been attending to. Who is that?"

"Mr Patrick O'Rourke, your humble servant, Sir," said a slurred voice from inside the cell.

"Mr O'Rourke," said Joe, half laughing as he spoke. "Do you mind if I finish off the job you started yesterday and continue to represent that young solicitor you spoke up for in court?" At this point Christopher's cheeks started to generate as much heat as a thermo-nuclear glow.

"Not at all," replied Paddy O'Rourke. "I can manage handsomely on me own in any event, especially since I be teaching you everything you know, Joe Bailey."

"Then God help us, Paddy, since I'm not sure anyone else here can." Joe turned to Christopher, exuding confidence from every pore as he spoke, "Now, let's sort these young police officers out, shall we?"

CHAPTER ELEVEN

"Devvy" wrote to me. I got his letter today. He reckons that Bindi's a stupid git for stabbing Mukker. There's no reason for it. How much?" Bender, or Parminder Mangat as he was properly called, looked questioningly at the perspiring, plump, pudding-cheeked, countenance of Joshi: "the dealer."

"What? Oh, say five pounds a frame." Joshi reached out, with a hand unnaturally weighted with heavy gold rings, as he pulled a club cue down from its wall holder. He held the tapering shaft up toward the artificial strip light and carefully inspected the leather tip at the end and then he balanced the shaft, slightly away from the middle, on the back of his fat hand. "I don't want to take all your money off you," he concluded without conviction.

"Don't make me laugh Joss-stick. I'll go a tenner a frame with you any day," Bender, bent over the green baize table, was bouncing the coloured balls off the felt cushion by using his own specially-made cue, designed accurately to reflect his size, "'cept you haven't got the balls to run to a tenner with me, despite all your cash, 'cause you know, you'll admit it in a moment, that I can thrash you any day." Bender whacked the blue ball with the white so that it bounced off one cushion onto the cushion just in front of his own fingers and then it rolled back across the width of the table again to a stop: only inches away from the centre pocket. Clearly, Bender had intended it to drop down the hole but he didn't concede as much. He merely grimaced and reached out to roll the blue ball, underneath his palm, back into its central position again. "Put the pink back in front of the reds. You better use the rack."

"The frame you mean," replied Joshi picking up the wooden triangle to re-align the red balls and place the pink at their apex.

"Whatever you call it here. I'll stretch you on it anyway," he gave a forced laugh as he swaggered around the table.

"You play with different names Bender and by different rules too. We'll play our rules here."

"No sweat Joss-stick. I'll beat you by any rules you want. Now, you break if you like. You're bound to set me up if you do," Bender reached inside the stomach-high flap pocket of his brown leather jacket to produce a coin. "On second thoughts, we'd better toss for it, you might just get lucky and drop a red. Here you do it. You're good at tossing. Haven't I heard that Jossy tosses all the time? Here haven't you heard that Kwaki?" Bender looked over his shoulder to a small, quiet figure who leant against the wall with a large litre glass of lager in his hand. Kwaki's large, orphan eyes flickered a sad smile which was strangely missing from his lips.

"I'll play the winner," he merely said but, after a brief pause, he added, "I can't understand why Devvy should say that about Bindi, or why he should write to you Bender and not to Bindi himself."

"What does it matter. I've got the letter here if you want to read it," he pulled at a crumpled piece of Home Office writing paper from his chest high pocket, after pulling back the zip fastener with a tearing sound. "Read it," he repeated thrusting the paper at Kwaki's face. "If you ask me I think Devvy's right. What's gonna happen now is that the Nung are gonna strike back, and, if you ask me, I think they'll have a rematch here. To get even for Mukker. Heads or tails Joss-stick?"

"You said I could toss."

"Yeah, but not a coin though. Here you are," he flicked the coin over to Joshi who immediately flicked it into the air.

"Heads or tails," he said as it was spinning.

"Tails."

"Heads it is. I'll break," Joshi handed the coin back to Bender as he palm-rolled the white cue ball on the green baize between one side of the white-lined "D" shape, which was at the opposite end of the table from the reds, and the other. He eventually lined it up between the brown and the green ball.

"Who've they got who'd dare attack us here now that Mad Mukker's on drip?" asked Kwaki.

"Jumbo?" queries Bender. "They reckon he did Kenny Kenth. Poor Kenny, ain't seen him around since. We should've done for both Sood brothers then if you ask me?"

"'Kay," snapped Joshi irritably. "In case you guy's hadn't noticed I'm trying to play a shot here."

"Well, play it then and stop pissing about," retorted Bender who continued his conversation with Kwaki: "Don't you agree?"

Kwaki waited until Joshi had played his first shot which broke open the pack of red balls and brought the white cue ball back three quarters of the way down the table: just in front of the brown ball. "They're just kids," Kwaki said. "Now Bindi's put Mukker away, what can they do?"

"Rumour has it Mukker's off the drip and that he's gonna be discharged," stated Joshi.

"Rumour has it you stick cue balls up your dirty fat arse Joss-stick," laughed Bender. "And that's why you're always moaning on account of all them cue balls. Mad Mukker ain't coming out of hospital for a long time, if at all. Not if Bindi's slit him up he ain't. But there'll always be another to take his place. That's what Devvy and I say."

Bender walked around the table to look at the lie of a red ball, which was close to a corner pocket although at an acute angle to it. He tried to line the red ball up vis a vis the cue ball by looking back down the table from the corner pocket in the direction he had originally come from. He put his face on the same level as the top of the felt cushions and closed first one eye and then the other. "If I miss this shot, I'll set you up to earn any number of points," he complained as he came to join Joshi again. He bent over and gently glided the cue shaft forward and back, forward and back, until he felt it was right: "click" - the tip hit the white cue ball - "clack" - the white cue ball hit the red - "thud - the red hit one side of the corner pocket and rebounded onto the other side and back again and again and again, like a Newton's cradle with only one ball, but, since it happened so very quickly, the thud was the culmination of the multiple impacts producing a conglomerate sound. "Shit!" complained Bender. "Who could credit that!"

When T.I. Barker had originally organised the arrest of Christopher Larkin; when he had, as it were, aimed his white cue ball at a renegade red, the Trainee Investigator had felt that nothing could go wrong. The pieces were all in position for him to clear them up with the maximum possible points. He had realised that the renegade red could be potted as soon as he had been told of Christopher Larkin's representations; he had maliciously misled the Ealing Magistrate's Court by pretending that Balwinder Gill had been with him in the lounge bar of the Glassy Junction Public House when, in fact, T.I. Barker, together with his colleague Chief Superintendent Manning, had seen Balwinder Gill themselves as he had crossed over from one side of Kings Street to the other. What clearer evidence could there be to refute an alibi? His Chief Superintendent even had a photograph. It was not just a question of one gang member blaming another any more; but of two senior police officers testifying to the presence elsewhere of Mr Balwinder Gill. And, since the alibi was put forward by a solicitor, the Great Conspiracy came to light at last. The reason why so many earlier prosecutions had failed became clear: bent briefs. Well, now they had finally caught one of them and the enthusiastic senior officer was determined to straighten him out: on the rack if necessary. Strictly in accordance with the Code of Guidance (Stretching of Prisoners) Regulations: half an inch a day with eight hours uninterrupted rest in between. However, Chief Superintendent Derek Manning had been less that enthusiastic when T.I. Barker had telephoned him. He had refused to sanction Christopher's arrest and had mumbled words to the effect of "the photograph is inconclusive" and "anyone can make a mistake" and "neither of us had a clear view of Gill" and "I wouldn't like to say I was sure it was him" and "you didn't even know it was him until I said" and "if you insist, let's wait for an opinion from the Crown Prosecution Service first."

T.I. Barker had ignored the advice of his "slug-a-lug" colleague, who seemed content to wear a snail's shell on his back; instead, he had rung Commander Godlove, who had immediately shared his younger colleague's enthusiasm, especially since his own raid on the flat of Douglas Spencer, the "alternative" journalist, had failed to produce anything upon which to base an Official Secret's Act prosecution except for an illicit breakfast menu, which had clearly been illegally transferred into private hands from the Department of the Environment, and, although the Commander would have happily prosecuted Spencer for anything that moved, even the keen Commander had to accept that a menu was at a stand-still, relatively speaking, and the principle of "bacon and eggs today: nuclear fission tomorrow?" may not sound as convincing to his more politically sensitive colleagues as it did to himself.

"I'm pleased you're pleased, Sir," T.I. Barker had grovelled. "But I feel I must mention D.C.S. Manning's reservations. He said we need the consent of the C.P.S."

"We don't need anyone's consent to arrest anyone at all," the Commander had happily replied. "Admittedly, we may need some Whitehall bugger to give us the green light to actually prosecute but not to arrest. It's about time we fought back against these busy body lawyers who are trying to rule the world and let them know that we're not here as their bloody doormat anymore. Try that new Criminal Justice Act while you're at it. I went on a course about it last month. Basically it says we can nick anyone for anything we like but there may be a little more to it than that, you'd better look it up first. Good hunting!"

The arrest of Christopher Larkin had been easy and even Archie Lord had acted as the Trainee Investigator had earlier anticipated: leaving T.I. Barker free to interrogate a completely inexperienced solicitor without anyone to hinder him at all. However, at the very moment of his near triumph the red had bounced around the top of the pocket from one cushion to the other but, alas, it had not dropped down into the pocket as required.

The interview rooms at the bottom of the corridor of cells had been constructed to be completely soundproof. Christopher's first problem was in trying to open the door to the interview room. He jerked the handle but it wouldn't open. He pulled harder but, just as the door opened a fraction, it seemed to pull itself back onto its frame again with a harsh clunking sound. Christopher refused Joe's helping hand, with a curt "I'm all right" - as in an earlier time and a different place he had similarly rejected his father's assistance - and he finally tugged the door free of its frame, although it made a sucking sound of protest in reply. It had felt like pulling back a steel door in a security strong room although the resistance, in this case, was in the vacuum rather than in the door weight. Immediately behind the door was - yet another door. At least the second door did not require a superhuman effort to pull it open. It merely required a superhuman push instead. Finally, when

185

all three of them had entered the interview room, the door closed itself behind them with a "whumpf!" sound.

The floor under Christopher's feet moved slightly, as if there were water underneath the floorboards, and, indeed, the sensation of being inside the totally insulated room combined both the intimacy of the confessional with the insulation of the diving bell. Christopher felt as though he were truly twenty thousand fathoms below civilisation without even the assistance of a radio to contact the outside world. He did however, have a friend. He showed himself to be indispensable within the first few minutes. First, T.I. Barker had explained the tape-recording procedure and then he had inserted two cassettes in a large square box, more reminiscent of a video recorder in appearance than a tape recorder, and, after he had switched it on, he read from a piece of card contained within a clear plastic cover, presumably to enable it to keep it's shape and remain reasonably clear, then he looked up at Christopher and continued: "I must remind you again that you are not obliged to say anything but that it may harm your defence if you do not mention when questioned something you later rely on in Court. Do you understand?"

"Yes," replied Christopher Larkin nervously: the word came out between two swallows.

"I advise my client not to answer any questions," interrupted Joe Bailey who seized the initiative immediately, "on the basis that we do not know the nature of the evidence against us."

Joe Bailey sat next to Christopher Larkin and immediately across the table from T.I. Barker. The two men stared at each other for a moment: gunfighters ready to pull words from their holsters swiftly and fire off a salvo of opinion before the other could reply; ever aware of the presence of Judge Microphone hanging ominously over them.

Joe Bailey, who now had no career left to protect and no reason left to protect one if he had - he was, in his own words, a nearly drowned survivor washed up from the sea of booze onto the beach of abstinence after the sinking of H.M.S. Broken Marriage - cocked his head on one side, folded his arms and just managed to repress the nearly overwhelming urge to laugh out loud, which all self-important policemen somehow always managed to induce within him. T.I. Barker felt distinctly uncomfortable. It was like facing a legal Buddha. He had to regain control of the interview.

"I would ask you kindly not to interrupt this interview again, Mr Bailey, or I shall have to ask you to leave, the code of practice states ......"

"In Annex B, paragraph 2, that a solicitor shall not be denied access to a Client solely on the basis that he may advise him not to answer questions. You may ask me to leave, officer, but unless you have grounds I intend to remain and protect my client's interests. Tell me officer," Joe Bailey spoke directly to the microphone through a wicked grin which he wore naturally upon his lips like an old, familiar and comfortable piece of clothing: "under what grounds are you detaining an officer of the Court, Mr Christopher Larkin, against his will." Joseph Bailey was clearly enjoying himself.

"I've told Mr Bailey and his client already," T.I. Barker pleaded to the microphone, "that Mr Larkin has been arrested for Conspiracy to Pervert the Course of Justice."

"But you haven't told us why and who with and until you do my client will remain silent and we would ask the Court not to draw any adverse inference from that silence because who can be expected to answer to nothing." Joe Bailey pulled out his briar pipe, which had a stained red leather bowl, and tapped it onto the desk in front of him like a judicial gavel.

"Mr Bailey is hitting the table in front of him with his pipe," spluttered T.I. Barker, who was anxious that a future court, listening to the sound of banging should not misconstrue the noise as that of the Metropolitan Police issue truncheon. "And I .... er ....," T.I. Barker decided to switch off the tape and then decided not to. It would sound too much like defeat if he did. Clearly he had to re-climb the moral mountain top from whose dizzy heights an adverse inference could safely be drawn against those who merely stumbled around, without any sense of direction, in the foothills below. "I can say, since you have raised this matter at an inappropriately early stage, that the incident relates to representations made by your client at the Ealing Magistrate's Court earlier on this morning when he told the court that he was an alibi for a certain Balwinder Singh Gill. He said he was present with him in the lounge bar of the Glassy Junction Public House at seven o'clock on the Friday evening when, in fact, we have clear and incontrovertible evidence that Mr Gill was not where Mr Larkin had said he was."

"What evidence?" questioned Joe Bailey in a sharp pointed tone. He placed his pipe in his mouth as he waited for the police officer's answer and simultaneously pushed some sweet scented, aromatic tobacco into the bowl.

"I don't have to tell you that," said T.I. Barker indignantly.

"And we don't have to answer questions," retorted Joe smugly.

"If you must know," said the Trainee Investigator churlishly, "the victim himself identified Balwinder Gill as his attacker."

"Ha!" gloated Joe Bailey as he struck a Swan Vesta and sucked his pipe into action. "Is that it? A member of a gang names a member of a rival gang. Not that old chestnut again! Your senior colleagues will tell you, officer, that the leaders of the Holy Smoke and the Tooti Nung will come to an arrangement before the case is tried. They'll all end up failing to testify in exchange for a quid pro quo or the payment of Danegeld."

"I know nothing of the sort," replied T.I. Barker snootily.

"Then you've not been around," rejoined Joe Bailey, who took the opportunity to blow a large smoke ball in the direction of the Trainee Investigator. "Is that the only basis on which you've made this arrest?"

"No, as it happens, it is not," countered T.I. Barker as he waved away the smoke bomb attack with a frantic hand. "The suspect, Mr Gill, was seen by Detective Chief Superintendent Derek Manning and myself at about the same time, or perhaps some minutes later, to be crossing Kings Street from the direction of the flats where the

189

attack took place towards the Glassy Junction Public House." T.I. Barker looked triumphant. "Now you're not going to say we're lying are you?"

"I sincerely hope not, T.I. Barker, since you corroborate my client's representations to the Court."

"Pardon."

"You have just said ......"

"I know what I've said Mr Bailey," interjected T.I. Barker, "but I also know what your client said to the Court. He told Dr Leen that his client had been with him in the lounge bar ALL evening. The fact that we saw him on Kings Street ......"

"Proves he was on his way to the Public House. Tell me, T.I. Barker, where's the evidence of agreement?"

"What agreement?"

"Precisely. Isn't there an allegation of Conspiracy here? As the Bob Dylan song goes: 'they got him on conspiracy they never knew who with'." Joe Bailey did his best to drawl out the vowels in a passable imitation of the great man's voice.

"Obviously, he conspired with Balwinder Gill."

"Has Mr Gill said as much?"

"He doesn't have to."

"Ah, I thought as much. He hasn't said so, has he?" Joe Bailey unfolded his arms and took his pipe out of his mouth and, holding it by the bowl end, he pointed the stem at T.I. Barker: "You are skating on very thin ice Trainee Investigator. My client is an officer of the Court. You are holding my client when there is no reasonable cause to suspect that he is involved in any crime. Hence, he has been unlawfully arrested and falsely imprisoned. I want to say

190

clearly and unambiguously that I consider that there is insufficient evidence to provide any kind of case against him. Not even grounds for an arrest! A man who has done nothing has nothing to answer to. We are withdrawing out consent to this interview from this moment."

"You may withdraw your consent but I can still ask questions if I want to," said T.I. Barker in an unnaturally high pitched voice. Neither the solicitor nor his client replied. Sweat glistened on the officer's forehead as he cleared his throat to speak again: "there is still a possible allegation of conduct to cause crime under the new Criminal Justice Act."

"Are you saying, T.I. Barker, that you can cause crime without committing it?"

"The section has not been tested yet. It could mean that," asserted T.I. Barker, who felt on the run from Joe Bailey's overweening arrogance.

"Well, if that is what you are saying in this case then you better arrest my client under the new Act then hadn't you?"

"I intend to conclude this interview for the moment while I seek advice following threats made against me by Mr Bailey here."

"I'm just advising T.I. Barker of the law to which we are all subject," parried Joe wearily. He pulled out another match from his Swan Vesta packet and relit his pipe, making an irritating sucking noise as he did so.

"I'd rather you didn't smoke," snapped T.I. Barker after he had switched off the tape recorder.

"Would you? How interesting." Joe Bailey blew another smoke cloud in the general direction of T.I. Barker, who glowered petulantly in reply, before he crashed his way out of the room leaving Joe Bailey alone with his anxious client.

"I couldn't do that if I tried," spluttered Christopher. He spoke the last word like "cried" as he started to. "Christ, how stupid. I'm sorry. What will my parents think? God, what a mess."

Joe Bailey sat back in his chair and said nothing for a few moments. He merely smoked his pipe and gazed into the middle distance thoughtfully. "I wonder how Paddy's getting on," he said eventually.

"Eh?" replied Christopher who was a little hurt that Joe's attention was not completely devoted to his cause.

"Well, you've got him to thank you know. I'd come out to see him and he waived his right to a lawyer so that I could attend to you," Joe pointed the stem of his pipe at Christopher as he spoke and then his fat face smiled benignly: "It does you good to think of others when you're down. There's always some bugger worse off and that's the truth."

"I suppose so," replied Christopher grudgingly; "but in two days, I've lost my career, my profession, I've been arrested, I've ......"

"Your career?" questioned Joe.

"Archie's suspended me."

"When?"

"I rang him, you see. I rang him to come down here as my solicitor, but he wouldn't. All he wanted to know was whether he'd been named or not and then that's when he told me that it'd reflect badly on the firm or some such if I came into work. Apparently, I'm still on full pay though. I

guess all this will put paid to me being a solicitor. Aaah!"
Christopher placed his head in his hands and bent forward
and, as he did so, he wailed disconsolately.

A fat hand reached out and rested on Christopher's
head: the Pope giving his blessing. "You've just been
baptised," he confirmed. "This isn't the end but the
beginning. I always say you can only help clients properly if
you've been nicked. It's the only way you can appreciate
the importance of civil rights - by being deprived of them
yourself."

"Have you been nicked once then?" queried Christopher
dubiously: no-one in the world had surely suffered as much
as he had.

"No," admitted Joe wearing a granite demeanour, which
however, suddenly cracked asunder as his face broke into a
broad-beamed grin. "But I have been nicked six times, I
think, or it may be seven if you count five minutes in a
police van during a miner's demo." Joe's loud yellow
checked jacket and dirty yellow string tie took on another
meaning for Christopher whose conservative view of the
legal profession had had to take account of some rather
unorthodox customs in the last few days. "I attend all the
demonstrations I can on principle," explained Joe with a
great fat upturned-banana grin: "to protect the right to
demonstrate. You may have read one of my articles on the
subject in the Legal Action Group Bulletin?"

"The ...... what?" queried Christopher who realised, just
too late, that he was being far from tactful.

"Never mind. They weren't very good. In these
situations, the trick is to ensure that you don't get
convicted."

"And how do you do that?"

"Know exactly where the line is drawn. Stay the right side of it, even by a hair's breadth. And, most important of all, don't say anything silly. Only the devil and the tape recorder knows what's in the mind of man! By the way," said Joe almost as an aside, "you're going to be all right, you know."

"I am!" shouted an astounded Christopher Larkin and to celebrate this unexpected opinion, which, incidentally, he believed instantly, such was the confidence inspired by the fat man, he gave his nose a congratulatory blow: "snoooort!" he filled his threadbare paper handkerchief which nearly came apart in his fingers because of the effort he exploded into it. He glanced up at Joe, sheepishly returned the split strands of tissue paper into his pocket, and rubbed both eyes with the knuckles of each hand. "It's a good job you were here," he continued shakily.

"Yes, isn't it," agreed Joe, who had never been infected by the rampant modern virus of false modesty, leading men ultimately, to deny themselves, "I stopped the crime creation scheme all right," he sucked on his pipe but drew only fresh air in reward. He frowned in mock irritation: the constant attention required by his pipe was, in fact, a major source of pleasure to him. "The only way they can get home on these nebulous state crimes is to pin down the butterfly's wings and, by the device of leading questions, to hammer out your words into firm answers of criminal intent, to mould your multifarious thoughts into a design of their own making. I've seen it done many times."

"I might get my job back," Christopher started to think more positively. "What do you think?"

"You might. On the other hand you might want to work with me instead of for Archie. The police may take some time to realise that they've mis-cued."

"How long?" Christopher felt his anxiety returning.

"I'm not an Old Testament prophet," laughed Joe. "I just act like one."

"I feel a fool: crying and everything."

"Don't, it released the emotions. I wouldn't have stopped that if I could. It'll probably take you years to work through what's happened today. At least you've started the right way and not tried to suppress it."

"Perhaps you act more like a psychiatrist than a prophet," smiled Christopher and Joe's heavy hollowed-out eye sockets, with their layers of creased and folded skin, closed momentarily and opened again to complete an almost embarrassed facial expression, or, perhaps it is more correct to say, that it would have been embarrassment on anyone else but Old Joe.

"If I did, then the first person I'd sort out would be myself and I can tell you for free that I'm not likely to make it before the reaper makes me."

Christopher felt Joe's last admission like a slap around the cheeks. Surely this man was the epitome of certainty? How could he lay claim to the same self-doubts and general bewilderment felt so sincerely by Christopher Larkin since Joe had, apparently, marshalled his emotions and reason together so successfully in his many dealings with authority. He knew where he stood, didn't he?

A rude noise of displaced air like an elephant's fart, heralded the return of T.I. Barker. The door closed behind him with a wet "whumpf" sound.

"We've decided not to do anything, for the moment," said T.I. Barker magnanimously.

"In other words," gloated Joe Bailey between loud and contented sucks on his ostentatious pipe with its glaring red leather bowl, "you find yourselves snookered."

"How YOU could manage to do that to ME, dickhead, I'll never know," grumbled Bender.

"I think you've found yourself snookered," said Kwaki quietly.

"That's a two frame advantage in best of five and a cool ten pounds you owe me. I wish I'd taken your advice and doubled the frame stake," gloated Joshi.

"Hold on, you've not won yet," retorted Bender bitterly. He had to recognise that he had a serious problem to contend with; he was eighteen points down with eighteen points left on the table and Joshi had allowed the white cue ball to gently kiss the black and completely obscure his view of the blue ball. He needed a snooker to win this rack and fate, with its dash of irony, had allowed his opponent to snooker him instead. "If this had been a Toronto table I'd have licked you easily. Here, let me see," Bender bent over the table and tried to work out an escape route by calculating angle shots off two cushions. Finally he whacked the white ball hard, more in frustration than skill, and it shot clean off the table towards Kwaki who caught it, without emotion, in one hand.

"It looks as if I'm playing Joshi," he said coolly.

"A manful piece of fielding near the boundary," laughed Joshi.

"Steve Davies couldn't have hit that blue ball from that position," complained Bender. "Snookered by a Joss-stick! I guess I'll concede that game."

"At least you've not been snookered by a mad mukker like poor old Bindi," replied Kwaki who started setting up his first game with Joshi. "You know he's been banged up for that stabbing."

"That's not his only problem, he's upset old Marway," added Bender. Kwaki turned around to face his friend Parminder Mangat with a questioning look, which from Kwaki's large disc-like eyes, posed a very large question. Joshi raised his eyebrows and allowed his mouth to sag open.

"Did you say Marway? Marway Sidhu? The Sidhu brothers?" interrupted Joshi stupidly because, of course, he knew the only possible answer to the trinity was "yes."

"What I heard, but I didn't know how true it all is so don't go shooting off your mouths about it. What I heard is that Marway isn't very happy with our Bindi. I heard it from his cousin just now at the bar; but keep it to yourselves."

"And keep your voice down," urged Kwaki, "because he may be in here somewhere."

"No, he's at a booze convention. Some rep' somewhere is getting him pissed on a brewery credit card. Anyhow, you know how Bindi went off to India an' all that. Well, so it's said, Marway gave him some money to give to his great-uncle in Amritsar. His great-uncle being a kind of holy man of one kind or another. Well, Bindi never gave it to Marway's great-uncle and that money ain't been seen since by Marway or by anyone else 'cept perhaps by Bindi."

"What are you trying to say?" asked Kwaki slowly and deliberately.

"Let's get this clear, Kwaki. I ain't saying anything. I'm just telling you what was told me. That's all. And if he's got his problems, then we still have to carry on an' all, don't we? Till he gets out that is. I mean, someone's still got to lead the Smoke, right?"

CHAPTER TWELVE

Eleanor sat behind a wide expanse of glass-covered desk in an office that sprouted indoor plants from every conceivable angle, corner and crevice. In front of her were four male secretaries waiting patiently for her to speak, each one of whom had a small notebook in one hand and a large telephone receiver in the other. She pointed to one of them with a long, carefully manicured finger and said, rather curtly: "buy."

"Miss Redfern says buy," the little lackey dutifully relayed her message before looking back to his omnipotent mistress for a doggy biscuit of a kind pat on the head. However, by this time, Eleanor's finger had moved on.

"Sell," she said simply.

"Miss Redfern says sell," repeated another secretary eagerly.

"Boy," she beckoned dispassionately.

"Yes, Miss Redfern."

"You're fired," she smiled coldly as she spoke the words like a ruthless television heroine on a low budget TV movie. She had started moving her finger again, when the office door violently crashed to the ground and Archie Lord came galloping towards her on a wild, white stallion, which snorted angrily sending all her secretaries scurrying for cover. He was dressed like the Bedouin King Farouk: his hook nose, high brow and noble countenance looked down on her disdainfully. His horse, impatient at being bridled to a standstill, snorted and turned his head. Lord Archie had to change position in his saddle and, as he did so, his proud eyes danced with pleasure at Eleanor's smile.

He reached down with one hand to pull her up behind him. She was pulled up through one layer of sleep into another.

Now, they were tumbling over the white linen sand dunes, with the cool sea breeze to fan their hot desire, as naked together they rolled together lustfully. He entered here gently as first, taking her with him at a deliciously slow
pace to a sweating, fever-ridden desire:
"Aaaaaaaangalanaglangalangalang."

A hand reached through Archie's fading will-o'-the-wisp body to grasp the shaking brass alarm clock. "Shit," she said as she lay on her back feeling both bewilderment and disappointment in equal measure. Her eyes were stuck together and painfully sore. "Christ, my contact lenses," she exclaimed as she reached for her eyes. "Oh no .... damn and fuck!" she swore uncharacteristically as she belatedly removed the tinted lenses from her eyeballs. Although she had naturally brown eyes, a deep hazel tint on the two lenses, with an almost hint of red, added depth to her colour and complemented her fiery hair. She rubbed her now lens-free eyes and cursed as she climbed out of bed. Boddington on Everest had had it easy by comparison. She sighed as she made base camp: the bathroom.

"Hello Monday," she grunted at the bathroom mirror before immersing herself in the heavenly hot shower: the stinging spray taking away, momentarily, the pain of arriving once more on the cold door step of consciousness.

As she climbed out of the shower she wrapped her body in a fluffy pink towel and coughed. Once she had finished coughing, she coughed again: courtesy of Embassy Silk Cut. Of course, she was going to give up smoking - of course. In the meantime she needed her morning cigarette. "Fight it," she muttered to herself as she wandered back to her bedroom with a small pink towel around her head and a large one around her body.

Eleanor sat down in front of her Victorian style dressing table and, with a brush in one hand and a hairdryer in the other, she set to work to set herself up for the day. Her experienced hands quickly applied the brown/black eyelash mascara, "Warm Coral" eye shadow, chestnut eyeliner, "Coral Cloud" lipstick and Nail Enamel and, finally, the Arabian Blush. The latter had a romantic advertisers image of a Bedouin warrior on horseback: she turned the picture around, only to see its distorted reflection in the mirror. She slipped out of her expensive low-cut vermilion silk camisole and into the expectant low-tar variant of silk cameo: an advertiser's cigarette. She estimated that each one gave her approximately six minutes pleasure.

Once Eleanor had put on her bikini briefs and underwired bra she stepped, fagarette dangling from her mouth, into her maroon skirt, with vivid carmine strands, and she buttoned up her lacy pure-white blouse. She had a beautiful and dangerous scarlet shawl which she sometimes wore with this skirt and blouse, but not when working. Instead, she found a brick-red cardigan which did not quite match the maroon but played off the carmine strands and highlighted her hair.

"You look like a lightship, darling," grumbled Rita, over a breakfast of black coffee in the kitchen. "A beacon calling stray men. Why do you bother? You and I have enough of a problem fighting them off as it is."

"Speak for yourself," retorted Eleanor, who was banging pottery around in a futile effort to find something that didn't need washing. She gave up, with a sigh, and hand-rinsed a mug which wore the logo: "liberate a woman: kill a man." Fortunately, Rita had already filtered the extra strong roast coffee beans through boiling water and the rich dark smell had lightly touched her with a bouquet of longing when she had been dressing earlier in her bedroom. She poured the coffee eagerly into the mug while Rita spoke.

"What about your Christopher then," she teased.

"Do us a favour," replied Eleanor and she closed her eyes to fully appreciate the first stimulating mouthful of bitter juice from the black, beetle-like grains.

"Why not?" queried Rita.

"He's a wimp, that's why not and, well you know."

"I know a real wimp and if you ask me......"

"Which I didn't," reminded Eleanor.

."..... Archie fits the bill," continued Rita. "Oh, he's got a lot of front, I'll grant you that, but he has the guts of a tortoise: one touch and he's hiding in his shell. He's only thinking of himself: a wife to slave for him and you to ...."

"Rita, please. I don't need this first thing on a Monday morning."

"I just don't like seeing my friends being hurt by wimps like that. And he is a real gutless wimp and you'd see it yourself if you weren't expecting him to carry you off like the dashing knight he isn't."

"I don't think that at all," replied Eleanor guiltily, as she thought of her earlier dream. Well, she told herself, I didn't exactly see him as a dashing white knight although, she had to admit, the difference was really rather marginal. "Look, you live your life Rita and I'll live mine."

"Fine, but I'm living your life each time you lean on my shoulder for a good cry."

"Which I won't in future," snapped Eleanor.

"It's not that I mind, darling, it's just that I care."

"Yes, but even caring friends shouldn't interfere."

"REAL friends should." Dud, dud, dud-dud, duuud. A car horn hit the same note as the last syllable of Rita's last word and seemed to continue it onwards like an echo.

"I'd better go," said Eleanor simply but before she finally left Rita she kissed her on the cheek. "I'll never have a better REAL friend."

"Nor I," she replied touching Eleanor's hand with a delicate brush of her fingertips. "I'll keep my mouth shut in future."

"And maybe the sun won't rise," smiled Eleanor as she waved farewell.

Archie Lord sat impatiently drumming his fingers on the steering wheel of his turbo-Porsche sports car. He was like a dashing German pilot in the cockpit of a Messerschmitt fighting machine although, he had to concede, he did not usually go faster than fifty miles per hour since speed scared him. However, although he loved the beautifully orchestrated machinery, which hummed away inside the beautifully designed body work, he, nonetheless felt that it was not so much a car he had chosen himself as a car which had chosen him. Everyone expected him to own a Porsche and so he had. It was almost as if it was written into his partnership deed or into the genetic make-up of all assistant solicitors or, perhaps more realistically, into their aspirations: organised climactically by thrusting advertisements. The problem is that the climax, when reached, is never as much fun as the thrusting it took to arrive there.

Archie pressed his horn again, just as Eleanor appeared out of the rambling foliage. She stuck her tongue out at him in response.

"You're thoughtful," he said as she dropped into the seat next to him. The door snapped shut, with a well engineered, metallic click. Archie gently touched the gear lever, which smoothly flowed into first gear, and he released the clutch to unleash the engine: it gave a deep-throated, low-toned, mean growl as it pulled them away.

"I can think, you know," she retorted.

"Sorry," he exclaimed when he knew he wasn't.

"Is this it?" She gazed out of her side window as she spoke, not looking at him, while he went through the gears to third and then back down to negotiate a junction; a lorry made him drop down to first gear with a flick of the wrist.

"Is what what?"

"This." She looked around the interior of the car and then directly at him: "is this the only time we're able to see each other? In this car?"

"Don't you think it hurts me as much as you," he let his hand drift from the gearstick to her right leg which she ever so slightly pushed towards him - an invitation. "Christ, I've missed you."

"And me," she leant towards him, intending to nibble his ear, but he turned his head in her direction almost simultaneously so that her lips touched his right nostril instead. She pulled back and they both laughed. "Let me elope with you. I'll never let you go out without me. I'll keep you on a lead."

"Whoof, whoof!" His smooth, almost leather face broke out in an all white smile. His pointed chin became rounded as his skin stretched and his eyes danced with pleasure. "Take me away on our magical carpet."

"Your Arabian rug! It hasn't worn through yet. I mean, you haven't been using it when you've not been seeing me."

"Ha! Ellie, don't be silly. Look at me. Women like you don't come a man's way more than once in a lifetime."

"Liar," she laughed, "lovely, lovely liar. Tell me more, before I eat you up."

"I want to kiss every part of you: slowly, softly. To lick you. To enter you. Christ!" He slammed the brakes down hard and they both jerked forward to be stopped suddenly by the inert reel on the seatbelt. A lorry driver, whose lorry Archie had just missed hitting, stuck his head out of the driver's window.

"You stupid old fool! Pensioners like you shouldn't be allowed cars like that. Couldn't you bloody see me. I mean, I'm only a bloody fifteen tonner!"

Eleanor had looked first at the huge lorry and had gasped in shock; but as soon as she had realised that the vehicles had not actually collided she turned to look at Archie, whose bottom lip had dropped and whose eyes stared back at her like those of a three year old who had just had his ice-cream snatched away, and she laughed: she tossed her red head back almost arrogantly and let him have a blast of both unrestrained lungs. He sat still like an injured baby for a teaspoon of time or so - laughing at himself did not come easy to Archie Lord - and then he felt his own body tremble; he looked at her and his lips broke into a chuckle, then a chortle and, finally, a full-blooded guffaw: he threw his head back and hooted like a klaxon, with a silent drawing sound between the bellows of awkwardly expired air which he sucked in uncontrollably in large lungfuls, in a paroxysm of laughter. Eleanor heard the insane notes of his ludicrous convulsions and, like a virulent flu virus, they infected her, immediately changing her laughter into a frenzied furore; the physical fall out of both the occupants shook the Porsche in a belly-laugh vibration, so that it seemed, to the truck driver, as if the very car itself were laughing at him. He did not laugh in return.

The driver climbed down from his cab, slammed his door with a laugh-stopping crash, and marched purposefully towards the defiant sports car. As soon as Archie heard the crash, which had an effect on him similar to that of an upturned bucket of ice-cold water over his head, he flicked his gear lever into reverse and released his clutch but, alas, not before the lorry driver had swung his foot backwards in a wide arch and brought it violently forward again, like the steel ball on the chain of the demolition crane, the full impact of a steel-tipped Doc Martin boot on the glass cover of Archie's front, right-wing car headlight gave an almost satisfying crunch. It was the lorry driver's turn to laugh.

"He's smashed your headlight," said Eleanor helpfully.

"So he has," replied Archie, who wondered about stopping his car and pursuing one of three options: (a) telephoning the police, (b) forcefully remonstrating with the truck driver: the exact details of this alternative were a little vague in Archie's mind, or (c) noting down the truck driver's particulars including the registration of his vehicle and the identity of his insurance company. The problem with all of these options was that it gave the truck driver an unholy trinity of alternatives also: (a) thumping Archie on the nose, (b) kicking Archie in the testicles, or (c) stamping all over Archie's face. It should be carefully noted that there were, however, a number of subtle variations to each of the truck driver's possible options and he was, by no means, confined to simply one of three but could, if he wished, implement each one in turn culminating, or course, in the facial tattoo. Archie sped away.

"Aren't you going to do anything?" questioned Eleanor.

"Like what?"

"Like sorting him out. You can't let him get away with that."

"You mean I should have given him a good thrashing with my riding crop or challenged him to a duel or something."

"No, but you could have exchanged particulars or called the police."

"Well, yes, I suppose so darling. Provided I was wearing a suit of armour at the time."

"You were scared of him," she accused.

"I didn't see the point in trying to speak rational Queen's English to an orang-utan, that's all," replied Archie with a drooping smile.

They travelled in silence for the remainder of the journey although Archie, who was conscious that he had in some way failed her, kept glancing in Eleanor's direction hopefully. It was, however, difficult to look proud when your Arabian stallion had tossed you onto your arse.

Archie made an effort to be bright and buoyant as he bounced into the offices of Messrs. Crawley and Dodgers ahead of Eleanor. "Good morning, lovely day," he chimed to the elderly white-haired receptionist.

"Yes, very cold," she shivered her reply. "You wouldn't think it was nearly summer."

He looked at her askew. "Yes," he replied. "Or rather, no. Or rather, I don't know anymore."

"You never did, Archie Lord," retorted Eleanor bitterly. "You never bloody did."

"Perhaps I know a little more than you give me credit for," he replied as he climbed the stairs a few steps ahead of her. He placed his empty long thin stemmed pipe into his mouth, after he had finished speaking. When he reached the top of the stairs, he simply strode into his office without giving her his customary, over-the-shoulder, reassuring glance. It was strange how much a simple gesture like that could be missed or how much of a stir its absence could give to Eleanor's emotional cauldron. She slipped her handbag off her shoulder and half kicked it underneath her desk. She unveiled her typewriter by pulling off its' plastic sheeting, which she promptly screwed up violently and threw into a corner, then she stared at it's enslaving keyboard; she let both of her hands crash down on two thirds of the alphabet but, of course, nothing happened. She switched the machine on and it buzzed into life. She switched it off again. A cup of coffee was needed before she listened to his master's voice. She recalled that on the previous Friday morning she had made Christopher a cup of coffee and so she dropped two Lyon's medium roast coffee bags into two cups and covered them with boiling hot water. Eleanor tried to avoid instant coffee whenever she could and since Messrs. Crawley and Dodgers begrudged its' staff either a coffee percolator or, indeed, coffee bags, she kept her own personal supply; usually Archie warranted a morning cup but that was before he had failed to give her any kind of priority on the previous Friday night.

Archie Lord, however, had failed to appreciate that his mandatory morning coffee would be yet another casualty of the emotional war of attrition, which had already involved aspersions being cast on his manhood; so, when he entered Eleanor's office, he viewed the presence of two filled coffee cups as a sign of conciliation. He walked over to Eleanor and picked up a spoon. She snatched it from him angrily.

"It's not for you," she snapped

"Then who?"

"Christopher. If he's in. If not, he'll be here in a moment."

"Ah!" he sighed. He put his hand to his brow and swept back his fairly long grey hair. He turned to walk out of Eleanor's office again but then he stopped, as if he had just realised that he could not simply leave it there, as if he were suddenly struck stationery by a thunderbolt thought. "He's not coming. Didn't I say," he tried to make it sound innocent.

"Say? Say what, that he's resigned already? That he's had enough of you after one day to last him a lifetime. I wouldn't blame him either. Well, is that it? Is that why you're so sheepish, Archie Lord?"

"Am I?" he gave an embarrassed grin like a schoolboy who had been caught masturbating. "No, actually I've had to sort of suspend him," he caught her reaction like an electric shock, "with pay," he added hopefully.

"You've what! And what on earth does 'sort of' mean?"

"But I'm still paying him," he repeated hopelessly.

"That's big of you. What's the poor sod done wrong: not enough spit on your shoes, is that it?"

"Eleanor, please. You don't understand," Archie paused and looked down his hooked nose at her, creasing up his eyes into diamond shapes as he did so, he tried to make her understand by telepathy but it didn't work. He really didn't want to tell her too much since, with the benefit of hindsight, he realised that his own role was not exactly a glorious one. "He was arrested because he lied to the Court," lied Archie Lord. "He probably made some money out of it too," he embroidered. "He's been charged with some heinous crimes and will probably find himself banged away for some time," Archie's embellishment wove on fancifully.

"Good God, no!" Eleanor stepped backwards as she spoke as if trying to dodge the words flying from Archie's mouth. "That can't be so, can it?"

"Yes it can, I'm afraid. He was arrested Saturday afternoon ......"

"But he was with me Sat ......" interrupted Eleanor.

"With you!" exclaimed Archie: interrupting Eleanor's interruption.

"Yes," she replied defiantly, putting her curled up fists into the woollen pockets of her cardigan. "What's it to you anyway. YOU were with you wife at the time," Eleanor's eyes spoke through her hazel-tinted contact lenses, framed by chestnut eyeliner, "warm coral" eye-shadow and brown/black mascara, "J'accuse" they said.

"It's up to you what you do," Archie felt a little foolish. "I ...... what I meant to say is that ...... oh, never mind, it doesn't matter."

"Are you going to get Christopher bail today?" she asked, picking up both cups of coffee and handing one to Archie Lord. "Here, you may as well have this now."

So the little monkey can jump into bed with you when my back's turned, he felt like saying. Instead, he took the offered cup and replied: "No, it's better he has independent advice in a case like this."

"Like who?" Eleanor asked.

"Well, to tell you the truth, I'm not sure," Archie was hesitant. "Let's go for a pint tonight, shall we?"

"I don't know," answered Eleanor who genuinely wasn't. "You do know he's up today don't you? I mean the poor bloke comes down here to start work on Friday and finds himself nicked on Saturday facing very serious charges. He must appear in Court today surely. I mean you will try and help him if you can won't you Archie?"

"Do you have to ask me that?" smiled Archie - I hope the little sod does ten years, he thought, but then, with a twinge of regret, he calculated that even if Christopher did serve a ten year sentence, without remission, he would still be much younger than Archie was now. Nearly all my chips have been cashed in, he decided, and I have just enough for one more spin of the wheel, before I must finally leave the casino and settle for a long game of patience. The Waiting Brief for the Final Judgement. "Talking of Court," he said aloud. He swallowed the rest of his coffee in one long draught and put on his happy face. One last effort to impress Eleanor and fire his own hesitant cylinders into action. "Tally Ho! And all that. Must be off. See you tonight for a LONG drink?"

"Perhaps," she replied but her goodbye smile somehow lacked conviction.

When he had gone, he stayed behind; or at least, his voice did. Eleanor put some headphones over her ears and then placed a small cassette in a playback machine and heard him tell her to open a new file on the case of Elroy Washington. She obeyed his command-by-proxy. She typed the client's name and address on a self-adhesive label and then stuck the label over a pre-existing label, with a different name and address, on a manila folder. Messrs. Crawley and Dodgers believed in recycled waste, or, indeed, in anything which could save them money.

It had been Christopher who had seen Balwinder Gill last Friday, thought Eleanor, poor, poor Christopher what have you done? If you have lied to the Court then that can surely only be through your inexperience. Eleanor felt an overpowering urge to find out if Christopher was all right. She picked up her telephone, dialled Ealing Magistrate's Court and asked the telephonist to put her through to the listing office. No, they had no-one called Christopher Larkin before the Magistrates today. No, not even in the

Special list. She put the receiver down. Was he still in the police station? They wouldn't tell her that unless she was a solicitor.

Eleanor closed her eyes, leant back in her chair, and galloped frantically down the Uxbridge Road on her wild Arabian stallion. Somehow she succeeded in galloping through the public waiting area of the police station, over the front counter in an effortless jump and down into the custody complex where Christopher was waiting for her, bare-chested and wearing leg irons, she reached down and with ease, helped him onto the back of her horse, the leg-irons having somehow melted away in the meantime, together the two lovers galloped off into the world of sun and sand where she could show him the sights of her Arabia. He had reached out to her already and she had let him clutch only air. In her imagination she felt his head laying on her breast again as she had lain laughing on the floor except that this time she no longer laughed. This time she stroked the head that needed her. This time ...... the telephone buzzed through her attempts to rework time.

"Hello, Eleanor," croaked the receptionist.

"Hello," she replied.

"Hello, Eleanor," the voice repeated.

"H.E.L.L.O.," shouted Eleanor.

"Hello. Is Eleanor there?"

"Y.E.S!" she shouted. If Messrs. Crawley and Dodgers had been less concerned about cashflow and more concerned about quality then they may have acquired a receptionist who could actually hear the spoken word.

"Good. Then will you tell her that some nice policemen have arrived. Apparently they want to have a quiet word with her down the police station about some leaflets she was handing out. Tell her to be quick. She shouldn't keep policemen waiting."

CHAPTER THIRTEEN

"For the thousandth time, I can't tell you one thing for certain Christopher. All I can say is it's unlikely you'll be prosecuted. I can say no more than that."

Joe Bailey sat, with his arms folded across the top of his great fat tum, his square head attached to a square body looking at Christopher from the other side of his square "camping" desk - the whole image seemingly indebted to Picasso - as he wriggled his backside to find a more comfortable posture: only to shake the floor beneath Christopher's feet in the process. It was not every criminal lawyer who practised from the lower deck of a double-decker bus which blazoned the words "Bailey's Battle Bus" to the outside world in striking red letters on a virgin white background between the upper and lower floors, but then Joe Bailey was hardly a conventional lawyer. He looked at Christopher, through the hollow, wrinkled sockets that hid his eyes, across the gulf of experience which divided them. "One thing I do know, young Christopher, and that is this. You'll never receive a letter on Metropolitan Police notepaper saying: sorry about all this. We've decided not to prosecute. Perhaps if several years drift by without a word you'll realise you're safe but, until then, you'll have to live with it. Life in the pressure-cooker - with the rest of us dumplings! Prosecutions are all the rage these days so anything is possible. Hardly a day goes by without some poor sod or other gets potted. It's an American disease. Prosecute anything that sticks it's head above the parapet and then sue the rest! Come on now, Chris, if something does happen, which I doubt, I'll stand by you whatever.

We'll bring in Liberty and issue press releases. We'll make you a cause célèbre ......"

"I don't want to be a cause célèbre," complained Christopher plaintively. "I want to be a respected solicitor." His words, which had little to commend them if reduced into written form, took on a new depth of meaning once hammered into shape on the anvil of his tongue: they braced a sagging backbone and heartened a sinking spirit.

"You're a Waiting Brief, so wait and learn. If they dare to prosecute they'll most surely fail. That I can guarantee. But only, only if you brief me. I know some lawyers who can safely and satisfactorily lose cases which cannot be lost. I've seen Archie Lord successfully create a case against his own client by cross-examination of police officers, when there was not a shred of evidence against the poor sod before his lordship had unleashed his silver tongue. I must admit his voice sounds grand but he's more interested in his own bloody eloquence than in what he says. When the poor sod, who he was misrepresenting duly got convicted and banged away for six months, do you know what Archie said? Do you know what the old bastard actually said? He had the audacity to whisper to his client: see, you would've got twelve if I hadn't represented you! What an arse-hole Archie is."

"That surprises me. I mean that you should think that," replied Christopher who was sat on the other side of Joe's desk with a bacon bap and a hot mug of Khat tea: a Bailey breakfast.

"Why? I told him to his face when you were there, remember? Just after he'd set you up to do Paddy O'Rourke's remand without telling you how. And now he's dropped you in the sewer without a pair of wellies. Though I must admit he's done you a favour by not acting for you," Joe lent back on his chair and placed his elephantine legs on his desk, which creaked in protest; he pulled out his comfortable pipe, with its red leather bowl, and forced in a palm-full of tobacco: sprigs of which hung over the sides. He lit a Swan Vesta and held it tantalisingly over the bowl as he were about to light the fuse for the Gunpowder Plot. He had either paused for thought at a dangerous moment or else he had a natural flair for histrionic gestures. Christopher suspected the latter, especially after he had lit his pipe with the dying flame, and in that, at least, he resembled the rather more flowery affectations of Archie Lord. "Tell me, do you think I am exhibiting signs of professional jealousy?"

"No," said Christopher who simultaneously thought: "yes."

"Good, because you see before you the genuine article. Honesty and poverty go hand in hand in this business," Joe Bailey slowly stretched his body like a lion after a siesta and then, pipe in mouth, he stood up and squeezed past his desk and his huge body glided by Christopher, like an aircraft carrier by a small dinghy, his hands then locked onto Christopher's shoulders from behind and crushed his bones like balsa wood in a steel vice. "Believe me, I'll see you through this all right, for sure."

"Thanks Joe," replied Christopher diffidently. "I do believe you will."

Christopher felt Joe's grip long after he had released his hold. It was a physical confirmation of support from someone who understood the temporary paranoia induced by an arrest and the sudden upsurge of vulnerability of which continual glancing over the shoulder and sleepless nights were symptomatic: to help unbend all reasons and replace rationality with fear. Joe's strange distorted shape, in his strange eccentric clothes, waddled down the corridor of his strange office to the platform at the base of his spiral staircase. Rich red curtains, which were spread down both sides of the lower deck, created an illusion of warmth. Joe's law books, most of them apparently dating from an age when Sergeants had exclusive rights of audience in the Court of Common Pleas, hung from the ceiling in an ingenious web of knotted white rope. The two long seats, on either side of the corridor near the platform where Joe stood, were all that remained of the original lower deck. Joe was halted in his efforts to climb upstairs to his flat on the upper deck by the rude electronic buzz of his cordless telephone on his desk.

"Answer that, Chris. And tell them I'm not here."

"It's the Court Joe," smiled Christopher. "Balwinder Gill wants to know if you'll act for him in place of Archie Lord?"

"Ahhh," sighed Joe happily. "Tell them, no wait. Tell them this, that W.G. Grace is coming to the crease. That the prosecution are about to be knocked over the boundary. Tell them that ...... Tell them, yes!"

"Yes," said Christopher to the piece of plastic. "He's on his way."

Joe Bailey stood on the rear platform of the bus, his lips grinning like a fat upturned banana, while he pretended to knock cricket balls for six. And, as he did so, his faded nicotine-yellow tie flapped about like a distress flag around

218

the outside of his yellow-checked sports jacket. Christopher almost asked him whether he had slept in these same clothes, but, fortunately, he stopped himself just in time. Could anyone really be that excited about addressing the unsympathetic tribunal of the Ealing Magistrate's Court?

"You're not really pleased, are you Joe? I mean, I know it's work an' all that and everyone needs the money ......"

"Money, bah! I won't get the legal aid transferred for at least a week. In the meantime, I'll work for a penny an hour. How's that!" Joe pretended to whack an imaginary cricket ball out of his imaginary stadium to tumultuous applause heard only by his imaginary self. The force of Joe's fantasy was such that, when he realised Christopher was seriously and innocently concerned, he placed his cricket bat down carefully on one side before he addressed him, arms akimbo, as if he were addressing a judge. "Winston Churchill once said that a good soldier has a sincere desire to engage the enemy. Well, the first qualification for this job is not a sincere desire to hear yourself talk otherwise Archie would fetch home the laurel wreath every day. No, it's fire in the belly. And I've got a huge bellyful ablaze!" Joe winked and climbed down from the rear platform of his house-cum-office.

Christopher saw Joe Bailey's back as he walked from the rear platform around the bus and pulled himself into the driver's cab. His pipe was sticking out of his mouth, like Popeye the sailor man, although his physical constitution was more reminiscent of Pluto. The bus vibrated into life. It chugged, clattered and clunked into action with Captain Bailey at the helm.

Christopher's thoughts drifted homeward once more as he thought of his father and of the daily bus ride from Afetside to Bolton. The bus had been in no better condition than Bailey's Battle Bus and, perhaps, a little worse. In addition, it was a single decker. A double decker could never climb those small, winding, windy moorland roads. Christopher had been confident then that he knew everything there was to know - at the mature age of five and three quarters. He could recall his father holding his hand and sitting down next to him on the weekly trips to watch the Trotters perform at Burnden Park. It was as if the bus ride had contributed to the magic of it all. His father then being free to concentrate on his son instead of his wife. They had been alone together when his father had cleared his throat before speaking to little Christopher in those slow, measured tones of certainty. The speech of a man for whom life held no surprises. "Now then, tha knows old Worthy may be the wrong side of thirty for a footballer but he's plenty of commitment has that man. That's the secret, tha knows: commitment. And I'm not just talking about soccer either."

"No Dad," Christopher found himself saying to his past just as Joe's mobile office rolled to a standstill.

"Right then," Joe's jovial pumpkin head pepped around the partition that separated the lower deck from the rear platform. "Let's give them hell."

"I feel like a soul in torment myself," grumbled Christopher. "I don't think I'm cut out for all this. It all seems sleazy somehow."

"Don't dodge life, Chrissy. Besides what's sleazy about ensuring that a human being has a fair trial. That's the most anyone can do you know. I mean, in the absence of God as a judge and jury we cannot always guarantee the just result I'm afraid. Come on, a little more battering and we'll soon have you knocked into shape."

"Eleanor!" shouted Christopher as he climbed off the platform onto the tarmac of the Magistrate's Court car park. "That's Eleanor," he repeated to Joe's bemused face. "In that police car, see!" Christopher pointed to a marked police car which was stationery at the traffic lights on the main road beyond the car park.

"Who's Eleanor?" queried Joe without enthusiasm.

"E-L-E-A-N-O-R," he shouted to her glum face, half hidden by an embarrassed hand, behind the rear near-side, passenger window of the patrol car. She looked up as she caught a faint drift of her name in the air. All of a sudden she started waving frantically at him. Christopher needed no written instructions to realise that she needed his help. The lights changed to green and she was gone. "That was Eleanor," he repeated foolishly.

"Eleanor who?" Joe asked.

"Eleanor Redfern," answered Christopher stupidly as he tried to think but his thoughts raced ahead of his ability to make sense of them.

"Is that some tart you met in a local boozer?" retorted Joe bitterly. "Getting our young end away were we?"

"Chance would be a fine thing," replied Christopher as he forced a sick, unnatural grin in return. He did not want to upset Joe although he felt the chemistry between them was now turning the litmus paper of friendship into an acidic red.

"Come on, let's go a courting and I'll show you how to make a real bail application."

"Right," agreed Christopher but almost immediately he asserted his true feelings. "No, I mean hold on Joe," Christopher actually grabbed big, bad Bailey by the arm in order to restrain him physically as well as mentally. "I must find out what's happened to Eleanor."

"Stuff Eleanor," growled Joe. "Are we doing a job of work here or what?"

"Stuff you," exclaimed Christopher. "You don't own me Joe and if I have to lose two jobs in one day then I shall. This really means something to me."

Joe shook his arm free and glowered at his new recruit with terrible propensity. Christopher swallowed hard but, nonetheless, held Joe's mental stranglehold without giving ground. It was almost as if Joe's huge consciousness had enveloped his will but then suddenly it backed off. His face creased into his large, chubby, banana smile although his eyes remained as humourless as stone. "You'll do," he said finally. "I was beginning to wonder but not now. Well, it looks as if I'm going to Court on my own then, doesn't it? If you need me, let me know."

It took Christopher nearly fifteen frantic minutes and six urgent telephone calls to establish that Eleanor was at Southall Police Station. It took him quarter of an hour to arrive there by taxi and quarter of an hour to wait for an audience with His Illustrious Highness, the most exalted custody officer.

"Not you," he grumbled when he saw the young solicitor of slight build and black moustache arrive in his custody complex. He loudly smacked a key of his keyboard

222

in protest and complained: "why do you always come here on my shift. I guess I'll have to put up with big mouth Bailey now as well. Okay, empty your pockets. Who's your arresting officer?"

"Pardon?" asked Christopher politely.

"Who's nicked you, sunshine?" shouted the custody officer impatiently.

"No, no," Christopher's face turned from an uncomfortable deathly pale into an even more uncomfortable crimson red. "You don't understand. I'm here as a solicitor for someone here, for a client I mean; for Eleanor, Eleanor Redfern," there was a pause while the custody officer regarded the young solicitor with disbelief. "I mean she is here, isn't she?"

"Oh yes, she's here all right but I don't think that's any concern of yours. Let me say first, I'm surprised anyone would be stupid enough to want you to act for them in the first place and, in the second place, even if they were that stupid: I'm not and you won't. So, as the prophet said to the messiah, piss off pronto."

Christopher felt as if he had received a karate kick to the stomach. The custody sergeant did not even bother to stare him out but rather returned his eyes to the more important concern of his keyboard. Christopher was no threat to him at all. He was nothing and therefore could safely be ignored. Christopher almost turned away to leave but his feet stuck to the floor as if something deep within him was taking over from his conscious, bodily control. What would Joe Bailey do? The thought floated upward through a maze of myriad, jumbled, inconsistent and alternate meditations. He certainly would not leave. If

Christopher left now he was somehow no longer a part of father Bailey's world. He would be destined to do conveyancing for the rest of his life in some large Building Society or within some other monolithic monopoly. If he was to lose he would, to use a Bailey-ism, "go down fighting."

"HOW DARE YOU!" he surprised himself by saying after an amazing amount of cogitation had, finally, produced an amazing response. "I am a solicitor requesting to see my client and if this is refused then I demand to speak to a senior officer, NOW."

"DON'T," the custody sergeant looked up from his typewriter and pointed a loaded forefinger at the impertinent young descendant of the lowly scrivener's trade, "you ever RAISE you voice at ME," he snarled in a raised voice. "I eat youngsters like you with my morning coffee. NOW, I doubt your first assertion but I suppose I must accept it. Standards having fallen all over the country; we'll be having toilet cleaners and bog brushes in here next, all covered in shit, demanding to see their clients. BUT, as for you saying that you have in here a client, I can categorically assure you that you have not."

"I can see her name on the board," Christopher's trembling voice was just under control as he pointed to the list of cells on a white board with the names of prisoners scrawled on it in red felt tip.

"But she hasn't asked for you, sunshine, nor for anyone else," retorted the custody officer.

"Look. I'm telling you I've received specific instructions from her before she arrived at this station. Now are you going to ask her whether that is so or am I going to speak to a Superintendent?" Joe Bailey's words sounded strange on Christopher's tongue but the very act of speaking them strengthened his will.

The two men locked eyeballs. Christopher felt an inner strength surge up within his body as he imitated the Bailey hustle. He had to see Eleanor, he had to, he had to, he had to --- whatever it took.

"Wait there," snapped the sergeant as he suddenly stood upright, jerking his chair backwards in the process, with a macho-crash. He lifted up a bunch of keys, which hung from his belt, while he slowly and deliberately did the macho-march-two-step-with-hip-swagger down the corridor of cells. "Don't mess with me," he said in a body language as loud as words.

When the custody officer came back he did no more than jerk his thumb in the general direction of Eleanor's cell, but when Christopher started to walk in the direction he had indicated, the sergeant stopped him again with an open palm. "Wait," he stated simply. He picked up the telephone receiver on his desk and dialled an internal number.

"T.I. Barker? Custody officer. Your leaflet case has just picked up a brief. No, not him. Were you expecting Mr Lord? No, all right; but this brief 'ill surprise you. Remember that young man you nicked, "Loser Larkin" we called him. Well, he's here in front of me now. Yes he is. No, I can't really now can I? All prisoners have a right to a solicitor at any time; surely you know that T.I. Barker. It's all in PACE," the custody sergeant put down the receiver, with the sly smile of a man who had managed to turn an embarrassing loss of face to good advantage. He then simply jerked his thumb at Christopher again and returned once more to his computer keyboard. Christopher could hear the officer's irregular amateur tap taptap tapping seemingly echoing Christopher's own footfalls as his shoes clipped the polished tiles along the corridor leading towards Eleanor's cell. The bubbling cauldron of his emotions almost knocked him out of his self as his relief stirred around the boiling pot with excitement, fear and desire. It was nearly another person who said "Hello Eleanor" in a trembling, high pitched voice.

"Christopher," she replied simply, with a word made up of broken letters that did not quite fit together. And then she cried. "He didn't come for me," she tried vainly to catch her tears between her fingertips. "What did he say. He must have said something."

"I'm sorry," Christopher stood, stupidly male and unsure.

"He doesn't care."

"Oh, I see," he hesitated. "Archie. I'm afraid I don't ......"

"Didn't he know. When you saw him. You know, when he applied for your bail, didn't you tell him?"

"I haven't seen him Eleanor. I ...... that is ...... he didn't apply for bail. Joe Bailey came down to the police station Saturday night and that's it. They're not charging me, yet," he added. "I thought I was finished," he hesitated and looked away from her and then, feeling himself shaking with an upsurge of unleashed emotional stress, he reached out and, still standing, he cuddled her huddled, seated figure: "Eleanor, Eleanor, Eleanor, what's happening to us both? Why? What are you here for?"

226

"Those leaflets," she looked up at him. "I didn't know."

"Know what? Eleanor, what leaflets?"

"We gave you one in Southall. Remember? Rita and I? Rita! Is she here?"

"Her name's not on the board outside."

"Thank God. I promise you I didn't know it was wrong. Why have they only arrested me? They're her leaflets. I don't even care about them. I didn't know they were seditious."

"Seditious?"

"Yes, the officer said it carried the death penalty. The bastard, he thought it was a big joke. A big wind up. The bastard."

"You mean those leaflets about rioting? The voice of the unheard?" Eleanor nodded to Christopher's composite questioning. "Sedition, was that the reason given for the arrest or was that a joke?"

"Oh, I don't know. I don't know anything anymore. I was just trying to help," she spluttered out the last word and choked on her own intake of breath. She coughed out tears as she cleared her throat: "hold me, hold me tight. I'm scared. I want to go home." She became a little girl again as she spoke and Christopher was able to become her father for a fraction of time. He had never been a father figure before.

"Excuse ME." T.I. Barker stood, with his legs apart and his arms folded, in the open cell doorway. "I mean to say," he looked at the two, tightly embraced figures, "I wouldn't want to spoil anything," his contemptuous eyes said the opposite of his voice.

"My client is very distressed," replied Christopher.

"So would I be: if I had you for a lawyer," retorted the young police officer. "Never mind. Come along now for a quick interview and then we'll see about home time. Come along children."

"Don't patronise me," snapped Eleanor.

"One second, officer." Christopher started to stand but had to return to his seat when T.I. Barker invaded the space he was going to stand into.

"Trainee Investigator," he asserted.

"Whatever," said Christopher, who jumped up again suddenly so that the officer had to take a step back instinctively. "Why has my client been arrested?"

"She's been told."

"Sedition?" queried Christopher.

"Nonsense. Section Five of the Public Order Act 1986. You're familiar with the provision, I take it."

"Yes," lied Christopher. "But my client was told on arrest that she was being apprehended for Sedition and that it carried the death penalty."

"You told me that," Eleanor pointed at T.I. Barker with an outstretched arm so that the tip of her carefully manicured forefinger touched one of his tunic buttons.

"Nonsense," repeated T.I. Barker. He looked at Christopher and winked. "I would never use a word like apprehended. Now, do you want to remain here or can room service escort you to your en suite bedroom. I'm sorry but we've run clean out of torture racks and iron maidens," he threw a downcast glance at Eleanor. "Or perhaps not. Still, I dare say you'll still find something to complain about before you go."

"I dare say you'll give us cause to," rejoined Christopher who felt strangely threatened. He followed the officer out of the cell and, together with Eleanor, they walked down the corridor towards the interview room. His heart beat out an uneasy awkward rhythm as he relived his own experience of thirty six hours ago. He could still hear the echoes of tap taptap tapping from the discontented sergeant's word processor as his heart pounded out its own uneven tune.

Christopher was in the interview room with a subdued Eleanor sat beside him, both of them facing T.I. Barker, before he realised, too late, that although he had comforted Eleanor he had not yet advised her at all. Her unexpected vulnerability had had first claim on his own unprofessional but all too human resources. T.I. Barker had already started the tape recorder, cautioned Eleanor, and was into his first question before Christopher had awoken from his new found fatherhood and recognised his own short-comings as her solicitor.

"Why did you hand out these alarmist leaflets," asked T.I. Barker as he placed one of the pamphlets on the table in front of his prisoner and her solicitor.

"I advise you not to answer that question," snapped Christopher Larkin.

"Mr Larkin, may I remind you that you have already had an opportunity to advise your client in private and your behaviour is now interfering with the proper conduct of my interview." T.I. Barker spoke in calm, measured words for the benefit of the microphone. "Therefore, Sir and Madam, I shall now conclude this interview and seek the authority of a more senior officer on how best to proceed at this juncture," T.I. Barker leant over, switched off the machine and, as soon as the "click" indicated that they were once more in the region of unrecorded space and time, he released a crooked smile and said: "Let's see if I can have you booted out of here, shall we?"

T.I. Barker left the room and snapped his fingers at a passing constable whom he required to stand just inside the double doors of the interview room while he was gone. Christopher looked up at the elderly, bored police constable who smiled warmly in return. Christopher nodded towards Eleanor and the officer instantly understood. He nodded in reply, smiled again, but shook his head in the negative.

"Thank you, Chrissy," said Eleanor warmly. She made his name sound feminine and soft. "It's great to know that someone's sticking up for you," she clasped his hands in her own while Christopher received her praise with a guilty conscience. Had he done his job properly in the first place then the confrontation would not have been necessary. "Will I be allowed bail?" she asked.

"Of course, I'll make sure of that," replied Christopher with an assurance he really did not feel. If things went drastically wrong he had a vague, unplanned notion that he could always bring in Joe Bailey. Joe would sort things out.

"Good," her nutmeg brown eyes held him gently but firmly: weary but slightly wanton. "Come around to see me afterwards. I must talk this through. Have tea. Perhaps even something stronger."

"I'd like that."

"You've been a great help. I hope you don't find yourself in any kind of trouble now," she said with a trace of genuine concern.

"Life in the pressure cooker," he said as if thinking the words only.

"What?"

"Sorry, something someone said."

"Mr Larkin." A human teddy bear padded into the cell in front of T.I. Barker. "My name's Chief Superintendent Derek Manning. I've just received a complaint from T.I. Barker here concerning your conduct and he has requested that I be appointed to investigate whether you should be excluded from this interview. I've heard T.I. Barker's account of what happened and now I would like yours. I may then listen to the tape but only if your account differs. Right then," Chief Superintendent Derek Manning clapped his hands and rubbed them together like a scoutmaster.

"Can I speak to you privately," requested Christopher.

"No," replied T.I. Barker petulantly.

Chief Superintendent Derek Manning twiddled his moustache thoughtfully while T.I. Barker blustered in the background. "Please leave us," he said finally to his more junior officer. "Please," he repeated to show an element of contrition. T.I. Barker slammed the heavy inside door as he left. The outside door of the "airlock," soundproof entrance to the interview room was also slammed shut; but it sounded more faintly. "Right then," the Chief Superintendent repeated in a lower-pitched, calm tone.

"Well," Christopher thought quickly. "I interrupted the interview because my client was asked an improper question. The officer asked if my client had handed out

231

alarmist leaflets. My client couldn't possible answer that without either admitting that the leaflets were alarmist or else denying that she handed them out," Christopher warmed to his theme as he spoke. In fact, he would have objected to whatever question had been asked but the reason sounded good in hindsight. "The officer should have asked first if she had handed out the leaflets and then if they were alarmist."

"Humph," Chief Superintendent Manning smiled. "And you would rely on the Code of Practice which stops you from being excluded merely because you have advised your client not to answer questions, wouldn't you?"

"Would I?" asked a surprised Christopher Larkin.

"Yes, I think you would," he smiled benignly. "So many young men blundering around in the dark. Colliding into each other," the Chief Superintendent sighed and shrugged his shoulders. "I think this whole thing is a bit of a nonstarter but then it's not down to me," he spoke frankly and, frankly, Eleanor was impressed. She had a weakness for father figures.

"Do you think I should answer?" she asked. "I mean, it's always all right to tell the truth, isn't it?"

"I think that depends upon the charge," smiled the Chief Superintendent. "I think young Christopher may have the right idea. Indeed, if you decide to advise your client not to answer any more questions and you, Miss Redfern, decided to take that advice then I can see no point in continuing the interview and perhaps you should be released at the earliest opportunity. I'll advise T.I. Barker accordingly."

Christopher felt suddenly very tired. The stimulating effect of the Khat teat, which Joe Bailey had given him for breakfast - the Catha edulis leaf being the only non-controlled "street" drug left in the UK - was beginning to wear off. The termination of the interview sounded a very attractive option indeed and one eagerly grasped at by Eleanor.

"I'm not saying a word to police," she stated. "Am I, Christopher?"

Why does it have to be my decision, he thought wearily. How can I possibly guess at the weight a Court of Law will attach to a space of nothing? He was grateful for Chief Superintendent Manning's helping hand and the crutch it provided.

"That's right, Eleanor," he said. I hope so, he added quietly to himself, I do hope so.

CHAPTER FOURTEEN

"Bail! What do you mean bail? Am I hearing right? Did I hear you say Joe Bailey got Bindi bail?" Mukesh was speaking towards the hospital ceiling. He had little choice since his sides hurt terribly if he moved any part of his body. Therefore only his eyeballs could stare, out of the side of his sockets, towards Anil Sood and the somewhat blurred figure of Rat-face Jnagel, who hovered uncomfortably behind Anil. "He was granted bail! Balwinder Singh Gill is on the streets so soon, before me. The fucker! Was it that arsehole Archie again?"

"No," Anil spoke through a heavy walrus moustache at a slow and considered pace. "Some other brief. Old Joe Bailey, I think. Anyhow, he's out. I don't know how, but he is. I saw him myself."

Mukesh did not answer for a moment but, instead, he turned his eyes towards the ceiling and sighed, then he flashed his lively restless eyes at Anil once more. "Give me a cigarette. Now. Before sister comes back. The man in the next bed, his friends lit up and let him smoke theirs while they visited. Come on!"

"I don't want to be in no trouble," replied Anil slowly.

"I don't believe this. Light a fucking fag," ordered Mukesh and Anil duly obeyed. He took a short draw himself before handing it to Mukesh. "At last! My grandfather, he just visited me, just before you came. He wouldn't give me no cigarettes, no booze, nothing. Just these," Mukesh waved towards a white cardboard box containing a variety of Indian sweetmeats. "I ask you! My father was all heavy the day before yesterday because the police claimed they found some drugs on me. I told him they were planted but would he listen?" Mukesh continued and neither of his friends stopped him to remind him that his father had died some time ago. "I'm telling you, if I don't find some kind of job when I'm let out of here I may not have a home. I don't need a job, I've plenty of money; but I can't tell Mum and Dad that, can I? I can't tell them because they'll want to know where the cash comes from. Talking of cash, what did you make on the last ...... don't tell me. Don't tell me. I mean, you did sell it, didn't you? Don't tell me you didn't."

"No-one will help. Honestly. We can't find no-one no more," Jnagel spat his words out in a staccato manner with a rapid spurt of sound for each sentence. "What do we do? When no-one helps no more. You can't blame us?"

"Shit," growled Mukesh. "See, if I'm not around it all falls apart. Why don't you do something Anil?"

"No-one's told me to do anything," Anil's sleepy, heavy lidded eyes betrayed no emotion. Whatever was stirring within the depths of his mind was rarely released onto the surface of his placid face except when, periodically, he erupted into a frenzy of violence. On those occasions it was as if he had stored up his buried resentment in a super-charged battery of energy that, once unleashed, drained him once again and left him abnormally calm and deceptively tranquil.

"Do you have to be told everything? When you have a shit, do you have to be told to wipe your arse? You saw Balwinder Singh Gill?"

"I told you," replied Anil with downcast eyes.

"Yes, you told me. You told me. What you didn't tell me is whether you did anything about him or not? You didn't tell me that. And I'll tell you why you didn't tell me, aaah," Mukesh grimaced suddenly with pain, closed his eyes momentarily, and then opened them again to fix Anil with a contemptuous stare. "You didn't tell me because you didn't do fuck all," his voice faded away and was replaced by the rasping sound that soon deteriorated into a fit of coughing. "Give me some of them pills. And some fucking water. Quick. I don't want them nurses sending you away. We have to sort something out first," he took the pills out of Anil's hand with his lips and swallowed them with a beaker of water held by his friend. "That is, if you're man enough to sort it out, that is," he looked at Anil expectantly. "I mean, Balwinder Singh Gill. If anyone's going to take any notice of us any more. If anyone's going to help us instead of the Smoke then we've only one possible answer. I mean would you deal with the losing side if you can deal with the winners? If we don't hit back now then we're finished."

"How can we? I can only count on ratface here," Anil's voice was deep and heavy as it it's tone had been depressed by it's content.

"I told you, Mukker. I told you we couldn't count on no-one no more," chipped in Jnagel like a loyal parrot.

"Well, I can count on you two and a raid on the Snooker Hall ......"

"Against twenty of the bastards as least," interjected Jnagel in astonishment. "Come on!"

"But I've a gun," smiled Mukesh. "A big fucking twelve bore."

"No guns," replied Anil Sood. "The last time we used a gun it all went wrong and we left with nothing. Remember?"

"That was only a sixteen bore."

"It was an eight bore automatic," retorted Anil.

"No, I only told you that to make you feel big. It was sawn off, that was the problem."

"It cut me fucking hand," Anil spoke with injured innocence. "Three stitches in the palm of me hand. I only fired it once. Then I had to have three stitches. I've had it with guns."

"That's because it wasn't sawn off properly. This one ain't sawn off at all. Just walk in the Snooker Hall with it. Point it at Balwinder. Bang! No more Balwinder and no more hassle. They'll be shitting themselves. You can wear a stocking over your head like a bank robber. Ratface here can drive. Bang! We're back in business. It's as simple as that, you know. All they want is some proof that we've got the bottle."

"I don't know," Anil shook his head.

"Here," Mukesh rummaged among some personal effects which were scattered across his bed within easy reach of his right hand. "Ratface, I can't see what I'm doing. Hand me the blue silk bag with my toilet things. Thanks. Undo it. That's it. Pull out the flannel and stuff. Hold on a nurse is coming passed ...... She's gone ...... Pull out the soap-box. Not that one, that one really has some soap in it. No, cause I don't want soap. The other one, the green one. Yes, that's it. Open the box. But carefully, don't pull out the contents. Is the man in the next bed still

237

asleep? Is there any nurses about? Good, have a look Anil."

"Where did you buy them from?"

"Anil! Do you think I walked into a shop and said: can I have some twelve bore cartridges please? What happens when we use them then? The Met' will trace them no trouble. They'll trace the gun too - all the way to Southall. It's stolen from some geezer who didn't have a certificate 'innit. Screwed his house years ago with Manjit, before he was sent down. They may even arrest him for your shooting," Mukesh smiled happily.

"What's these numbers? There's a number five on this one and an SG on the other."

"You know shit!"

"Use the S.G. It tells you what sort of pellets are inside. I told you all this the last time, don't you remember Anil? I'm an expert on guns."

"I don't remember you firing that sawn off!" complained Anil Sood.

"Did I want a cut hand? Besides it might have blown up or something. I read all the stuff on guns though. *Fortune Hunter* and *Soldiers of Fortune* and so on. By the way, you can buy me some of them while I'm rotting away in here. I like to keep up to date with the real world."

"You still haven't said what these letters and numbers mean," said Anil suspiciously as he remembered the deep wound he had received on the last occasion. "Does that mean the gun makes a bigger bang? I don't want to lose my hand this time."

"No, stupid. It just means the pellets are bigger and so there's less of them in a cartridge. That one," Mukesh pointed to the number five, "has about two hundred smaller pellets. Whereas the S.G. has nine big ones. Each about nine millimetres which is the biggest you're able to buy. It'll tear a man's head off at close range. I bought if off a bloke in a pub. Don't know him and he doesn't know me. That's the way to do business in arms. I've saved it for a special occasion."

"Yeah, but there's a few problems here. I'm the one taking the risks," said Anil uneasily.

"Haven't I taken risks?" queried Mukesh. "You an' Rat-face know the risks I've taken. Didn't I use that small poacher's gun on tubby Chowla. Right up his backside," Mukesh put the forefinger of one hand against the clenched fist of the other to demonstrate. "Bang!" Right up his arsehole. Well, now it's your turn Anil. It's either that or we may well give up. Come on, he did for your brother Jasbir, you know that, so it's down to you now. Are we just a bunch of women or are we real men? If you want to dip out now, that's down to you - don't come 'round me again, that's all. My friends have balls."

"Where's the gun?" asked Anil resignedly. "Is it at your house?"

"Oh yes." Mukesh started to laugh but ended by choking: his tongue protruding violently from his lips as he did so, spots of blood mixed in with the spittle which dribbled down his chin. Anil offered him the beaker of water but he waved it away. "Oh yes, just go to my Mother and say - can we have Mukesh's double-barrelled shotgun please, we want to go out and blow someone away! I mean, Anil, what do you think or do you think at all?"

"Give me those cartridges," Anil spoke to Jnagel and did not answer the taunts of Mukesh. His face was calmer than usual although this belied the fact that underneath the surface of his rippleless pond he was deeply disturbed and hidden waves were sucking his thoughts down, deeper and deeper, until they dwelt only on death. "I'll do it tonight," he said firmly.

"I've got his all worked out," hissed Mukesh. "The gun is where we hid them knives. In the hollow piping on the wasteland next to the railway track. The other side of Ealing Broadway tube station. It's wrapped in oil cloth and covered in polythene," Mukesh paused and let his eyes dwell on the ceiling for a few moments while he caught his breath. "As I said earlier," he spoke more slowly now as if losing some inner power, "do them at the snooker hall. It'll be easy between seven an' eight but check Balwinder is there first," he closed his eyes and started to drift away. His lips were still moving but nothing discernible was being said, until he pulled himself back into their circle of conscious communication once again. "Between seven and eight the fire exit at the back is open. The cook opens it when he's making the evening's food. Later he uses the microwave, so the door's closed after eight. Put the S.G. in the right hand barrel. That fires first. All the big pieces of shot will stick together at first in a loose ball. Blast Balwinder with it. Then fire all the little pieces of number five from the left hand barrel: the shot will scatter around and stop you being followed. Then drive off. You can walk past the kitchen without being seen but coming back, the cook may come out - stab him if he does."

"Or just wave the empty gun at him. Waving the gun should cause him to run off. If he's any sense that is," volunteered Jnagel in his three staccato bursts of quick-fire words. However, by this time Mukesh was no longer listening to his friends but he was, once more, riding happily on top of a pile of soggy sand in the front of a dumper truck. His aunt was about to call him in again for tea as the relay of distorted memories started to replay themselves with the same scenes from which he would never escape until the day he died. Each time, however, when he awoke from his dreams, his father became more whole and substantial so that he could hold long and detailed conversations with him and, although his father still did not approve of what he did, he now understood him as he had never done before.

"Hospitals, courts, prisons and police stations," grumbled Jnagel in a rapid under-voice spoken as much to the floor as to his thick-necked companion who strode on ahead of him while he darted from Anil's left side to his right side in a vain attempt to be noticed. "Hospitals, courts, prisons and police stations, that's where we always end up. Always in the end. Visiting and waiting and suffering. It's not good."

Anil ignored his companion who looked up at him expectantly, his point ears and inquisitive, sniffing nose seemingly reminiscent of the rodent he was named after: Jnagel had difficulty in keeping up with Anil's huge, purposeful strides which had taken on a certainty of movement formerly lacking in them. Jnagel pulled out his car keys as much to remind Anil of his own importance as for any practical reason. Anil's eyes were attracted by the rattling aluminium alloys. "You're going to drive," he said simply.

"I'll drive you home."

"You know what I mean."

"It's no good," repeated Jnagel. "I've had all this. You and Mukesh forget that I did a three year stretch, I don't wanna do that again. You forget."

"You did barely eighteen months with parole," sneered Anil as he opened the double door exit into the hospital car park. He flicked the door back with the fingers of his left hand to try and catch Jnagel's face but the latter slipped through the gap too quickly for him. "And if you pull out now then what else are you going to do. Be a waiter in the Star of India for thirty fucking pounds a week - with free meals thrown in, like a beggar?"

"I might go back to college," Jnagel sounded singularly unconvincing, even to himself. "I might," he added as if by repetition he somehow found reassurance.

"All right," Anil blew the words at Jnagel through his moustache filter. They were meant as a gesture of conciliation: Anil would not stand on his companion's dream, "but for now you'll drive me to the tube station and then to the Snooker Hall. I'll blow Balwinder away with this S.G. cartridge and then I'll scatter the other bastards with the other barrel. Bang! Bang! I'm ready to do this job. Bang! Bang!"

"Here's the car," Jnagel sounded less than enthusiastic. "It's nearly six o'clock now. We'll have to leave it today. I'll come for you tomorrow."

"No way," Anil opened the passenger door as soon as his companion had turned the key in the driver's door and, by central locking, unlocked all four doors simultaneously. The doors opened with a gentle metallic click. "You wouldn't be able to keep a car like this at college."

"A BMW's a necessity," Jnagel smiled his reply. "Besides I'd work in the evenings. I always work hard. Everyone knows I do. No-one can say different than that," Jnagel rattled his words off like worry-beads running through the fingers of a young, sharp, prostitute in an old Delhi brothel. He drove faster than he spoke and he spoke very fast indeed. The bright red BMW did a two wheel skid before travelling from 0-60 in the flutter of an eye. He took the car in and out of the traffic down the Uxbridge Road and then through some back streets so that he travelled nearly twice the distance necessary but in half the time, by virtue of his having avoided the Iron Bridge at Hanwell, where traffic moved so slowly that the pedestrian pavement was the overtaking lane. They dropped from 60-0 in a heartbeat and a half. The men had arrived.

To reach the wasteland it was necessary to climb the barbed wire fence and half roll, half fall down a rugged hillside with old broken prams, rusty cans and jagged glass from broken bottles breaking their mutual descent with the efficiency of hidden land mines. Down, down, down they went, crashing painfully down not through snow but through the chemical waste product of detergent foam. Finally they broke through the dense jungle of sharp-thorned twigs, forming part of a natural motte and bailey, on the other side of a small ditch and mound, at the very bottom of the hill. Once out of the broken foliage, they faced the railway line.

Immediately opposite them was the long, deserted, platform and their eyes naturally followed its length from their left to right where it tapered away into an infinite line of pallid, broken stone on which ran the dull, leaden railway track. To the right of the track and parallel to its course, on the same side as their roving eyes reached a drab line of hoary bushes, their leaves made whiteish grey by industrial disease. As a ceiling to their vision stretched the sunless sky: overcast with heavy threatening clouds of black and grey. Into this ashen frame came mechanical movement heard first through the vibrating track and then seen as a mere speck which became elongated into a long tube of distinct grey metal seemingly released from the cheerless clouds floating on the distant horizon.

"Wait 'till it's gone," mumbled Anil as he pulled out a packet of American cigarettes. It was the one the cowboys always smoked when herding cattle in Texas. Jnagel took one with his long, delicate fingers and slipped it into his small, mean mouth the long white tube nearly pure white against his dark skin. The tobacco was a relief, a purity of breath when compared to the sulphur, carbon and lead which his lungs were used to inhaling.

"How long," he grumbled between draws of tobacco. "I mean it's quarter past six already. Let's leave this for tomorrow, or Wednesday. What do you say? Am I right or am I right?"

"The train's gone," replied Anil ignoring his friend's question. "Just wait 'till that passenger pisses off and then, that's it. Wait here and make sure no-one sees me," Anil walked towards an indentation in the ground as nonchalantly as he was able: his big body swaying slightly at the hips as he did so. He stopped, crouched down and then looked back towards Jnagel who put a thumb up in return, then he bent over the hole: his whole arm and shoulder disappearing from Jnagel's view. When he stood up again he held a long piece of black cloth covered with polythene which was itself wet and dirty. "Come on," he said. "Let's not hang about with this fucker. Look my whole pissing arm is filthy now. Give us the cartridges."

"You had them last."

"No, I didn't .... Oh yes ... hold on, I know .... I left them in the car. Let's go and do it.."

"What about a stocking?" asked Jnagel as they clambered back up the hill again. "For your face. So no-one knows it's you."

"Perhaps I can use one of yours."

"Funny. Very funny."

There was a long silence punctuated by grunts, sighs and curses as the two young men cut and bruised their bodies on the journey back towards the car.

"I'll buy a mask on the way," he said finally.

"You'll never have time. It's nearly half past six. You'll never have time now. Besides how will you know if Balwinder's in there."

"That's a point," agreed Anil who looked at his watch. "We were going to wait outside and wait for him weren't we."

Jnagel unlocked all the car doors simultaneously with a touch of the remote buttons. Ten tons of explosives could have gone off as easily. Doors and death were equally

245

instant. Jnagel now knew that he could persuade his friend to delay the enterprise if he wanted to. And he had consistently wanted to all the time until the moment that he was able; when he felt a crazy and deep desire to the contrary. He had not wanted any part of this business at all; but he would never feel more able to assist in it than now. If it was not done tonight then he knew that the thought of it, in the darker moments when he was alone with his prison memories, would freeze him out of action entirely, making the deed impossible by the very consideration of its possibility. Thus he would lose the regard of Anil and Mukesh and there would be no role for him at all. What else could he do? Where else would he be successful? Ideally as a rally driver but then skill was not qualification enough and the barriers of sponsorship and regulation put a mental block before his ambition so that he, in common with so many young men, did not even try. "You can try the telephone," he suggested knowing that he was now finally committed. "I mean you could ring the snooker hall and ask for Balwinder. His friends call him Bindi. That's it, if you ask for Bindi. When he comes to the phone, put the receiver down. Do that when you buy the mask, then I'll drive you round the back. If the door's open: straight in and out. Simple."

CHAPTER FIFTEEN

"It was simple. Really it was. Nothing to be grateful for, really," said Christopher who was, nevertheless, really grateful to receive Eleanor's real gratitude.

"You were wonderful. I'll buy some champagne to go with dinner or shall we eat out? What time is it? Half six, just time to bath first. Oh, I'm so glad to leave that place, so glad you came, so glad you helped me, so glad to be free," Eleanor clapped her hands together like a happy child. "Here you sit down, I'll put on some music. Whisky? It's a fine malt. Would you like to go to an Italian Restaurant? It's my treat .... Oh, what am I saying? Christopher you will think me an absolute fool," she put her hand to her mouth and bit the nail of her middle finger. "An absolute idiot," she laughed and then looked at him like a naughty girl. "I haven't any money."

Christopher laughed with her and then suddenly stopped as the implication of what she had said sunk into his consciousness. He patted the outside of his pockets. "Neither have I," he confessed feeling ashamed. He was sure Archie Lord had never been driven to the extremity of such a confession.

"Never mind. It's my treat and I'll cook you a curry you'll never forget."

"Is that a promise or a threat?" laughed Christopher.

"You tell me. Afterwards," she smiled with a twist and a curl to her lips which, somehow, lacked precise definition as the corners of her mouth blended into shadow. She handed him a squat crystal tumbler and, as he took it from her hand, the tip of three of her fingers ran down his knuckles. He recoiled involuntarily and her hand darted back swiftly, like a lizard's tongue, while her smile broke up on the rocks of uncertainty. "Sorry," she said.

"No," he replied. "I mean ...."

"I'll make the curry," the smile again; but this time a trace duller than before; not so sure. "Help yourself to drinks."

When she had closed the door, Christopher stood up and paced the room - several times. It was as if he had to burn up the latent energy and try and walk out of his own stupidity. Why did he pull back from her so firmly? Why did he always seem to do the opposite of what he really wanted? He wanted her and yet had rejected her, without thinking. He paced the floor from one end of the living room to the other while, in the background, he could hear the clatter of utensils, the clunking sound of Eleanor chopping vegetables with a knife followed by the fainter sharper "click" of the knife hitting the cutting board after slicing, then the sizzling as the vegetables hit the pan; he turned on his heel and walked back along the path he had forged for himself across the Axminster. His emotions began to fall into some kind of shape. He heard the music for the first time. It was Oasis singing "D'you know what I mean." "I wish I did," said Christopher to himself. "I wish I knew what I meant."

He passed the bookcase and cast an impatient eye across the volumes: "Getting Here," "The Wisdom of Bones," "Climbing Mt. Improbable," Paul Foot on Enoch Powell, Richard Ellmann on James Joyce, Hemingway on himself in Paris. Christopher pulled out that volume because it was the slimmest. He opened the cover: "to my

moveable feast, love to darling Eleanor, Tony the tonic."
Who was Tony? It was strange but it never occurred to
Christopher that Eleanor might have known other men
besides Archie Lord. Perhaps that was because he had
known so few women himself and none of those intimately.
What did "Tony" mean by a moveable feast? That he ate
her? Quickly Christopher returned the volume unread.

"*The History of the Russian Revolution*" seemed a far
safer bet but the sheer size made him feel weary. "*Crime
and Punishment*" seemed apt but his eye fell on an even
more appropriate title: "*Awakenings.*" He was about to lift
the book from the shelf when Eleanor awoke him.

"Found anything interesting?" she was behind him. How
long had she been there?

"Sorry, just looking." He felt himself colour.

"No, I don't mind," she added. She looked at him from
the corner of her eyes; her body seemed to take up the
whole room. Christopher felt both intimidated and,
simultaneously, annoyed with himself for feeling so.

"Can I lend a hand?" he asked.

"What? Oh, the curry. No, it's all right. All under
control. I hope," she sat down, crossed her legs and picked
up a magazine. She seemed to ignore him.

Christopher swallowed the last of his whisky and
poured himself another. That was what Joe Bailey would
have done. The question was, what did he want to do or,
rather, not so much that since the answer was clear; the
problem was how to achieve it. Not only by the
manipulation of social skills but also by the conquest of
himself. He cleared his throat.

"Did you say something?" she asked hopefully.

"I just wondered how long dinner would be?" he lied,

"Isn't that a question to ask mother?" she retorted; her earlier enthusiasm for him had clearly waned as she felt more in control of herself again.

"Pardon," he said surprised at her aggression.

"Never mind," she answered.

"Have you lived here long?" he attempted to change the subject.

"Ever since I split up with Tony. We didn't get on, finally."

"Tony?" Christopher raised the word into a question.

"You wouldn't know him."

"I could fill a thousand volumes with what I don't know," Christopher stumbled over the words as if they were boulders along a rocky path. Fortunately, Eleanor laughed.

"You and me both," she held out an outstretched hand, languidly. After her earlier rebuff, she didn't want to appear too keen and it was as if she were merely experimenting with his emotions or with her own. He reached out to touch her fingertips. "I'll have one of those," she nodded to his drink.

"Yes, yes, of course," he swallowed his own and poured them both a large Scotch each. "Do you want anything with it; just ice - there you are."

She caught his roving, embarrassed glance and moved up on the settee, patting the side next to her with her free hand. As soon as he had sat down next to her, she coiled her arm around his neck and delicately turned his head towards hers. She kissed his lips lightly, with a stern, serious look, then she kissed him again. This time her lips

250

did not go away after first touching his but rather stayed to move his head backwards and forwards in time to the beating of a heart.

Once she had moved her head backwards to look at him but he, not liking the lack of contact, immediately moved forward to feel the intimately textured warmth of her lips again.

"Christopher!" she said between mutual lip contact. "The curry."

"I love you," he said.

"I thought you loved my cooking instead," she jeered playfully, much more relaxed, however, now that he had made himself vulnerable to her.

"I love your red freckles and your lovely hair. It smells of
flowers in Spring-time," he held a fistful of her hair in one hand but as he bent down to kiss it, she flicked it gently out of his grasp with a twist of her head and he was left kissing his own palm.

"What foolishness is this," she teased.

"Is it foolishness? I ......" he stuck on the one word and looked down towards the top of her maroon dress. His eyes entranced by her calm stillness.

"I'm going to put on my shawl. I feel much more comfortable wearing that about the house. This cardigan smells of police stations."

"Of course," he replied and started to rise from the settee with her but she pushed him back down with a cool hand.

"I'll be but a moment," her eyes sparkled suggestively. "And then we can eat."

When she returned, wearing the shawl, she was also carrying two plates of curry. "I'm starving," she said simply. "I'm not letting this go to waste."

"It smells gorgeous," replied Christopher.

"Here, you hold mine a minute. I'll pull up the coffee table. Hold on. Just a second, I'll bring the wine - cold and white." She left the room to return with an open long-necked bottle. "The glasses! Where are the bloody .... oh, here they are. That's right, tuck in, don't wait for me. Now then, let's pour the wine. One glass for you. Is the curry that hot! I'm used to the taste of chillies because Tony always used to make strong curries. Here, have some more wine. It'll cool your throat down. Now let me eat mine: mmmmm, that's what I call a curry."

"Cor," sighed Christopher. "this is more an experience than a meal," he fanned himself ineffectively with one hand. "But a pleasant experience," he added. "A very pleasant experience: to share it with you."

"I'm not used to cooking for company these days. It's usually just Rita and myself or, more often, just me," she smiled coyly. "But I'm glad you like it."

"I love it. I love it," exclaimed Christopher eagerly as he swallowed two large mouthfuls with a gulp. Tears started to stream from in his eyes as the chilli-devil began to rub his tender throat with a painful coarse brand of sandpaper.

"Tony used to make even stronger ones than this: Jamaican Hot Pot he called it."

"We have a Lancashire Hot Pot," said Christopher between gasps. "But it's nothing like this," he looked up and caught a hurt expression in a remote corner of one eye: "nowhere near as good," he added quickly. "Tony, he was a Jamaican then?" Christopher tried to sound nonchalant: the words "we're all liberals here," were not exactly tattooed across his forehead - he just acted as if they were.

"Mmm," replied Eleanor.

"Were you close?" he asked stupidly.

"We still are," she retorted with a whiplash answer which stung him more than the chilli. "I mean we're married," she raised two hands to forestall an instant heart seizure from Christopher. "That is, we're technically married. Don't die on me! Do you think I would have kissed you like that if I'd been happily married; but then I suppose there're some women who would. Still, I'd hardly be sharing a house with Rita now, would I? When I was living with Tony he was my everything and more, just like the song says. I would have done anything for him. Come to think of it, I probably did."

The room within which they dined and talked seemed to close in around them as darkness blurred the edges into shadow creating a new intimacy: the closeness of the confessional. It was an environment which engendered confidence in Christopher. The combination of scattered darkness, cast into corners by a solitary table lamp, and a sympathetic ear, which clearly knew the meaning of pain, encouraged him to be forthright.

"I've never been close to anyone. I seemed to miss out somehow. All my friends coupled off as soon as they were able, leaving me stranded to soldier on through academia to a so-called promised land. I seem to have fluffed that as well."

"A promised land?" Eleanor scratched the top of her head allowing several red strands of hair to cascade tantalisingly over her eyes. She stood upright as she did so and then moved the coffee table back to the wall. Christopher stood to help and was tempted to move the offending hairs which were annoying him more than they were, apparently, bothering her. "That's it," she said as they pushed the table back underneath the bookcase. "Out of sight is out of mind. Is that what they promised you at University? A land of milk, honey and Porsche motor cars," she teased. "It must have been quite a let down coming here," she simply slid down onto the rug she had been standing upon, making no effort to return to the settee. Christopher knelt down beside her as she stretched back onto her elbows. "No, you can't sit down," she kicked him gently with a stocking foot as she spoke. "You've yet to obtain the chilled claret. Go to it! Some wine waiter you've turned out to be!" She snapped the fingers of one hand while her eyes sparkled with the cheekiness of command.

"M'lady," bowed Christopher in mock ceremony. "I vill ensure zit is zist best claret in the 'ouse with a red colour to match m'lady's fiery hair."

"Does that mean you'll pour it over my head," laughed Eleanor. "What kind of wine waiter are you anyway?"

Christopher returned with the open bottle of claret in one hand, a towel over his other arm and two clean crystal glasses held delicately by the stem. "Zis is to m'lady's pleasure?"

"Freedom is to my pleasure," she said quietly and then drank a glass in one draught. "I've never been so frightened. It was Rita's idea. I didn't really think I was doing wrong. Was I doing wrong? It was only some silly old leaflets. I don't even know if I believe in what they say anyway. I was helping a friend. Am I in trouble?" Eleanor looked up at him like a little girl as the defences of womanhood fell from her shoulders like her shawl, which accidentally fell away in his protective embrace. Christopher squeezed her softly and rubbed his forehead against her ear in reply. "I'm in Court tomorrow and they want to make an example of me, don't they?"

"You'll plead not guilty," said Christopher firmly.

"And you'll represent me, won't you?"

"Archie ......" started Christopher.

"Is a self-regarding peacock. I've been a fool to waste my time on him," finished Eleanor bitterly. "After Tony I thought .... but never mind. Here I am moaning about myself and you are in the same position or even worse. They may prosecute you for Perverting the Course of Justice, even yet. Oh, I hope they don't, Christopher."

"Do you?" replied Christopher surprised.

"Of course I do," she laughed as she picked up the bottle of wine and topped up their glasses. "I'm just thinking. We're a right pair of soggy dumplings aren't we? I mean your regular Bonnie and Clyde, I don't think. We could both end up convicted and out of work."

"Joe's promised me a job, I think."

"And me? Who wants a burnt out, drunk out, bum for a legal secretary. Not Archie Lord, that's for sure. Cheers." She raised her glass but Christopher didn't clash crystal. He stared thoughtfully into the deep red liquid instead.

"You're not convicted yet," Christopher said bravely in a Bailey gesture of defiance. "And if I've anything to do with it you won't be. I'll ......"

" do your best," finished Eleanor. "I know you will. But I'm not denying I've handed out the leaflets. Is that a crime in this green and pleasant land? When I was a little girl everyone used to hand out leaflets all the time from the religious freaks to those collecting for the miners."

"We have a new order now," mused Christopher. "Some thing we once thought of as fundamental, no longer are so. They're now casualties of the new way of looking at things." He tried to put into words some of the things Joe had earlier said to him but somehow he lacked the vocabulary or, rather it is more true to say that he lacked the experience of life which went with the words to make them resound with conviction.

"I feel like a casualty," she replied pathetically. "Hold me close and kiss my wounds."

Christopher wrapped both arms around her, awkwardly at first but she adjusted her position so that her back rested in the crook of his arm. She gazed up at him longingly, tenderly, half in act and half in earnest, half a mockery of earlier embraces with other lovers, half altogether his. He, however, gave her his wholeness, unencumbered by any history.

His lips pressed hers, soft then hard, she guided him backwards, using her additional height as a lever, he felt himself go back, fall back, lose himself backwards into a scented garden, the parameters of which was her perfumed entirety. It was her arms and body which were the walls and the boundary of his world and he wanted no other. No courtrooms to fall down in, no policemen to drag him away and no man's law to indict him.

She covered him with her blouse as she removed it from her shoulders and with her breasts as she slipped off her bra. His tongue traced the line of a vein from the sweet sweat in her crevice to her swelling nipple which he then felt, rubbing slowly, against the roof of his mouth. She fell over to one side pulling him over as well, still sucking with his eyes closed: his turn to be the infant now.

Time may have still ticked resolutely by; but for these two lovers, within a womb of mutual desire, their passion took them curiously out of joint with the harsh demands of the clock-face and the chimes of every man.

She touched him so delicately, like a spider's web falling to the ground, and softly her more experienced hands freed him from the constraints of his own clothing while freeing herself also with a wriggle and a squirm. She pulled him on top of her and then to the side as they rolled under and over, over and under, roly-poly across the creaking floor. He did not worry about entering her - although that had earlier been an inhibition of his - it just happened naturally as they rolled happily around: up and tumble down, naked and free.

He thought at first that he was someone else and he believed, at first, that he would not be able to please; that he was not big and black and moving with rhythm. That old phallic, and far from liberal, mythology had eaten away momentarily at the roots of his psyche and, had she not made the first move, he would have remained, emotionally self-emasculated: by his own repressive act, far from proved to be in fact.

As it was they played together in their adult nursery as they had never expected to do, the lack of prior

257

expectation was an important factor in their uninhibited fun, their freedom from the repression of "ecstasy by numbers." She did not feel that she had to come to please him as she had, stupidly and mistakenly, tried to please other men in the past by pretending to come at the same moment that they did. She had temporarily replaced her fantasy of subjection with an unplanned game in which no role was required of her. His tongue sought out her soft, excited state and then the pressure of him deep inside her, but with him, unlike with Tony or Archie, she could hold him still, both hands cupped around his buttocks, and rub on his pelvic bone: harder and harder. Her breathing faster and faster, the muscles inside pulling together until she felt them go away and then tighten again, an ebb and flow of tidal tingling, a release, that when it came, swelled through her body like a wave of relaxation. A sigh, that was internal, for her own pleasure only, like the last note, echoing in the mind and not the concert hall, of a primitive, primeval and entirely pleasing symphony. She looked down at what remained of him and, while she still smiled contentedly, she secretly missed the subjection which had been fun in a different way. In this case, however, she had undoubtedly been in control and Christopher seemed so puny now that it was all done. Perhaps she should eat him up as certain female spiders did once they had had their wicked way. She laughed at the thought of this, rolling off his crushed body. He seemed all skin and bones, his ribcage like a xylophone, compared to her healthy flab, which was saved from being fat by her larger size and proportion.

Indeed, it's fair to say that he felt himself intimidated by her as she pulled away and lay on her back like some huge, becalmed whale. He brushed down both sides of his moustache simultaneously, nervously seeking some kind of assurance from that traditional sign of man-hood. She looked beautiful as she lay next to him, all smooth moist skin, red hair and sleek confidence. His own body, unclothed, was clearly smaller, thinner, frailer than hers. he tried to find his boxer shorts, which had slipped off as if a skilled choreographer had carefully orchestrated the steps to cause minimum fuss, but his efforts were restrained by the palm of her large right hand, fingers stretched out like the ribs of a Japanese fan, which seemed to cover his entire chest and hold him back as her head leant forward to block out the light from the table lamp and cast her face into sinister shadow. Perhaps she was going to eat him after all.

She was somewhat annoyed that he wanted to dress again so soon. He had been lucky to have her at all and he should be grateful. She would make sure that he was. He cowered back as she leant over him, her unleashed hair splashing all over his face, she shook her scented locks across his eyes, his nose and mouth: to wake him up to how lucky he had been. Looking for his clothes, indeed! She had no false modesty about her own attractions - she had fought off too many men for that - and would not normally have even considered the likes of Christopher as a potential lover - was it not just this morning that she had told Rita he was a creep? And yet here she was lounging next to him (he was the lucky one) and he, obviously unenamoured with her charms, was about to search for his clothes. The worm!

Christopher had never worn his boxer shorts over his head before. It was a little difficult to conduct any kind of serious conversation with your nose sticking out of a fly-hole, then there was the smell ......

"Have I done something," he mumbled through the cotton curtain which had been forced over his face.

She started to laugh and so he left the boxer shorts on and tried to chase her across the carpet, wearing them over his head, until she pulled them off and, in between a fit of giggling and gasping for breath, she kissed him again and again and again, wrapping him up in her body like a cloak as she did so.

"I think I like you," she said as he commenced to kiss her breasts.

"We're going to be all right, aren't we?" he asked, blissfully happy in that moment but very unsure about the mountain they had inadvertently climbed. The next moment, he thought of the next until the future seemed to twist and turn, a stream winding its way across the floor of a steep sided ravine, which he could only glimpse at hazily through the valley mist from the edge of the precipice. He snuggled his limbs together with hers and they both shuddered as, together, they felt the cold chill of the west wind.

CHAPTER SIXTEEN

"Are you really going to blow him away then, for fucking final; I mean you're really going to use that an' all, Anil. Are you? Are you?"

Anil looked over his walrus moustache at Rat-face Jnagel, rather like a python peering over a hedge, giving him the dubious benefit of a controlled stare by two hard, cold, glass pebble eyes. Hence, having received no direct answer to his question, Jnagel persisted and, as he did so, he drummed his fingers along the outside of his steering wheel, each finger-tapping burst being drummed out in conjunction with a short-fire question of nervous propensity.

"Well, I rang the Snooker Hall, didn't I? I asked for him and he answered, didn't he? Bindi here, he said and then I put the phone down on him which was the right thing to do, weren't it. Fuck, it's hot in here, aren't you hot? The gun's loaded now; isn't it? What happens now, don't you have to slide the safety catch off: they come on automatically now. Did you hear Mukker say that a number five cartridge has about two hundred and thirty pellets in it? I don't know how many an S.G. cartridge has, do you? Oh yes, it's nine big ones isn't it? Well, it's better I stay in the car and keep the motor running, eh? I should be a bloody rally driver I should. I'll do a wheeley and we'll burn off like a bloody moon rocket:- Brrrrrrrrrrummm! You watch me when I really wanna fucking drive: Brrrrrrrrummm! I'll burn up the fucking tarmac. You ain't seen me really drive yet, have you?"

"Shut your face," retorted Anil and the words were dropped out of his mouth like anchors over the side of a ship, deep and heavy. "Drive round the back. SLOWLY."

Marway Sidhu was drinking whisky. That was not unusual. Marway Sidhu was not talking to anybody. That was very unusual. In particular, he ignored the customary greeting from the customary gang of boys, who entered in triumph, bearing Balwinder Singh Gill between them; but he did stab the latter with a jagged glass stare. Indeed, it seemed, for one fraught and frightful moment, that Marway would actually object to Bindi's presence by telling him to leave. Needless to say a serious incident would have certainly ensued had he done so. Instead he grunted, like he was clearing his throat of phlegm, and stared into his whisky as if about to spit into the glass.

The gang members pushed Joshi towards the bar, one of them kicking him up the backside as he ordered a round of lagers, then they left him to wait on them as they all congregated around one snooker table at the far end of Southall Snooker Hall. No-one was actually playing.

"Joe Bailey's a good brief, for sure. He must be, to talk you back onto the streets again," Parminder Mangat, known as Bender because of his ability to bend laws, was tossing a coin into the air as he spoke.

"I've known Joe a long time. I just went to Archie Lord because Joe has this habit of lecturing you. I don't always want to hear that. It gives me ear-ache; but it doesn't stop him being good though. He must be good to make my bail but I still had to find a ten grand surety. No problem. My dad shits that much every day," Bindi swaggered as he flashed a smile. A cue for the others to laugh. They all did except Bender who merely nodded instead.

"What's the evidence like?" he asked, putting his coin in the top zip pocket of his brown leather jacket, and producing a thin packet of Lucky cigarettes. He deigned to accept a touch of flame from Kwaki's gold lighter. He ducked his head back to avoid the first, involuntary cloud of smoke which he exhaled after lighting his long and distinctive cigarette. "I mean, that's the first question we asked in Canada. That's what it's all about, you know."

"Don't give me all that," Bindi pointed a double-barrelled middle-cum-forefinger at Bender, with a cocked thumb to show a loaded, angry intent. "Canadian crap! We're on the streets of London here and you know fuck all. I know what fucking evidence will convict me and what won't. I've slipped out from under more criminal charges than you'll ever wet yourself dreaming about."

"I doubt it," said Bender simply.

"Don't come the hard man with me. We ain't ever actually seen you do anything here 'cept move your lips."

"I've brought stuff over."

"Everyone's brought stuff over. So fucking what. You've pulled off a hoist in Canada, so you say. I happen to have heard that from someone else otherwise I'd blow you out. But over here you're starting at the bottom and so you can quit trying to crowd me all the time. I'm fucking sick of all this "I know" business. In fact, I'm fucking sick of ......"

"All this crap, eh Bindi?" Satish Brar interjected diplomatically and brought up his hands in a characteristic gesture to cool down his friend's notorious temper. His gesture was a strange combination of calm, openness and surrender. Bindi knew it well and responded by changing down through his emotional gearbox. Satish fluttered his deceptively feminine lashes at his friend as if to say: it's all right, we're on your side, we know he's overstepped the mark.

"Yeah, yeah," agreed Bindi grudgingly after a short pause in which he and Bender exchanged eyeball strengths.

"The beers are on me, 'kay?" Joshi ambled into the group carrying a tray of drinks. Somebody pinched his fat bottom and he almost dropped the lot. Everyone laughed and goodwill was restored, almost immediately.

"Someone better feed the table otherwise miserable Marway will come over moaning again," suggested Satish who looked at Joshi after he had spoken.

"Oh no, why me? Haven't I just bought the drinks?" whined the fat gang member as he fiddled nervously with his gold rings.

"Pull your money Joss-stick," snarled Bindi. "You make the most on dealing by far. Pull it out and I don't mean your plonker!"

"He couldn't find that anyhow. Not unless you gave him at least a week," jeered Satish as he slapped Joshi's face playfully.

"'Kay, but just this once. It's always me," Joshi grumbled as he placed a fifty pence piece and four tens into the machine. He jerked the lever angrily and, for his money he heard a satisfying rumble of balls. Satish started scooping them up into a wooden triangle on the green baize-covered table.

"Fucking ace," said Bender who pushed Joshi out of the way to pick up both snooker cues. He threw one at Bindi who just managed to catch it in a fast reflex snatch before it hit him in the face. "A fiver a frame," he challenged.

"No problem," retorted Balwinder after a low, chest-deep, snarl.

"The phone for Bindi!" a voice, shouted from the bar room, carried across the tables to reach the group as a faint echo.

"You're not off the hook," snapped Bindi as he slapped the cue onto the table with a crash. "I'll be a minute."

"It's your hook," laughed Bender.

"We'll see. Hold this frame." Balwinder marched off with aggression surging from his sinews as he swung his arms out to purposefully strike each table that he passed. After he had disappeared from sight, Bender swaggered confidently around the table making ghost shots with his snooker cue. Balwinder, surprisingly enough, did return in less than a minute as he had promised. "No fucker there 'innit," he complained as he took his cue back from Satish.

"Fucked off for waiting," smiled Satish Brar.

"Fuck should I know," replied Bindi. "Right, let's have your cash then," he taunted. "You can break if you like."

"No, you," retorted Bender.

"Okay, I know I won't fluff it. Hope you came with plenty of fivers - best of five do you?"

"Here," Parminder Mangat handed out fifteen pounds casually to Joshi. Bender's eyes were half closed by his own cigarette smoke and, as he leant his head backwards, an observant artist could have traced a line from the tip of his cigarette to the top of his forehead: the hypotenuse; the right angle being where the brown filter tip met his upper lip. "You be bank."

"That's a great idea. He owes me fifteen anyhow," Bindi unzipped his lips as he spoke to display two rows of sharp, white teeth.

"What!" Joshi exclaimed before Satish ground his toes into pulp with a sharp, twisting heel. "Aaah! 'Kay, 'Kay, I remember. Shit, that hurt."

"I don't know why that guy puts up with you," observed Bender in slow, measured tones.

"Why? Do you intend to do anything about it, Mr. Canada Wet," sneered Bindi.

"If I do, you'll be the first to know."

"Look," Bindi pointed his snooker cue at Bender as if it were a rapier. "Joshi does all right because I'm the boss. He makes money and we all make money. Any problems and I've the bottle and the wherewithal to sort them out. Now. Mr. Canada Cunnilingus Wet-face, you are rapidly becoming a problem to me. This is not good news from your point of view, unless you're partial to hospital food - on drip."

Parminder Mangat was largely an unknown quantity from the physical point of view but an almost imperceptible tremble around the knees and thighs of his designer label jeans would have revealed, to the acute observer, that he was not entirely confident of a successful outcome following any kind of violent exchange with Balwinder Singh Gill. He was, however, still determined to receive far more respect from his peers than hitherto, especially since he had formerly occupied a revered position as an astute and uncaught car thief holding a reasonable reputation with

266

the blade. In his last hoist, of a garage on the outskirts of Toronto, he had held but not fired, a sawn-off. He therefore liked to think himself a touch above the Junior League of London Brits. Unfortunately, for his own self-image he knew little about the local drug trade and virtually nothing about the complicated infrastructure of importation and street sales, which in the Asian Community at least, had yet to reach the multi-million dollar limits of it's Jamaican equivalents. It was, however, too complicated for him to simply soak up by osmosis from street-talk and jive. For the moment, at least, he needed to know and a battle with Bindi, which he was not at all sure he could win in any event, would simply cut him out of the charmed circle: whatever the outcome. It may hurt his pride to back down but Parminder had the intelligence to realise that he had no choice.

"There's no problem Bindi," he pulled the cigarette stub from his mouth after he had finished speaking and dropped it on the floor just in front of Balwinder so that he had a legitimate reason to take a step forward, invading Bindi's territory, in order to crush out the dying embers of flame from the gleaming ash-tip. "No problem," he repeated tensing his leg muscles in order to kick Bindi in the groin should the latter try to strike him with his snooker cue. Parminder didn't want to fight, because of the rational and carefully thought out fear of isolation; but, almost simultaneously, he did want to slash Bindi to satisfy a far more primitive urge than mere reason. Indeed, it was this ambiguous cocktail of emotion and intent which caused him to attach a question to his meek reply: "Is it?" he added to confirm his strength.

Yes it fucking is - Bindi felt like saying but he stepped back from the brink. He had nearly killed both Jasbir Sood and "Mad" Mukesh and, while he greatly enjoyed the power of the thrusting blade, he, nevertheless, feared his own pleasure in equal measure to his enjoyment of it. His hesitancy was an exit visa from his own personal hell and, while the excitement had been almost enough to keep him: a lonely, shaking terror would not let him remain. He could crack open Bender's skull with a sharp wrist-whip of his cue. However, he merely lined up the white ball on the straight line of the chalk D-shape instead. He avoided saying anything for fear of saying too much. He was about to break the pack of reds when Anil Sood scattered his thoughts in a far more successful mental break. Fortunately, he was still on an adrenaline high from his earlier confrontation with Bender and he started to move his body almost at the very moment Anil spoke his solitary word.

"Die," he said simply and discharged the first, right hand barrel, of his gun.

Despite Anil's exclamation, Balwinder had virtually no fear that he would die at all. He thought of all sorts of things, but not that. He thought of Jasbir Sood, Anil's brother, although not in any reasoned way: he simply created an image of Jasbir's face by pressing the playback button of his own mental video recorder. He thought of the strange yellow colour washed onto the steps together with many pints of Mukker's blood after he had plunged in the knife: now it was his turn to donate. He thought of his father and of how he had failed him. He thought of Marway, who momentarily replaced his father's face;

"well, I'm paying now," he thought finally as a gutter wound was bloodily furrowed across his chest. Then the pain soaked his whole body blood red.

When Anil had previously planned the future in his own mind it had been a cold, clinical and, above all else, organised endeavour. It was more real somehow when it was actually being imagined; whereas, when it happened, it passed by as if in a dream. The problem was that Anil was not a Mafia contract killer, he was merely playing out the role, with insufficient rehearsal of the part. Consequently, the boom of the discharge, the painful and unexpected kick from the gun and the nearly overwhelming smell of powder caused him to panic. Contrary to what Mukesh had told him, he had intended to fire the first barrel to scatter the gang members and then calmly and stonily approach the cowering body of Balwinder Singh Gill and, from a range of two feet or so, blast off half his skull. That would be for Jasbir. A debt repaid. But, when the gun fired, causing threads from Balwinder's jacket to be torn out in a graceful arc together with pieces of flesh and blood, he decided that he had done enough.

A pull of the trigger by his forefinger blew away Anil's personality. Before he had actually fired the gun he had been in control of both the external situation and his own internal emotions. He had stood, legs apart, some four or five yards away from Balwinder Singh Gill, with Jnagel scurrying behind him somewhere, and then he had shouted, which was not part of his plan at all although, perhaps, was indicative of an escaping emotional pressure bubbling away inside his body, before the pull of the trigger gave him a much needed and heady release from tension.

At the range of four to five yards the pellets had not quite reached the stage where they had spread out to resemble more a swarm of bees than a bullet, nor, however, were they a tightly packed wad, but, rather they sliced scythe-like through the air at the speed of sound: a one ounce mass of ball bearings about two to three inches long followed by several pieces of plastic wadding from inside the cartridge's casing. Had Bindi not instinctively turned to his side the entire contents of the cartridge, including the wadding, would have hit him dead-centre in the chest, smashing into his rib cage, but not passing through his body, and, in the absence of any heavy clothing, almost certainly killing him. As it was he had turned enough to take the discharge almost side on and, as a result, he had managed to duck the delivery of a free sample of "death to go." Not, however, without cost.

"I'mmmm EEEEEEE!" he screamed as his knee-caps simply slid out of their joints and his left arm, nearest both the snooker table and the direction of the blast, reached out feebly, and unsuccessfully, to restrain his bodily collapse. His head hit the side of the snooker table as he fell cutting his forehead with a three inch gash while his left arm, in its abortive attempt to support the rest of his body, was broken as it became a mere frail, trapped limb of human weakness rather than the steel lever of support he had, in vain, desired.

Once Bindi had screamed - more like the calling card of a psychical nightmare than a material occurrence in the physical world of cause and effect - Anil panicked and, as part of an emotional eruption, he bellowed out his brother's name - "J A S B I R!" - as he lifted up the shotgun, so that it pointed towards the ceiling, he had the vague and inconsistent motive to avoid hitting anyone with the far deadlier S.G. cartridge, as he did so, he pulled the second trigger. He disappeared almost immediately underneath the deluge of plaster, roofing felt, tarmac and even some small splinters from the wooden beam support. A small two inch hole appeared in the ceiling as the sand and lime dust caused everyone to cough and rub their eyes.

"For fuck's sake - Go!" barked Rat-face Jnagel as he pulled on Anil's arm and led him, the choking, crying blind man, out of the area where the snooker tables were and into the corridor, which led to the fire doors. The cook blocked their path, swinging a meat cleaver, an insane glint partially revealed from a squinting eye. Anil, who was holding his gun with one hand and covering his eyes with the other, had immobilised himself and could only cough up dust, cry and utter "Jasbir." Jnagel, however, had an overriding urge to reach his car which exhibited a far stronger will than that possessed by the cook to resist it.

"I'll kill you," Rat-face Jnagel shouted although, had he been required to do so, he would have had to admit that he certainly didn't have the means to do so. The cook, who from that day would always swear that the second man pointed a pistol at his head, simply dropped his meat cleaver, ducked and dashed back into his kitchen again.

"Jasbir!" shouted Anil again as his friend pulled and pushed him towards the car. Fortunately no-one was at the rear of the club to prevent them from leaving. The rubber from their wheels was torn rapidly across the roadway as the Tooti Nung departed from the scene leaving the smell of burning rubber behind.

271

Balwinder Gill felt himself to be in a dream where there was no pain but merely the fear of it. There was nothing to hold onto in that blankness save for the skipping, periodic moments of remembrance: still photo-frames, all that was left of a moving film.

Bender, the bastard, smiling as he leant over him to unbutton his shirt. Something wet and cold put on his face. Blood - was that his? Too much to be just his. Vomit and bile down the front of his shirt. When did he do that?

Ambulance men telling him that it was all right. Yes it was. He had paid his dues now. It was when he was first moved that pain skimmed in and out of his consciousness: sometimes coinciding with images but mostly not. Stabbing invitation to scream - until the injections came.

CHAPTER SEVENTEEN

He returned to consciousness with a happy smile. It had all been a dream. All his life, up until that moment of waking, had been merely the restless, disturbed hallucinations of a long repose. Now he awoke into an ethereal existence, only glimpsed at during his lengthy hibernation – until another night's sleep gave him another life to live.

The room was not the one he was accustomed to call his own. It all seemed curiously out of joint with his prior concept of time and space. It was as if someone had placed all the molecules into a great atomic blender, a Master Chef of matter, and thus created an amorphous jelly which was then allowed to set, like its fruit equivalent, into a solid mass of an entirely different structure from that it had previously assumed. One thing was abundantly clear: his mother would not appear with a cup of tea and a slice of toast.

Why no mother? The answer was all wrapped up snug and warm in the bed of Eleanor Redfern.

Christopher sighed and time started to move less slowly.

Eleanor appeared in the doorway full clothed, carrying a tray on which was balanced a pot of tea and a plate of toast. It all slid into a scrambled jumble, albeit still safely on the tray as she sat down on his side of the bed. "Good morning," she said.

"I'm in your bed," he replied.

"Who's a lucky boy then," she retorted cheekily.

"I am," he grinned.

"You'll need all your luck today," she confirmed wearing her serious mask, "Otherwise I'm going to jail and definitely not collecting the two hundred pounds."

"Talking of money," said Christopher as he poured two cups of tea – there was an emotional energy flare up as Eleanor momentarily opened the wrong envelope and Christopher was nearly blamed for a letter he did not send: requesting money for his legal services. "I mean" continued Christopher quickly "whether Archie is still your boss. I mean," he stumbled on to avoid any ambiguity at all "whether you are still working for him. Still being paid."

"Not by Archie anymore. He's a selfish coward," she answered finally. "A glamorous, selfish coward admittedly. But, nevertheless, his instinct is to save his own butt and to kick any other available arse he can find. First it was yours and now it's mine. It's taken me a broken dream or two to understand Lord Archie's attributes; but now I know. Now I finally know," she spoke down into the rising steam from her own tea-cup rather than to Christopher himself, a cascade of unbrushed and knotted strands of topsy-turvy red hair tumbled down from her forehead, like a waterfall to hide all of her face save for the tip of her nose.

"I'm not exactly Rambo myself," laughed Christopher uneasily.

"No, but you're honest and true," she replied.

Am I, he asked himself. Surely not, he replied, pleased but unsure. "You're beautiful," he mumbled half aloud and half in dialogue with himself.

I know that, she smiled privately, her mouth unseen.

274

"I'll do anything for you," he continued as he reached out with a possessive hand that stopped short of contact as her head turned to reveal a face with a maternal scowl.

"Pretty lies," she sneered. "Are lies nonetheless."

"But pretty still," replied Christopher.

"Pretty stilted you mean," she rejoined.

"It's how I feel," he fumbled for his glasses as he spoke in order to bring her features into sharper focus and to try and see her as she really was, a difficult endeavour. Finally she handed them to him and they both sipped tea. Christopher looked over the rim of his cup for an answer and, after he had eaten a large chunk of silence, he continued: "I'm being honest and true about my feelings," he confirmed, hoping to keep up the character which she perceived him to be.

"As much as any man can be, I suppose," she conceded ungraciously.

"Will you marry me?" he asked after a moment.

"Don't be silly," she replied. Her hazel brown eyes went nearly black with opaque opprobrium.

"I'm serious," he said, wondering whether he was.

"I don't know. A man screws you one minute and wants to possess you the next. You'll be asking me if you were good in bed next. Male insecurity and a desire to own go hand in hand."

"That sounds like Rita talking," retorted Christopher in a rare flash of perception as his glasses slipped down to his nostrils.

"Perhaps it is," conceded Eleanor. "But does that make it any less true."

"I sometimes wonder whether any of us really think for ourselves," he said after a short pause and he pushed his glasses back up to the bridge of his nose as he continued: "or whether we don't go on repeating what we've heard from family and friends generation after generation. Of course we put our own personal stamp on an idea but the basic wax remains the same, handed over by someone else, heated up to melt his seal and then pressed down securely with our own, as if no-one else had ever used it before. We're all such liars Eleanor. I wonder if Rita arrived at her political principles by careful and calculated thought," posed Christopher as he bit thoughtfully into a piece of cold toast.

"No, by screwing a full-time official of the SWP," laughed Eleanor bitterly. "So you admit you were lying then."

"About marriage?" asked Christopher between swallows. he rubbed some butter from his moustache before he continued: "No, I wasn't actually."

"Oh dear," replied Eleanor. "You seem to know so little for one who knows so much."

"Meaning I don't know much about relationships," he postulated as he finished his tea and toast and tried to avoid thinking about the rest of the day.

"Am I being unfair?" she queried. Her whole face opened up, like a newly revealed stage, as she raised her head to allow her hair to fall to each side of her face as if a theatre curtain had been pulled back to announce the start of the play.

"No," he admitted laughing. "I confess to a lack of experience of relationships or, indeed, of life. I'm a blank page of total innocence, burnt a little at the edges maybe. I sometimes wonder if I know anything about anything at all."

"Is this man defending me today!" teased Eleanor and she dazzled him with a brilliant smile she did not feel: a mere decorative façade.

"Ancient Athens was my field at University," confessed Christopher dreamily to Eleanor's fading smile from lips which first stumbled and then finally broke in dismay. "I mean, the law of Classical Athens."

"Christ," she mumbled. "So if I were Socrates I'd have a fighting chance."

"Probably not," he mused thinking of Plato, "since he chose to defend himself and although it was stirring stuff, he was his own worst enemy. Everyone is. Take the ...."

"I was joking," interjected Eleanor. "Or perhaps partly serious. I was thinking of myself, I'm afraid and of today in particular."

"Oh," replied Christopher feeling a deep foreboding gather like an ominous, grey, granite cloud, over the remains of their tea and toast. The anxiety over what was to come had diluted the ecstasy over what had passed.

The threads from the past led them, two coloured strands in a careful tapestry of pain, towards an inevitable future of, to them at that time, an entirely uncertain outcome. Christopher was worried and Eleanor was worried that he was worried which, of course, worried Christopher.

"You know I've never defended anyone before," he said.

"I've got no-one else," she replied.

"It'll go over for trial if you plead Not Guilty and I'll fix a date which Joe Bailey can do," he said with quivering words which fell out of the sentence the moment he spoke them making that simple assertion appear both complicated and disjointed.

"Is that what will happen?" she asked.

I hope so. Oh God, I hope so, he did not say. "Yes," he answered in a negative tone.

"Good," she replied feeling bad. "I've confidence in you," she continued. And I lie a lot she thought unhappily. Archie, you're an awful bastard and I wish you were dead but, before you die, come and defend me. I wonder if Christopher will wear "L-plates" she thought unkindly and she conjured up a picture of him in court with the words: "I've just started, please excuse," tattooed onto the back of his head. On second thoughts he could wear a pair of "L-plates" in bed as well. She smiled as she pictured them, hanging around his neck, flapping against his naked chest as he attempted to perform: wicked, wicked lady, she nearly laughed out loud.

Christopher misinterpreted her full beam smile. "Thanks," he said sincerely. "I won't let you down."

"No, but I might not let you up," she goaded placing a hand on each respective shoulder in playful torment.

"I'll be your prisoner for life," he laughed.

Don't say that, she thought, fight me and we'll have some fun. Christopher did not respond as she had hoped and she released her hold. He could tell that her mood had petered out but he put that down to the forthcoming trial.

"We'll be all right," he said in an attempt to reassure her but somehow his words had a hollow echo: an almost imperceptible absence of meaning.

"Will we?" she queried. The "we" was sprayed with so much sarcasm, courtesy of Irony Aerosol Inc., that it nearly wiped out the ozone layer single handed.

"I better dress," he said in a hurt and puzzled manner. "And I'll try not to say anything to offend."

"Can a giraffe try to roar like a lion?" she mocked.

"No," he paused and gave her a shy smile as he climbed out of bed naked. He felt vulnerable since she was fully dressed and although he did not mind that feeling and, indeed, in some curious childhood way it was quite pleasant; nevertheless, he knew now that she would not like the fact that he liked it and so he kept his feelings to himself. "But giraffe's are fine if you like long necks," he replied after a moment.

"Perhaps I should stick to the King of the Jungle," she gibed as she moved from her bed to the stool in front of her dressing table and after fiddling with various articles and seemingly rubbing her eyes, she commenced brushing her hair.

"Not if you're in the city," he returned pulling up his trousers as he spoke.

"Giraffes are pretty useless in the city too," she taunted and Christopher could see her eyes as she gave him a sly look. They seemed somehow different: more brownish than before with a vague touch of red. How did they change colour like that?

"I don't know," he said out loud. "Us city giraffes are a good head and shoulders above the rest."

"I like that," she smiled openly and Christopher could tell it was a genuine response. He was beginning to understand her or, at least, appreciate when her smile was a true reflection of her emotions. Her facial muscles were somehow more relaxed and free. "You're a funnyosity you know. I could quite like you," she tormented.

"What do you do with men you quite like," he smiled as he tucked his shirt into his trousers and tried not to notice that it smelled.

"Share a bath and a bottle of wine," she giggled like a little girl. "But only a good wine. It must be French and from Bordeaux. Apart from that I don't mind."

"In the bath?" he queried as he made a mess of knotting his tie.

"Oh yes. The best place to share an intimate bottle of plonk. Then if he starts mentioning rings, bells or banns you can either drown him or pull the plug: depending on how you feel at the time."

"Will I receive a baptism?"

"The Order of the Bath with oak leaf cluster," she replied wriggling her nose.

"An oak leaf won't cover very much." he protested.

"Who wants anything covered?" her head bobbed playfully from side to side in the mirror as she spoke causing her hair to fall forward in fiery strands. "That's the other reason for drinking in the bath."

"Did you say drinking the bath?" he questioned with mock severity.

"Only if he brings Spanish wine. Some brands of bath-salts have a more distinctive palate."

"What about vintage Spanish?" he questioned in jest.

"No-one keeps a bottle long enough to find out. Besides it's a contradiction in terms like," she pondered as she stood up and her face disappeared from the glass to face him in the flesh, shadows casting its features into relief. "Like," she repeated. "Young Conservative."

"Or Socialist Worker," rejoined Christopher thinking of Roger from the Jimmy Joyce Public House. They both laughed.

"Or poor solicitor," she teased.

"That's no contradiction," he protested. "I'm the living proof."

"Only until you sign a partnership deed somewhere. Probably with a corporate or commercial company: coining in money by the lorry-load," she needled and while she surveyed his face carefully and slow: as if the answer would be important to her.

"I just want to help people," he pleaded in his own defence.

"An innocent man," she mocked..

"Honest and true, you said," he retorted holding onto her assessment like a life-raft in a stormy sea.

"They are not mutually exclusive," she smiled sadly.

"Is it better to marry an innocent man than a guilty one," he stated hopefully.

"It depends what they are guilty of," she laughed.

"Loving you," he said.

"If you love me, then beat this public order rap. Be strong for me, like you were in the police station. Be ......"

"A hero," he interjected, finishing the sentence on her behalf. "It's just that it's such hard work sometimes," he laughed and she caught the giggle germ too and they both fell into each others arms. "I'm so happy with you though," he whispered. "And I don't want to be at war all the time."

"Well," she breathed back to him. "We can wash off the smell of battle when we return – over a bottle of wine," her features melted with human warmth and then became hard as she grinned again: "talking of smells," she sniffed at the air around his shirt.

"What do you mean?" he retorted although he knew very well what she meant. "Anyway, I've had this on all yesterday," he complained. "And I didn't expect to stay the night."

"I should hope not," she teased. "Now take it off while I show you my range of men's shirts," she put her hand to her mouth to stop herself from bursting out into a belly-laugh. "The Cosmopolitan woman," she teased herself. "Actually they were left here by Tony. He's the same build as you, roughly. What are you? Size 16."

"15," he answered.

"Well, try one on. It won't hurt to try."

"Have I a choice?"

"Most definitely not. I don't believe in choice," she teased "People end up doing things they don't want to do."

He undid his tie and peeled off a distinctly damp and smelly shirt. She took it off him by holding it between her thumb and forefinger. She screwed up her nose in distaste. "Ugh," she said as she dropped the shirt in her own wash basket.

"Do I smell as bad as the shirt?" he questioned as she turned back towards his half naked body.

"No you smell quite nice," she confessed as she rubbed the palms of both her hands up and down his chest. She laughed shyly: "you smell of me," she said.

"Then I'll never ever wash," he smiled happily.

"People can smell love-making you know," she stated as he felt himself falling forward into her face. Their lips touched, parted, touched and then pressed together – moving as if in tune to a timeless, unthought, rhythm. I want to be her, he thought. I'm Eleanor as well. She dug her nails deep into his shoulder blades causing a joyful pain. He screwed up his already closed eyelids and the pain became a bright redness before it turned into a dark purple ecstasy. He wanted to enter her. To roll over in bed in a hot, sweaty, mutual surrender. To spend the rest of the day
....

The rest of the day! He opened his eyes and gently pulled away from her. She opened her eyes and then screwed them up again as her body swayed in a dreamy, melting, languorous pose.

"Darling," he said as softly as he could.

"Mmmm," she replied. "I like smelling me on you," she giggled, "let's ....."

"..... remember that we're a 'courting today," he interjected in a melodious manner.

"Courting?" she opened her eyes suddenly and then twitched her nose at him as she caught his double meaning together with the unhappy shower of freezing cold droplets of unavoidable reality. "Fuck!" she exclaimed.

"Unfortunately not," he complained.

"Why tell me?" she vehemently accused.

"Shouldn't I?" he answered confused.

283

She pulled a small hair from his chest by digging out the root with a sharp fingernail. "Not if you love me more than your profession," she insisted as he made a manly attempt to muffle a moan.

"That hurt," he looked down at the red blotch on his chest. "Anyway," he said sulkily. "I hate my profession at the moment and I love you ......"

"At the moment," she added to torment.

"No for always. For ever," he protested. It's because I love you that I stopped. It's my love that's putting you before my needs which, at the moment, are ...."

"To go to Court," she finished his sentence as he had not intended.

"Only to represent you," he reminded her. And I'm frightened. My God, I'm frightened of that, he didn't say. After all, she had confidence in him and, in consequence, he owed her his best effort: howsoever inadequate that may be.

"Oh yes," she replied. Am I really going to go into the dock? She felt puzzled and unsure. Of course I am, she recalled. Why me? Can some silly leaflets make such a difference to my smart, efficient persona of legal secretary? Why couldn't someone tell me it was so? Rita should have helped me; but did she know? "Rita doesn't know I'm in court today."

"So?" questioned Christopher. "I'll tell her," he added.

"No, no, don't. Oh God, I don't feel prepared for this," she stopped and cast her eyes up and down his half-naked body. "You're not even dressed," she complained.

"You were going to find me a shirt," he reminded.

"Oh, I'm sorry," she said as her words cracked open like the shell of an egg allowing an embryo of emotion to sprout into tears. "I'm so sorry, so bloody sorry," she continued. "So bloody stupid," she added.

"Everyone has the right to be stupid at least once a day," he said, for something to say, as cheerfully as he could manage.

"No they don't," she retorted, drying her eyes with a small silk handkerchief, which displayed a Japanese lady hiding behind her fan. "Not anymore. You have to march down the long straight road these days. If you step off they won't let you on again, unless you're lucky or rich."

"Do you feel you've stepped off then?" he asked as he placed a wad of talcum powder under each armpit and rubbed another handful into an imperceptible, perfumed nothingness on his chest. It was quick dry wash before he donned another man's shirt.

"Pushed off more like," she complained and then she twitched her nose apologetically. "No, that's not fair on Rita. The truth is that I didn't think I did anything at all. I should have thought it out. The consequences, I mean. One has to be so careful these days. I wonder if this is how all political martyrs are created: People who don't know what they're doing; tried for things they didn't know they'd done."

"You're hardly political, Eleanor, and I hope I don't make you a martyr today."

"No, I suppose I'm not. I was just helping Rita, believe it or not. With some vague notion of trying to educate people as well, I suppose. Now, that was the stupid, conceited bit. Anyway, will I have to give evidence or what? Aren't you supposed to explain these things to me?"

Only if someone explains them to me first, he thought, but aloud he said: "No, it's only a remand today. Not much will happen. You'll just say not guilty and a date for trial will be fixed then and there," Christopher repeated what he had said earlier as if it were a lawyers litany which confirmed his faith. "Simple," he added with a sick grin.

"Oh," she replied unsure and then she laughed wholeheartedly. "That shirt fits you like a made-to-measure bin-liner!"

"Thanks," he retorted unhappily. His diseased grin deteriorated rapidly from mere invalidity to the death-bed where it was replaced by the crumpled broken lips of humiliation. Tony had obviously filled out his shirt in the regions that Christopher's chest could not reach. "It's too big for me," he said.

"No-one will notice if you tuck it tight into your trousers and wear a jacket over the top," she tried to control her mirth. You could always wear it as a dress instead, she just prevented herself from saying. "Here let me do your tie," she took over the task naturally and easily as she dextrously flicked one long narrow piece of red material underneath a wider length and, with a quick, upward jerk towards his throat, she had fastened a fine knot. "This tie is stained," she complained.

"I did it on the train. Tartan beer," he rubbed the dull stain with a touch of spittle from his forefinger. "I'll have to buy a new one."

"Tony left ...." started Eleanor and she had started to move towards the wardrobe again as she spoke.

Christopher stopped her with an almost upraised palm. He was too deferential to let her have the full, traffic-stopping, "How" sign, reputedly once favoured by red-Indian tribes. "No, thanks all the same. I'd rather not. Thanks for the shirt though," he tried to sound genuinely grateful which was not easy when he felt foolishly phoney. Fortunately, he was saved from further explanation by the arrival of the bus, announced by a klaxon call.

"Christ, what was that!"

"Bailey's Battlebus. He's giving us a lift on his way to court. He must be the only lawyer to take his office to his clients like a workaholic snail carrying his place of employment on his back." Christopher was possessively proud of Joe Bailey. He felt somehow tied up with his success beyond the mere fact of his new allegiance as a new employee. He opened Eleanor's bedroom window just in time to see the rotund solicitor emerge from the foliage. Joe must have heard the window open because he looked up almost immediately. "You received my message then," Christopher shouted. "You weren't in when I called."

"No," he shouted back. "I went to the hotel first and only then did I play back the bloody answering machine. I've just hear that Balwinder was stupid enough to be blasted last night, I'd only just got him bail as well" he had his arms akimbo as he spoke. "Come on," bellowed the big solicitor, his black, national health framed glasses vibrating on his nose as he tilted his head backwards for a gratuitous roar. "There's a whole, wide world waiting outside and if you don't come to it, it will surely come to you!"

CHAPTER EIGHTEEN

Balwinder Singh Gill was going to die. That was a solitary certainty, the only absolute; the one thing upon which he surely could rely. The gutter wound across his chest had fatally poisoned his blood stream with unforgiving lead which, at that very moment, was being pumped through his heart valves and into his brain, coursing through his arteries and veins, hunting down his life, like a frantic hare. He had to pay the price for the lives he had taken – that was fantasy. Both Jasbir Sood and "Mad" Mukesh had lived. He had killed no-one – fortunately. Luckily, his victims still played the consciousness game. Bindi could die knowing that he had no man's death to answer to. Just a dearth of achievement to answer for.

As Bindi laid on the bed in his private hospital room, paid for by a frustrated father close to despair, he knew that it was the dearth which frightened him much more than the death, that, if his life were to fade into the shadows, he would have left nothing behind: no children, no business, no success of any kind. Zero was what he had amounted to. A void was his epitaph.

"I'm nothing," he said as death knocked upon the door.

"Do you want me to tell you what you really are?" queried Sister Mulrennon in a homely Southern Irish accent which had an echo of iron. She closed the door behind her as her question opened Bindi's mouth but silence was his first reaction as Sister Mulrennon continued tauntingly: "Quite frankly I'm itching to let you know."

"I'm going to die, nurse," he pleaded dramatically.

"Fiddlesticks," she answered. "And I'm ward sister and not a nurse. Now put that breakfast tray on one side and sit up."

"But my chest hurts and my arm. I'm in real pain," he grumbled.

"Your head will hurt in a minute from me attempting to knock some sense into it. Now sit up as I told you. I've just to examine you for a moment and then I'll let you see some visitors who have just come along to pay their last respects," she laughed wickedly. "You've had your mother and father worried sick with all your silly talk about dying. Stuff and nonsense. The surgeon's told you, the houseman's told you. If you want to see what people look like who are really dying then I'll take you to the Intensive Care and then perhaps you'd learn a thing or two about death my lad."

"It's the way I feel," he replied as a dash of stupidity was added to the recipe of his thoughts. "It's what I know will happen."

"Stuff and nonsense, let's have a look at those stitches now," she tugged off the bandage unceremoniously and poked about on Bindi's chest. "Mmm, they'll do," she mused.

"Shouldn't the surgeon or at least a doctor be checking that," complained Bindi.

"You're not important enough," she smiled sweetly with bitter lips. "In fact if you'd been on the ward I'd have discharged you today myself, so I would. You're a waste of time, space and effort my young man."

"And you're a pain in the bum," Bindi replied. "I should report you."

"Be my guest." She stuffed a thermometer into his mouth although Bindi was not sure whether her motive was to silence him or to take his temperature. "Don't let your friends sign your arm plaster," she commanded. She moved to the bottom of his bed and pulled up a board which held a sheet of paper fastened in position with a large bulldog clip which perched on the top like a black butterfly. She perused the board scantily before putting it back. "I'll give them thirty minutes at the most and if I hear any disturbance whatsoever I'll curtail their visit and I'll curtail you as well. Do I make myself clear young man?" she queried as she removed the thermometer and, after a cursory glance at the reading, she pointed the bulb of mercury at Bindi's nose. "I'll have no trouble and no noise on my ward," she stated and without waiting for any kind of response, let alone an answer to her earlier question, she left her resentful but subdued young patient. Bindi looked down at his plastered left arm and then across to his right wrist where a plastic identity tag replaced his former chain of white gold. I don't count in here at all, he thought grimly to himself, not as the eldest son of the Gill household, nor as a force on the Southall streets. I am simply nothing and I'm going to die.

"The Irish nurse with the steel tongue and the big tits says you're fine," blustered Joshi as he burst into the room in front of Kwaki and Satish Brar. "Fine and so I'm glad," he said unconvincingly.

"Fuck you, fat face," retorted Bindi "I'm dying in here."

Joshi's pudding complexion was stirred around in the open bowl of his cranium frame. The fleshy mixture changed from mock mirth through hurt pride to near tearful rejection. Bindi misinterpreted the last complexion as one of concern. "Thanks for coming though," he said and, uncharacteristically, he gripped Joshi's hand in a warm welcome. "How's tricks?"

"Without you – not so good," answered Satish loyally, not trusting Joshi to reply. "Bender thinks he's the boss already."

"Where is the git?" asked Balwinder who pulled himself up in bed to look over Satish's shoulder and, with disappointment lurking in his lashes, he stared into his friend's slate grey eyes. "Where's every other git, come to that?"

Joshi and Kwaki exchanged glances as Satish brought up the palms of his hands: "Don't burn yourself up worrying 'bout it but they're out and about buying and selling."

"What!" screamed Bindi.

"Cool it, the stuff had to be shifted anyway," Satish tried to sound reasonable and calm although he knew the consequences as well as Balwinder did.

"He's dealing with my . . . with our contacts. Do you think he'll leave well alone once he knows them?"

"What could we do?" moaned Joshi.

"The others wanted to move it along," Kwaki stated simply and his large eyes slowly surveyed Bindi's face as if expecting another eruption in reply.

"What else could we do?" repeated Joshi pathetically.

"He says he'll deal with Anil Sood, so he says," affirmed Satish.

"Who says he shall?" growled Bindi. "Don't I even have a say in my own vengeance anymore. I mean to say, what is this?"

"Bender says it's bad for business," Kwaki answered in low careful tones. "To that extent it's everyone's concern."

"You sound like you believe him," Bindi spat the sentence out in a word-phlegm of anger.

"Some things he says makes sense," confirmed Kwaki.

"But we're here ain't we?" Joshi beamed. "WE came to see you anyhow, 'Kay?"

"Okay. O-fucking-kay," Bindi looked over to Satish who stood silent and still. "Bender's acting like the boss you said. Well, sounds like you're right there Satish, for sure."

"Only to you come out innit. The doc' has told your father who told your brother who told me that you could be out at the end of the week," Satish looked at his friend as if he doubted it.

"The nurse said she'll discharge me today," laughed Bindi but there was no warmth or even humour in the expulsion of lukewarm air from his lungs. It was a bitter gesture.

"She doesn't like you, that one," smiled Joshi nervously.

"Did you work that out all by yourself," sneered Bindi. "Perhaps you should be leader of the Smoke instead, 'Kay?" he added ironically. "Seems like anyone can be leader now, even a wanker like you."

"Okay, I know everything's not okay," stated Kwaki. "But what's everyone to do while you're here in hospital. Even the peasant dungmen carried on without the "mad" fucker – what do you expect us to do? Less than them?"

"I expect you to ask me, that's what I expect. Do you think Anil did this without Mukker's say so?" he fingered his chest as he spoke. "No chance. Have they nicked the bastard yet?"

"Not that I know of," replied Kwaki, who looked at his own reflection in the first floor window instead of at Bindi's eyes and thus caught a rare glimpse of his own facial expression: defiantly chastised.

"They'll have him soon," uttered Joshi in an attempt to reassure.

"Do you think for one moment that I want that," Bindi hit his forehead with an open palm. "Has no-one been born with a brain 'round here or was I unique?"

"Mutually assured silence with 'Mad Mucker' is what you want," concluded Satish Brar thoughtfully.

"And why not?" questioned Bindi. "We've done deals before. The lawyers merry-go-round don't help no-one but the lawyers. It'll put everyone away. I won't testify against Anil if Mukesh doesn't testify against me – what's wrong with that?"

"Bender's gonna do Anil. That's what's wrong with that," reminded Satish.

"But he hasn't asked me first!" raved Bindi as he leant forward in his bed to emphasise his point. He then twisted from side to side in frustration. "For fuck's sake, Satish can't you do anything?"

"I'll try. I'll try," he replied. "I tell them what you say. Everyone wants the best for you."

"'cept Bender. He's just sorry that Anil didn't kill me. The bastard was grinning when I caught this little lot. He'll be grinning again when I'm dead and gone."

"What's this death wish stuff?" asked Satish severely. "Your mother was saying you had a death wish and now all I hear you talking about is death, death, death. And yet everyone says you're doing just fine."

"Perhaps if you were laying here in pain you'd have a death wish too. Perhaps Mukesh will come over here from his ward and strangle me with his intravenous drip, I don't know. Perhaps I'm going mad in here thinking about how all you bastards are carving it up out there without me. Without ME," he repeated in exasperation.

"Not for long," smiled Satish. "I even put your BMW through the wash in readiness. I'll come an' pick you up in it on your release date, like a bloody chauffeur," his mouth made an attempt to laugh but it was not joined by his tombstone eyes. In any event, Bindi was unimpressed.

"What is there to come out to? Canada Kid and the All Stars? No, thank you. You must sort him out Satish. For all our sakes. Otherwise we'll just have another round of stabbing and then everyone will end up inside. Those who ain't in hospital that is. If Bender won't budge then ask him to come and see me in here. In fact ask him that today. He can visit this afternoon. Ask him in front of the rest of them. He can hardly refuse then. Look Satish," he said after a pause. "I don't want to be squeezed out of things, I still want to do something really big and perhaps make us all a good business out of the profits, you know what I mean. I mean money by the truck load. If only I can cast some light into these shadows which are all around me at the moment. They're all swallowing me up in a kind of sickness where every other thought is of death. I need some help in here," Bindi reached out with his right hand to do what his words could not: he clasped Satish's arm and then his hand.

"I'll help in whatever way I can," said Satish who continued: "just stay clear of Marway Sidhu when we bring you home. He was not exactly sorry when you got your load. As for us, we're all on your side and will promise our help, won't we?" Satish stared at Kwaki and Joshi who said nothing in return.

"Do you want any help?" asked Joe as Christopher shook his head and pressed a button Joe's small Espresso coffee machine. It whirled, sighed and rattled profusely before it produced, under protest, a small brown splattering flow of liquid caffeine. "I can only take legal dope these days," Joe complained as he turned his back on both Christopher and Eleanor in order to produce a bottle of milk from the battery operated refrigerator. She looked at Christopher querulously and he raised his eyebrows and shrugged his shoulders in reply. Her body language seemed to express a sentiment along these lines: the problem with all these old, left wing, liberal relics of the nineteen sixties was that they could embarrass a girl with comments like that. Old Joe Bailey had an older Bob Dylan, who was not physically present, rasp the line: "It's not dark yet, but it's getting there," while those who were physically present preferred non-verbal communication.

Christopher's raised eyebrow was semaphore for: don't stand on my hero because he's not trying to impress you. That's just the way he is. Whereas the shrugged shoulders were a physical communication of: "He's all we have." As is often the case with tics, glances and other forms of body oratory, the communication was instant and unambiguous: more a mentally faxed message than a telepathic transfer.

Joe Bailey added milk to two cups but kept his own black. He wandered to the red curtains and pulled one back to gaze out of the window for a moment. "Sometimes the police try to move me on," he grumbled.

"Well," smiled Eleanor. "I don't suppose they have many double decker buses in here."

"Humph," growled Joe derisively. "The Metropolitan Police have no jurisdiction in the Magistrates' Court carpark."

Christopher had no idea whether Joe was right or wrong but he had no doubt at all that he sounded far too convincing to argue against. It was surely that ability to solidify his statements into seemingly unanswerable assertions, sculptured firmly in granite, that had won Joe Bailey so many cases before the courts. Christopher secretly wished that Joe were taking his place before the Magistrates' that morning. He dare not suggest that, nor even hint at it, since Eleanor had expressed such confidence in him.

"It'll soon be time to give 'em hell," asserted Joe heartily as if mocking Christopher's hidden fears. Joe stared at his young assistant solicitor for a few moments before he addressed Eleanor. "Do you like your coffee?" he asked.

"Yes," she confirmed without enthusiasm. "But I can't help worrying about today though."

"With Christopher at the helm!" he boomed and he winked at his very unhappy assistant. "We thrive on stormy weather, eh Christopher? Ideal for drowning our Uncle Bill in his own contrivances."

"It may be," said Christopher tentatively in an attempt to express something without actually expressing it. "That I've insufficient ballast for the voyage in hand."

"I must see Bindi today," replied Joe in an effort to deflect a possible request from his assistant solicitor. "I've an old style committal to prepare." And besides I'd rather you received your baptism of hot advocacy acting for "your" Eleanor than representing one of "my" clients, he did not add. Nevertheless he felt vaguely uneasy about the situation. It was a problem of Archie Lord's creation, he told himself, somewhat unfairly, and he added, to himself that he should not go around performing emergency surgery forever because of Archie's fouled up diagnosis. After all, Archie Lord was happy to enjoy her company while he was receiving satisfaction for his efforts; but now she needed help without reward he was nowhere to be seen. I haven't been to bed with her, thought Joe bitterly to himself. Let those who receive her favours do her a favour in return.

Joe had not been granted a seat at table of love for some time now and, alas, had not tasted her majestic feast for at least half a decade or so nor had he swallowed so much as an aperitif nor, indeed, sampled the delight of one miserly mouthful of hors-d'oeuvre, such that even the smallest titbit had been denied him. After tragic starvation on such a scale, a man develops, simultaneously, both a stomach for very little and a craving for a great deal more. Thus, when he catches the mouth-watering aroma from someone else's fare he considers it to be much less than fair. Joe was, inevitably, becoming much older, although he truly felt he had aged enough. Perhaps it was time to go backwards? The restaurants with the choicest food may then re-open to his importunity but, until that unlikely occurrence, he would refrain from waiting on the other happy diners. At least his desire would not be tempted by their delight.

"Anyway hadn't you better go," said a grumpy Joe Bailey to an empty coffee cup. He couldn't say it to his wife and children because they had already left, leaving their empty space behind to torment him. "Well?" he looked up to face his two young lovers.

I don't suppose I can put this off any longer thought Christopher fearfully. However, he smiled a message of confidence to Eleanor, which he did not feel. "We're on our way Joe," he said.

But where will I go to? Eleanor's mind questioned the future of her body. Is it too late to run away? "Thanks for the coffee anyway Joe," she kissed him on the forehead like the father and protector he wasn't.

I should protect her, mused Joe. "ANYWAY," she had said. It echoed around his mind like a tune which both annoyed but would not exit. It was accompanied by a sharp stab of his jealousy which had itself, so strongly, shackled his intent. She had kissed him too.

It was too late. Admittedly, Christopher should not be conducting a trial so soon in his career and Joe conceded that he could have helped more than he had, so far, assisted. Admittedly, Archie was not really to blame – or was he?

It was a somewhat desolate, albeit decided, Joe Bailey who did not wave goodbye as he drove away from the

Ealing Magistrates' Court, chewing at his pipe and trying not to think.

Balwinder Gill awaited the arrival of his solicitor with the self-satisfaction of someone who has happily achieved a reversal of roles. Most people had to visit their solicitor. Bindi's solicitor came to visit him. This he had previously told his departing friends with glee. Actually, it was in the nature of Joe's practice that he came to visit everybody but, as that detracted from Bindi's all enveloping ego, he chose to close his mind to that unflattering fact. It was true, of course, that Bindi's brain was also boiling in the juice of many other worries but he would be able to unburden most of those on Bailey's cogitation. The fat man oozed confidence and self-assurance. A heavy-weight fighter battling from Bindi's corner. It would be good just to see him again.

When the door opened Bindi smiled. Mukesh did not as, knife in hand, he kicked the door shut behind him. Bindi then did something totally unexpected. Indeed, any other reaction would surely have been the last conscious gesture for fate to allow. He farted! Loud and long. The nervous gesture was like the discharge from a shotgun where mud and not cartridges had fouled both barrels. Balwinder's backside seemed to float a few inches to one side, like a self-induced Hovercraft, as the blast subsided into smell.

Mukesh threw his head back and roared with laughter as he was instantly incapacitated by anal amusement. Bindi, who caught Mukesh's infectious laughter, held his own nose in a mock resistance to the offensive from his nether regions. "Is that," Mukesh said finally, after drying the tears from his cheeks and rubbing his own eyes with a knuckle forefinger handkerchief. "Is that," he repeated. "What they mean by Holy Smoke?"

"No," laughed Bindi in return. "It's what they call: A Ragged one!"

Mukesh even managed a laugh at the pun on "Tooti Nung" as he fingered the point of his knife and looked down with disdain on the small cut he had made in his own hand. "I came here to finish off Anil's job," he said as if still undecided. "He seems to have screwed it up."

"Not really," Bindi's mouth dropped into a bitter grimace. "He did as good a job on me as I did on you."

"No, you did better," confirmed Mukesh. "You nearly killed me, you know."

"That was the idea," retorted Bindi as he held Mukesh's eyes with his own. He was such a young, arrogant man, decided Bindi – like me, he thought smiling to himself, like me. A mirror for my conscience: to see how far I haven't grown.

"If I had held that gun, you wouldn't be here," rejoined Mukesh grimly.

"Like Chowla?" questioned Balwinder.

"You have said," returned Mukesh.

"Are you going to kill me now?" asked Balwinder in a matter of fact tone. Somehow he knew he was safe and that his own death was no longer on the agenda.

"Just so I can be banged away on remand," he replied. "I think the fun's over for a while. What do you say?"

"I'm not sure I've had any fun."

"No?" queried Mukesh.

"I might go back to college," he continued thoughtfully, surprising himself as his tongue lurked in ambush on his brain and gave voice to a hidden agenda.

"Then you can't deal?" the high note of the last word signified a question to which Bindi responded immediately.

"Of course. Ignore me, I'm thinking out loud. We have to get this sorted for sure," he paused. "We won't testify against Anil if you don't go against me."

"Or me," added Mukesh. "If anyone's arrested I mean. I'm not saying Anil would talk or anything but the last thing I want is any kind of conspiracy rap on my shoulders."

"Look," Balwinder pulled his legs from under the bed clothes and dangled them over the side of the bed, to put his body in a sitting posture as he watched Mukesh's swinging legs and knife-fiddling fingers. "Let's keep it simple. No-one puts no-one else in court for anything done so far. What do you say?"

"Anyone who's summoned to attend court don't remember nothing. Nothing at all," confirmed Mukesh and both young men nodded sagely at each other.

"You're a man I can do business with," smiled Bindi as he held out a hand which Mukesh grasped. "We can cheat the law of its prison fodder at least."

"At least!" bellowed Joe Bailey who had heard Bindi's last words as he had opened the door to his private room. "At most you will make me bankrupt! A pox on you both," he laughed heartily. "I hope they haul you in for perverting the course of justice. That would last two weeks at the Old Namesake and make my bank manager a very happy man."

"Bollocks Bailey," snarled "Mad" Mukesh who balanced the knife carefully between fore-finger and thumb as his mind was similarly balanced between "do" and "don't."

"Don't be daft," said Bindi as gently as he could with his hand touching Mukesh's knuckles, "Joe's got a duty of confidentiality to me, haven't you Joe?"

"Alas, yes," affirmed Joe Bailey with a big fat grin. His huge bear like presence was as intimidated by Mukesh's knife as it might have been by a passing fly. "But if I could waive it, I'd probably wave you two goodbye."

"Don't you approve?" asked Mukesh lazily as if he almost didn't care. "It's better than murdering each other I guess."

"And it restores Order without Law," gloated Balwinder Singh Gill. "I've no problems. None at all. I'm immortal, didn't you know."

"Then you don't need one overweight, much mis-used and manifestly mortal lawyer. There's somewhere else I'd rather be in any event. Incidentally Bindi," Joe held the door open as he spoke with a false grin. "I hope you don't meet someone else who feels the same way you do." Joe stretched a mock scan across his own chest with a spatulate forefinger as he continued. "You already have, haven't you? See you Bindi. If you're still around, that is," he added with a cocky, contemptuous smile. "If you're still around."

CHAPTER NINETEEN

"Will I still be around after judgement day?" asked Eleanor of Christopher as together they climbed the steps of the Ealing Magistrates' Court, an unlikely solicitor and client, holding hands.

"You make it sound almost biblical," chirped Christopher with false bonhomie.

"Christ this place looks positively Old Testament," Eleanor paused to look up at the outside of the building. "Don't you agree?"

Christopher followed her eyes and, like Eleanor, he found himself bullied by the building, subdued and insignificant in comparison with its size, swallowed whole by the Gothic archway as if by a giant's mouth.

"Abandon hope all who enter here," whispered Christopher under his breath.

"You're supposed to be encouraging me," teased Eleanor with a hollow voice, which echoed into silence down her own throat.

"I was only joking," he rejoined, wearing a rather jagged, battered and broken smile.

"Come on," she urged him towards the old fashioned, wooden framed door, which was tugged open, just before they touched it, by a uniformed attendant.

"Messrs. Crawley and Dodgers, out in force today?" he smiled. "I've already said good morning to Mr. Lord."

"Oh God," retorted Eleanor.

"No, just his son," quipped the attendant with a cocky grin. "You'll find him …."

"We're not looking, thank you," interjected Christopher. "And we're Messrs. Joseph Bailey and Co.. Or at least I am. I mean ...." he stumbled.

"He means I'm the Defendant, George." she touched the attendant's arms as she spoke. "I've handed out some naughty leaflets so they say."

"You miss," the attendant stepped back and cast his eyes up and down the length of her body as if he were trying to see through her clothes. He almost made a quip about naughty but nice but then he remembered that a joke said at twenty is an insult said at seventy. "When they come after the likes of you then we know none of us are safe," he shook his head from side to side. "What a state to be in," he sighed.

The foyer of the Magistrates' Court had not seemed nearly so large the last time that Christopher had attended. However, he still felt more like an ant than a hero. He was, however, an ant with work to do. He brushed his antenna and sharpened his mandible because whoever he was: he was all there was. And Eleanor needed him today.

Christopher knew that whatever else he did or did not do he must always strive towards that which his father had told him: "Try hard, lad. Th'rest in't up to thee."

Whatever the result might be, Christopher was determined that the effort would not be lacking; albeit an ant was not the ablest of advocates. It was, however, with the determination to give of his very best, as if his own liberty were at stake, that he approached the usher with a jaunty air.

"I'm Mr. Larkin of Messrs. Crawley and Dod ..... I mean, of Messrs. Joseph Bailey ...." stumbled Christopher.

"The barrel!" gloated the elderly woman usher happily. "Bailey the barrel they call him here. An' I didn't know he had any assistants either, no I didn't," the usher looked beyond Christopher to Eleanor. "Don't I know you, dearie?" she asked in a busy-body manner. "I'm sure I do," the usher adjusted her cloak and pulled out a lace handkerchief. She removed her matronly glasses in order to give them a wipe, as if the very act of polishing the lens would aid her memory. Strangely enough, it did just that; so that when she came to place the glasses on the bridge of her nose again she had the answer to her own question. "Eleanor, isn't it. I saw your name on my list but I couldn't believe it was you. Well I never. I didn't think I'd ever see the day. Tut, tut, whatever have you been up to."

"Just handing out leaflets, Betty. That's a crime nowadays, you know."

"Well I never. Still, at least you'll know now not to do it again, won't you dearie?"

"Perhaps it's important we should learn the opposite," postulated Christopher petulantly. "Anyway, have we a few minutes before we go into court or what? I'd like to speak to the Crown Prosecution Service."

"Oh no," smirked Betty. "You're on now you know."

"You're joking," retorted Christopher shakily.

"No, I'm not. Not unless you want me to explain to Sir John Joust that you've only just arrived now." Betty turned her wrist to face her eyes and allowed her glasses to slip down to the end of her nose as she did so. Clearly she needed her glasses for distance only and she looked over the top of the frame to tell the time. "A few minutes past ten o'clock. Sir John will be very interested in that, I should warn you. You're the only case we have ready on our list at the moment although I'm expecting some detention warrant shortly. Better go in dearie, don't you think?"

Christopher steeled himself by auto-suggestion before he entered the courtroom. "I'm as good as they are," his mind repeatedly told itself as he led Eleanor from the spacious foyer into the cloistered Spartan environment of courtroom number four. It was not the same courtroom in which he had ineluctably blundered into the state's domain, but it was no less intimidating; although strangely, it was more by virtue of the fashionable contemporary interior design, which aimed to recreate the colonial court atmosphere. As if a Magistrates' Court in the heart of an immigrant sub-culture should somehow be reminiscent of the English Raj. Complete with large and completely unnecessary ceiling fans. Was the Home Office trying to make up for what the Foreign Office had lost. There was also a complete lack of windows which to Christopher's mind, signified the current trend towards a different and more sinister kind of privatisation. It would not be long before the "no access" signs were placed on the entrance to the public galleries of the court and the dispensation of justice became an entirely private concern. Indeed, it would be very shortly indeed: since the warrants of further detention, next on the cause list, could now be heard only behind closed doors.

Fluorescent lighting, air conditioning and central heating, none of which could seemingly be controlled from within the courtroom itself, were somehow stifling and not conducive of intelligent group contemplation. Perhaps the

306

very lack of any control over his environment contributed to a Defendant's lack of control over himself and caused a worry spiral to develop sending his thoughts curving continuously around with a progressive rise and fall in his emotions so that he could say: I'm merely the specimen here for the professionals to direct and make of me what they will. The sticky and tacky plastic seating, in row upon unused row, the arrangement of elevated wooden furnishing, the highest for the Magistrates, the lower benches were divided into two contesting platforms of adversarial intent, the all pervading smell of polish, cleaning agent and fly-spray were somehow more indicative of an ego inflation and Magisterial importance than of a serious effort to calmly and rationally protect the dignity of man.

The magisterial stage was entirely vacant although everyone clearly expected it to be filled at any moment. The clerk of the court, whose desk was in front and below the judgement seat, at a mere terrestrial level, made urgent facial signs to the young, incoming advocate while Miss Alison Pull, for the C.P.S., stood up from her seat, not of course to respect Christopher's lowly entrance, but in anticipation of the arrival of a greater being of judicial propensity. Christopher scurried to his appointed place, at the opposite end of the bench from the C.P.S and rummaged in his brief case for his books and papers. Poor Eleanor was left disjointed and alone, until the usher, with gleeful use of the meagre power attached to her office, unceremoniously half-directed and half-shoved her towards the dock.

Joe Bailey had obviously made out an important purpose from this earthly charade, thought Christopher, with something approaching desperation. Was it really any more than a superannuated crossword puzzle to stimulate the acolytes of adversarial combat? He could, however, live with that were he, like Archie Lord, to be granted membership of the privileged elite; although at that particular moment, Christopher, feeling very much the outsider, badly wanted the exit door.

"Pssst," he whispered across to Alison Pull, who gave him a condescending half glance of annoyance in reply. "Will you have a bind over?"

"For you," she smirked. "Or for your client."

There was, alas, no time to continue negotiations nor to lift them out of the mire of point-scoring sarcasm. God had arrived. There was, however, no fanfare of trumpets nor, perhaps unfortunately, did a great chasm appear to rent the ground asunder and swallow up the whole of man's mockeries. Instead, a dried up raisin of a man, with a crinkled complexion, shuffled into the court and begged a glass of water from the clerk.

"Good morning," he said in a surprisingly deep and mellow voice after taking a sip from his glass.

"Good morning sir," everyone replied more or less in unison.

He stared around the courtroom impatiently. "Well?" he asked finally.

"The first case sir is that of Eleanor Redfern, Mr. Larkin representing and Ms. Alison Pull for the C.P.S." the clerk smiled towards the attractive advocate for the Crown.

"Humph! Is this the Defendant," Sir John's alert eyes bulging from a thin and dried up face surveyed Eleanor.

"Yes, sir."

"Well!" he boomed.

"Sir," acknowledged the clerk humbly. He shuffled his papers unnecessarily and stared towards the dock. "Are you Eleanor Redfern?"

"Yes," she squeaked form a mouth which had lost its salivary lubricant.

"Do you live at the address shown on the information?"

"Yes."

"You are charged with having on Saturday last used threatening, abusive or insulting words or behaviour, or disorderly behaviour or having displayed any writing, sign or other visible representation which is threatening, abusive or insulting, within the hearing or sight of a person likely to be caused harassment, alarm or distress thereby namely T.I. Barker which offence is contrary to section five of the Public Order Act 1986. Do you understand the charge?"

"N....es. I mean ..... sorry ..... Yes sir."

"Are you guilty or not guilty?" asked the clerk.

"Guil ..... I mean Not .... I ..... sorry ..... Yes sir."

"Excuse me, sir." Christopher Larkin stood up in trepidation. He felt an indefinable anxiety quiver through his whole body from his loose knee caps to his trembling finger-tips. "I'm ..... er .... that is ..... if it pleases you ..... not entirely sure ..... that is ...... whether my client fully understands ....."

"She said she did. Have you spoken to her?" snapped Sir John.

"I have but not to her."

"Then you mean you haven't," snarled Sir John. "Be precise please."

"Haven't I?" replied Christopher completely confused.

"I think he means that he has not had the opportunity to speak to me, sir," Miss Pull smiled sweetly at the Magistrate.

"That would always be an excellent advantage outside of court," Sir John gave what passed for a smile on his shrunken lips. "But he's not representing you, is he?" queried Sir John.

"No, but," interposed Christopher.

"Sit down!" barked Sir John at the young male advocate.

"Perhaps I can help if I suggest to my L' friend that I have nothing to talk to him about."

"Capital," retorted Sir John. "then, let's proceed to trial."

"Sir," interjected Christopher with as much indignation as a wobbly almost uncontrollable larynx could muster. "My client has ... er .... not entered a proper plea as yet and there's also the q.... q.... question of mode of trial. And anyway," he concluded boldly. "We need a remand to prepare for a full hearing."

"Remand refused," retorted Sir John Joust. "First, this is a simple public order matter. Secondly, there is no mode of trial procedure since it is summary only – there is no right of jury trial. Thirdly and finally an ambiguous plea has already been given which will be entered as not guilty in accordance with usual practice."

"But sir," protested Christopher.

"Are you saying that your client will plead guilty?" queried Sir John.

"No, sir. I'm saying ..... er ....." Christopher who felt as if events were careering out of control, like a car without brakes on an ever steepening hill, had lost sight of what it was he intended to say.

"I thought not," smirked Sir John Joust. "Then let the trial begin."

"The trial!" gulped Christopher thinking desperately of Joe Bailey as if that very act of recall would somehow imbue him with the master's talents. "I would like a short remand to discuss the case first so that I know what I'm .... I mean .... sir, ... what I'm saying is this .... the case should be remanded in the interests of justice ..."

"It is rarely in those interests to remand anything, Mr. Larkin, since justice delayed means justice denied. We're talking here of a thirty minute trial, if that. It will fit in now, quite conveniently, before my warrants are due to be heard. Justice is contiguous with expedition and the needs of justice are best served by serving the ends of court-time."

And the new high speed courtroom production line has manufactured yet another high velocity verdict, Christopher thought but durst not say.

The Knight for the Crown lifted up her lance first and then galloped down the field with the sharp point aimed unwaveringly at Christopher's vulnerable and scantily protected colours. "The brief facts, sir, are these. Eleanor Redfern was handing out leaflets. On those leaflets were the words 'The riot is the voice of the unheard' in bold, blood-red letters. A hammer and sickle was next to the words sir. There was also a photograph of a policeman

311

being kicked in the head in the middle of the leaflet. As you are, of course, well aware sir, there have, alas, recently, been attacks on our officers in the London Borough of Ealing in which police officers have, amongst other things, been kicked in the head and, it is the contention of the Crown, that these leaflets were, as a result, a visible representation of a threatening or abusive nature. Of course it is open to you to find that they were merely insulting instead. The Defendant would, of course, still be guilty in any event. Further we allege that these leaflets were likely to cause harassment, alarm or distress to passing police officers and, indeed, they did so to T.I. Barker who was most upset as a result of reading one. I propose now to call T.I. Barker."

"T.I. Barker," the usher shouted through the courtroom door which she partially opened to that end.

The young smartly dressed officer, wearing a recently pressed white cotton shirt, marched into court swinging his arms as if he were on parade. His lean, muscular body seemed at odds with his face, which displayed features more at home on the shoulders of some minor clerical minion, than decorating the countenance of a law enforcement officer. His weak, dimpled chin below a baby's bottom complexion was somehow at odds with his macho uniform of military design.

"Yes officer," pondered Alison Pull for the C.P.S., after she had completed the formal preliminaries and identified the defendant as one of the leaflet pushers. "Is this the leaflet that Miss. Redfern was distributing and displaying to all and sundry?"

"I object, sir," interjected Christopher. "My learned friend's leading the witness."

"If my friend had listened he would have noted, sir, that I had already established those points earlier," she asserted and continued. "Can you remember my question?" Alison Pull queried of the officer. She was so confident of her authority and accuracy that she did not await any magisterial ruling on the objection.

"I can ma'am and that is the leaflet."

"What was your reaction on reading the leaflet officer?"

"I felt threatened, ma'am."

"And anything else?" Miss. Pull pushed.

"Oh yes, I felt most distressed and not a little alarmed I can tell you. Indeed, I think I can honestly say that the whole experience harassed me somewhat as well."

"Did Miss Redfern answer questions put to her concerning the leaflets?"

"No, she did not."

"Was she warned that this court could draw an adverse inference from her failure to answer?"

"She was."

"Thank you officer," replied Miss Pull "That is all we need to know. Perhaps you'll wait there in case there are some more questions for you."

"Certainly ma'am."

"Yes officer," said Christopher Larkin as he stood up, feeling even more smaller than he was when sitting down, "It is not true that you felt most alarmed and a little distressed it is?"

"No, it isn't," replied the officer smiling.

313

"There," started Christopher with one word of triumph – as if he really believed that life could produce such a success so simply – but T.I. Barker interjected to puncture his illusionary ascendancy.

"It was most distressing and not a little alarming, with respect," sneered the officer most disrespectfully.

"But I'm putting it to you that it wasn't," retorted Christopher shakily.

"But it was," replied the officer.

"It wasn't," returned Christopher in a loud, frustrated voice.

"Oh yes it was," asserted the officer louder than before.

"Let's ask the pantomime horse, shall we?" queried Sir John Joust sarcastically. "But, before we do, has anyone any intelligent questions to ask around here?"

"This officer is lying, sir," represented Christopher as forcefully as he was able.

"Mr. Larkin, have you heard of job demarcation?"

"Sir?" queried Christopher, whose face had started to emit heat from its glowing cheeks.

"It is my job to say whether he is lying or not. Whereas it is yours to prove it to my satisfaction. At the moment I can assure you Mr. Larkin that I am very far from satisfied."

Christopher looked around the courtroom as if hoping to find some lost inspiration lurking in a corner of the room somewhere. Instead his eyes fell on Archie Lord, who was sat in the back row, and in the spare second or so left to him, Christopher signalled SOS in Morse-code loudly and clearly from every pore in his body. Eleanor looked first towards Christopher and then following his eyes, she too saw Archie and sighed. Archie Lord, embarrassed, stood upright and caught the Magistrate's eye. He very nearly spoke, but, sensing that the ship had lost both her main mast and her rudder and was in imminent danger of floundering in the rough seas, with the consequent loss of all hands, he merely bowed instead, avoided Eleanor's pleading glance, and made a hasty dash for the door.

Christopher followed his former employer's exit with a mixture of anger and anxiety. The bastard is going to leave us both here to drown: clearly a preferable alternative for an image conscious egotist than the mild soaking he may receive at the expense of an attempted rescue. Joe Bailey would surely bulldoze down the court room doors at any moment and take over the helm from his inexperienced hands .... but no, in real life you rely on your own resources to become your own rescuer.

Christopher turned back to face the aged and cynical Sir John Joust and the contemptuous and arrogant T.I. Barker while he reflected upon an earlier conversation in Joe Bailey's Battlebus. Sweat dripping down his body in rivulets as he did so.

Christopher gulped, his own desert dry mouth provided only air to swallow, and he looked down at one of the offending leaflets because in his nervousness, he could not recall its precise wording. Of course! He could not see the leaflet unless he looked at it! That simple act of looking coldly down at his own papers provided him with a jemmy of words in which to probe apart the confident testimony of T.I. Barker. The man who had formerly asserted power over him and held him against his will, like a captive monkey in a laboratory; well, T.I. Barker was the prisoner now: locked in the witness box.

"Mr. Larkin," grumbled the testy Sir John. "Are you quite finished or would you like to assert just once more that it wasn't, so as to allow the officer to further reinforce his opinion that it was?"

"I am sorry, sir, for my own inexperience and sorrier still at your own failure to make allowance for it."

"Mr. Larkin!"

"May I please continue, sir?" replied a more assertive young advocate who suddenly felt not only that he had a role to play but also that he understood the point of playing it. "How did you obtain the leaflet officer?" questioned Christopher suddenly much happier, now that he had found both something to ask and the reason to ask it.

"From her," answered Barker cockily as he pointed his finger at Eleanor Redfern. Christopher Larkin followed the direction it indicated and saw, alas, that Eleanor's lovely red hair now had some much less lovely red and tearful eyes to match.

"Yes, the officer indicates the Defendant," mumbled Sir John Joust with a malicious smile.

It was, however, Christopher's turn to tilt his lance at the state's colours and, unflustered this time, he commenced a short galloping thrust of cross-examination. "You took a leaflet from a bundle she was holding?"

"I did. I took it from her. Without any doubt," sneered T.I. Barker, pointing at the Defendant.

"Did you know what the leaflet said before you took it?"

"Pardon," the officer felt a little unsure and, for the first time in his testimony, uncertain of his facts.

"Would you like me to repeat the question?"

"No, it's all right. Obviously I had to read the leaflet before I knew what it said."

"And you could only read the leaflet after you had taken it?"

"Obviously."

"Did the Defendant co-operate with you?"

"No, she was most unhelpful throughout and, as I have already said she refused to answer simple questions." He paused. "On your advice, I understand," he added acidly.

"So she didn't helpfully hand you a leaflet?"

"No, she did not."

"She didn't hand you a leaflet at all?"

"No, I had to snatch it off her because she wouldn't give it to me at first."

"Wouldn't she?" queried Christopher Larkin who was enjoying his job for the first time in his short professional life. "Tell me, officer, what adverse inference can you possibly draw from her refusal to answer questions?"

"That she was being threatening, abusive or insulting."

"By her silence!"

"By her not providing an innocent explanation."

"But regardless of any explanation by her you would still have prosecuted, wouldn't you?"

"No, not necessarily," the officer replied, slowly and unsure.

"If you had an innocent explanation you may not have prosecuted?"

"True."

"So the leaflet on its own would not have caused you to prosecute?"

"You're twisting my words."

"No, I'm not. You have just said that an innocent explanation may have satisfied you about the leaflet."

"Yes, but .... there wasn't any such explanation. She totally refused to co-operate. She was most unhelpful."

"True, and the lack of that explanation led you to believe the leaflets were threatening, abusive or insulting?"

"I suppose so, yes."

"The leaflets on their own were not threatening you, abusing you or insulting you were they?" Christopher paused for a half second, "That is until you caused yourself to be threatened by snatching one of them from my Client."

"Hold on. I haven't said that, have I?"

"I am rather afraid that you have," interjected Sir John Joust. "Any further questions, Mr. Larkin?"

"No, I think that's quite enough, sir."

"So do I. Miss. Alison Pull?"

"Well .... Perhaps not sir," she said finally.

"Very wise, as always Miss Pull. When in a hole, stop digging is my motto."

"Sir if I can just address you in my closing speech to one or two pertinent points," started Christopher with new found enthusiasm. "First, when the officer says he snatched the leaflet that shows....."

"..... that it was not displayed to him," interrupted Sir John Joust. "You don't become a stipendiary magistrate by being a complete idiot, you know. And quite frankly I can do without a lengthy speech about the liberty of the subject first thing on Monday morning. For that reason, if for no

318

other, I dismiss this case. The Defendant's free to go. I would ask T.I. Barker to convey my regards to his senior officers with a polite reminder that it is public money they are spending."

CHAPTER TWENTY

"Innocence has escaped intact. That must be one for the papyrus time sheets, least the future judge us too harshly," laughed Joe Bailey with a great fat, upturned banana-smile of yellow-green teeth. "The prisons are full of innocence, you know?" he continued provocatively. "The naïve short-change of today's much debased and undervalued coinage. That is an irrefutable fact, what do you say to that, Christopher?"

"That no fact is irrefutable," parried his young, newly confident assistant.

"Well answered but wrong. You've got the hots for Eleanor; that is an irrefutable fact and a different kind of prison. Or dare you deny that?"

"Joe!" exclaimed Eleanor indignantly. She would have gone onto retort: "how dare you!" Just like a television heroine she had once admired. However, she was not the sort of girl to naturally make a retort like that; so instead she became coyly embarrassed with lobster coloured cheeks. She was, also, not normally the sort of girl to feel such a confused mixture of self-conscious pride naturally; thus, uncharacteristically, she tried, unsuccessfully, to hide her red face behind some curly strands of her own bright red hair.

"I can deny it feels like a prison," Christopher looked to Eleanor who looked up to meet his eyes with a bold smile. "But I deny anything else."

"Take us home, Joe Bailey," taunted Eleanor wickedly. "Some of us have much better things to do than work for you."

Joe Bailey is a darling, darling," drawled Eleanor lazily to an eager, happy and relaxed Christopher Larkin. "Don't you think?" The sound of Van Morrison singing about a brown eyed girl formed a verbal back drop to her physical presence.

"Not if I can help it. Indeed I don't think I'll ever think again, unless that thought of itself breaks the rule. No. I'll just lie here, on your bed, forever, in a blissful state of awareness and tranquillity. The ultimate state of mystical union. It could become a popular method of transcending earthy cares."

"I hope not," she retorted. "There isn't enough of me to go round."

"Around and around," giggled Christopher, suddenly five and a half years old again, as he gently grabbed his Eleanosophy with both hands and took her tumbling over, over and again; until they reached the bed end. You're captured and enraptured in my arms."

"You'll be enruptured if you don't let me go," Eleanor pretended to knee him in the testicles but it turned into a tender tap, almost a massage instead. "I'm warning you," the "you" degenerated into an involuntary snigger as Christopher tickled her into a tittering tizzy by dancing his finger-tips underneath her arms. "Oohhhh Chrissy, stop it."

"I want you to always be laughing, always be happy, always, always, always, be with me, always," Christopher who was now sat astride Eleanor like a wrestler awaiting the first submission, lost his giggles in a single moment of contemplation of her soft, soothing and sensual eyes. Could he go to sleep in her face? Dream forward to the morning lights: follow her, stay with her, see the world through her eyes.

"You can't be always happy unless you are sometimes sad," she twitched her nose knowingly, breaking down the shadows of her sharp featured face. They re-formed once more when her nose stood still. "And I have had a share of sadness these last few days: lost my job, my lover and my liberty."

"And regained all three!" exclaimed Christopher.

"Thanks to you," her hazel brown eyes narrowed into a stare of concentration and regard. "I hope I don't hurt your feelings if I say that I doubted you for a sorry second or so, I won't doubt you again."

"I doubted myself too. And for more than a sorry second I can tell you," he caressed her delicate shoulders, like a fragile and precious replica of its own reality, seemingly at hopeless odds with her far from fragile, fiery red hair which blazed forth in open rebellion, dominating her feminine charm with an uncompromising spirit.

"I won't allow you to doubt anymore," she taunted.

"And what if I doubt that," he teased.

"Then you'll doubt me. And that is definitely not allowed," she freed one of her arms and tweaked his nose between her finger and thumb.

"Doubt you, never. Doubt that you doubt me is ....."

"Without doubt," she interrupted kissing him.

Doubtless doubt is all we have, was not spoken but remained within the very structure of the room as an ingrained uncertainty: the only true philosopher's stone.

"Eleanosophy for dinner, breakfast and tea," murmured Christopher playfully.

"No words," she ordered as she kissed him again and danced her fingers, like falling rain drops, on his erect penis.

He entered her so easily that, for a moment, he wasn't sure he had. He pushed in deeper as she pulled and scratched his buttocks, bit his rising neck and chest, sighed into his ear as a passionate female vocalist may suggestively suck a phallic microphone.

They rolled off the bed together, easily and for fun, head over heels across the floor, but still inside – only just: roly-poly, tumble and dive. Christopher's new, confident, arrogant erection possessed her and took her rolling with him until they crashed against the wall, too drunk with love to care, he came out to kiss her breast and body and she to lick his balls. He entered her and did not move as together they held time still and met each others searching eyes.

He slowly (ever so slowly) started to withdraw: out and then in, out and then in, out and in, out in. The vigorous vacillations of joyful sin.

THE END